CA

"If you haven't read this series yet, I highly recommend giving it a go. The mystery will delight you, and afterwards you'll be itching to start a knitting or crochet project of your own!"   —Cozy Mystery Book Reviews

"Good characters I hope to see more of."
                            —Kings River Life Magazine

"A cozy mystery that you won't want to put down. It combines cooking, knitting and murder in one great book!"
                                    —Fresh Fiction

"The California seaside is the backdrop to this captivating cozy that will have readers heading for the yarn store in droves."   —Debbie's Book Bag

"What a great start to a new series . . . A real page-turner."
                                    —MyShelf.com

Praise for Betty Hechtman's National Bestselling Crochet Mysteries

"Will warm the reader like a favorite afghan."
                —Earlene Fowler, national bestselling author

"Get hooked on this new author! . . . Who can resist a sleuth named Pink, a slew of interesting minor characters and a fun fringe-of-Hollywood setting?"
                —Monica Ferris, *USA Today* bestselling author

continued . . .

"Readers couldn't ask for a more rollicking read."
—*Crochet Today!*

"Fans . . . will enjoy unraveling the knots leading to the killer."
—*Publishers Weekly*

"Classic cozy fare . . . Crocheting pattern and recipe are just the icing on the cake."
—Cozy Library

Berkley Prime Crime titles by Betty Hechtman

Yarn Retreat Mysteries

YARN TO GO
SILENCE OF THE LAMB'S WOOL
WOUND UP IN MURDER
GONE WITH THE WOOL
A TANGLED YARN

Crochet Mysteries

HOOKED ON MURDER
DEAD MEN DON'T CROCHET
BY HOOK OR BY CROOK
A STITCH IN CRIME
YOU BETTER KNOT DIE
BEHIND THE SEAMS
IF HOOKS COULD KILL
FOR BETTER OR WORSTED
KNOT GUILTY
SEAMS LIKE MURDER
HOOKING FOR TROUBLE

A Tangled Yarn

BETTY HECHTMAN

BERKLEY PRIME CRIME
New York

BERKLEY PRIME CRIME
Published by Berkley
An imprint of Penguin Random House LLC
375 Hudson Street, New York, New York 10014

Copyright © 2017 by Betty Hechtman

ISBN: 9780425282687

First Edition: August 2017

Printed in the United States of America
1 3 5 7 9 10 8 6 4 2

Cover art by Patricia Castelao
Book design by Kelly Lipovich

Acknowledgments

This book was a lot of fun to write. My editor Michelle Vega's comments only made it better. Jessica Faust keeps helping me navigate the publishing world. Eileen Chetti did a great job of copyediting.

The patterns included in the book are favorites of mine and the one for the baby blanket has a special meaning for me. By the time I had finished the sample, my grandson Jakey had arrived and could put it to good use. Thank you to Shule and the team at Zoe's Yarn Studio for the help in figuring out the yarn and for teaching me the term "social knitting."

I have been part of a knit and crochet group for a while and never knew there was a term for what we were doing. Despite the fact that we lost our meeting place, our group has stuck together. Thank you to my friends and yarn advisors—Rene Biederman, Terry Cohen, Sonia Flaum, Lily Gillis, Winnie Hineson, Reva Mallon, Elayne Moschin, Anna Thomeson and Paula Tesler. I'm sure Linda Hopkins is keeping an eye on us from heaven.

Acknowledgments

Dominic and Roberta Maria have been my staunchest supporters.

It has been an interesting time for my family. Burl, Max, Samantha, and now Jakey—love you all.

1

DID I REALLY WANT TO DO THIS? IT WASN'T MY nature to lurk and eavesdrop. I was generally more direct, but this was different. It seemed like my only chance to get the truth.

And yes, I really should have been home preparing for the retreat I had starting later in the day instead of hanging around outside Maggie's coffee place. I could see the couple through the window. I didn't know them, but then Cadbury by the Sea attracted tourists from all over the world thanks to its quaint charm and position on the edge of the Monterey peninsula. Along with several coffee cups, one of my new breakfast muffins was on a plate in front of the man. At any moment he would take his first bite.

I'd been working on the recipe for a while, but this was the first time I'd offered them to the public—though only at two of the regular places I made muffins for. I had to know if they were a hit or a miss.

I slipped into the shop unnoticed and moved behind the brick-colored drapes Maggie had recently added. From here I had a slightly different view of the couple, though all I really noticed was that she had short dark hair and he was wearing a green cloth jacket. My eyes were glued to the muffin.

I'd had to come up with a whole new way of preparation and delivery since this new version of a muffin was perishable. But what with the popularity of breakfast items at fast-food places and the big chains of coffee places, it had seemed like a good idea.

Go on and taste it. I felt the tension rising as they kept talking instead of eating.

I felt my breath quicken as the man used a fork to break off a piece of the muffin and pick it up. All I could see was the back of his head, but I was pretty sure he put it in his mouth. When he replaced the fork, I waited for his reaction. But the woman kept on talking. "Nobody is expecting something like this in a small touristy town at the end of the earth. They could get careless when they make the exchange," she said.

"You're right. The actors think they're safe," the man said.

Okay, I got it. The muffin wasn't uppermost in his mind. I considered coming out from my hiding spot and simply asking him directly for his opinion, but only for a moment. Even if I could pull off a sudden appearance next to their table, what was I going to say? If I just asked what he thought of the muffin with no explanation, it would seem weird. And if I explained that I'd made it, I would most likely get a polite answer that might not be the truth.

"I'm just worried," he said. "This has to come off—or else."

A booming voice from across the coffee shop grabbed my attention, startling me. "You can't call that a muffin. It's that Feldstein woman again," the man said. "When will she understand that here in Cadbury we call things what they are. None of those cutesy names of hers, like The Blues for blueberry muffins. Calling this a muffin is absurd. Muffins are cakey even if they aren't sweet. This, this . . . ," he sputtered. He was standing at the counter holding a plate with a half-eaten one on it as Maggie looked on. "The only thing it has in common with a muffin is the shape. She ought to call it what it is—a portable frittata, or maybe a round breakfast mélange."

I'd forgotten all about the couple now and focused on the man at the counter. By now I'd gotten a look at him and recognized him as one of the members of the town council. They'd been on my case since I'd first started baking in Cadbury. You'd think I was committing some kind of capital crime calling my mixed-berry muffins Merry Berry, or the walnut ones Just Nuts.

It was all about the town wanting to be authentic. There were no ye olde shoppes of any kind, and if the buildings appeared to be Victorian architecture, with bright colors and fish-scale siding, it was because they were the real thing. I could definitely see the town's point, but I didn't see why giving my muffins clever names was a problem. To keep the peace, though, I had gone along with it. So, the Ebony and Ivory muffins were just called chocolate and vanilla and the Plain Janes became vanilla muffins; the Monkey Business muffins went back to banana. But I was drawing the line with my new creation. Calling them portable frittatas—no way.

But then he said something that made me calm down a little. "Well, at least it seems like a healthier option, and it tastes pretty good. My wife would probably approve." He stared down at the refrigerated glass case. "That is, if she found them."

So, I had gotten an answer about my new creation, but I wasn't sure what to make of it. I waited until he left before I exited my hiding place. Maggie looked up from behind the counter and seemed baffled by my sudden appearance. She had a bloodred bandana tied over her dark hair. Wearing something red was almost a trademark for the coffee-shop owner. Everyone in town knew it was her way of keeping a cheerful outlook after the tragedies she'd had in her life. She'd lost both her husband and her daughter in a short span of time. It had not ruined her, though, and she was a kind, giving person who doled out warmth with her coffee drinks.

"I guess you heard, then." She looked toward the street as the town councilman walked past the window. "At least he seemed to like them." I knew she was trying to spare my feelings. "Maybe we can figure out a way to present them differently. Nobody seems to understand what they are until I explain," she said.

I looked over to my couple, thinking of asking their opinion, but their table was empty and most of the muffin had been left behind. "Let me think about it," I said. "It's time for me to change modes now, from muffin maker to yarn retreat leader."

"No problem. Maybe things will pick up. You said these *muffins* will stay fresh all weekend." She offered me a coffee, but I said I didn't have time. "What's the plan for your retreat this time?"

"Arm knitting and finger crochet," I said, making my way to the door.

"Really?" Maggie said with a laugh. "Good luck."

This was going to be my fifth yarn retreat, and I was still dependent on my two helpers to come up with a program. Maggie's tone made me wonder if I'd made a mistake this time.

It hadn't been my plan to be running yarn retreats when I relocated to Cadbury. I hadn't really had any plan of what I was going to do when I made the move. It was more about avoiding moving back in with my parents. Their apartment in the Hancock building in downtown Chicago had a great view of Lake Michigan, but at thirty-five, living with them seemed like the ultimate sign of failure. I should add that my parents are both doctors and high achievers. Unfortunately, I hadn't exactly followed in their footsteps. I'd tried law school, but after one semester I knew it wasn't for me. I'd baked for a bistro that had gone out of business after six months—it had been their bad management, not my desserts. I'd been a substitute teacher at a private school, another profession that was not for me, and I'd been relieved when they didn't renew my contract. I'd turned to temp work, which at least wasn't boring. I'd handed out samples of a new flavor of chewing gums on a street corner, and offered to spritz women with a new scent as they came into a department store, among other things, but my favorite gig was working for a PI. I'd hoped it might have become something permanent, but he couldn't afford to keep me on.

Which brings me to why it seemed like my only alternative was to move back in with my parents.

My father's sister, Joan, lived in Cadbury, and when she offered me her guest house, I'd pretty much jumped at the opportunity. It was thanks to her that I'd gotten the job baking desserts for the Blue Door and started making the muffins that I supplied to the local coffee spots.

The yarn retreat business was all hers. She'd been an avid yarn crafter and had all the skills necessary, but she'd been killed in a hit-and-run accident. The only satisfaction I had was that I had managed to find the culprit and gotten justice for Joan.

My aunt was single with no children and had left her house and the business to me. To say I was a fish out of water was an understatement. I hadn't known the difference between knitting and crochet beyond that one took two tools and the other just one. But I had risen to the occasion and gotten some local help to handle the yarn part.

My job was to arrange it all and deal with the people during the retreat. By now I had learned how to knit and crochet and tried to make the projects along with the group. I also had come to understand the appeal of yarn craft. But I was nowhere near my aunt's level of proficiency, which was why I'd once again delegated it to my helpers to come up with the program for the upcoming retreat. I had a sinking feeling that I should have spent time seeing exactly how arm knitting and finger crochet worked.

It took about five minutes for me to drive my yellow Mini Cooper from downtown Cadbury to my place on the edge of town. I forced myself to stop thinking about the muffin flop and to focus on the retreat. When I pulled into the driveway, Julius was sitting by the back door waiting for me.

Julius was my first-ever pet—well, maybe I should say animal companion. If anybody was the pet, it was probably me. The sleek black cat had picked me out; that was for sure. I didn't know anything about his history other than that he'd seemed homeless before he came to my place. And he seemed to be doing a good job of training me.

"I can't stay," I said when I'd gotten out of the car. He blinked his yellow eyes and turned toward the back door with a tiny meow. "No, no stink fish right now," I said in my best impression of a firm voice.

Of all the foods in the world the cat could have liked, his first choice was a fishy cat food that had such a strong smell, I had to encase it in in numerous layers of plastic wrap and bags. Even then, a hint of its icky scent escaped. He let out such a disappointed meow, I almost relented, but then I saw the white airport van go by and turn in to the driveway across the street. How convenient to have Vista Del Mar, the hotel and conference center where the retreats were held, just across the street.

"Later, I promise," I called as grabbed my bag and rushed to follow the van.

It was April, but you wouldn't know it by the weather here. It was almost the same year-round—damp and never really cold or really warm. It was almost always cloudy, but after living here awhile, I'd noticed the variations in the sky. Sometimes the clouds were gauzy and the sun made an appearance through them, but at other times the clouds were spread across the sky in an even layer, like they were today. The layer was so thick, there was no hint of where in the sky the sun even was. When it was like this, the light stayed the same all day. And when the afternoon turned to evening, it was as if a giant dimmer made the light fade evenly across the sky.

Here on the edge of town, it was more rustic than the rest of Cadbury. There were no lawns, sidewalks or street lights, but when I crossed the street and started down the Vista Del Mar driveway, the landscape went to a whole new level of untamed.

The hotel and conference center had started out as a camp, and it still had more the flavor of a camp than a resort. It was more than a hundred years old, and the guest rooms were in moody, weathered-looking buildings spread around the sloping hundred or so acres. A narrow road built before cars were common looped around the grounds. The air always smelled of salt from the ocean mixed with smoke from the many fireplaces.

The grounds were all left to grow wild. If one of the lanky Monterey pines died and fell over, it was left to return to the earth on its own. I'd heard the same was true with any of the animals that made their home on the grounds. Ever since I'd heard that, I'd always avoided looking in the brush any more than necessary. It wasn't even an issue now since my eyes were glued to the van that had pulled up to the main building and was beginning to release passengers.

The majority of my retreaters weren't due to arrive until the afternoon, but I was going to greet the three early arrivals I called the early birds. They'd been to all my retreats and now seemed like helpers and friends. They had started coming early to have a pre-retreat. Usually it was for a day or two, but this time it was going to be more like a couple of hours.

I was surprised to see Madeleine Delacorte get out of the van. She seemed thrilled to see me and rushed over to give me a hug.

"Casey, you didn't have to come meet me," she said. I hugged her back, not about to let on that I was really there to meet someone else. Madeleine and I were friends, but not exactly on the same level. She and her younger sister, Cora, were like the local royalty. They owned tons of real estate, including Vista Del Mar, and were extremely wealthy. Madeleine had started coming to my retreats and credited the experience, as well as getting to know me, for the big change in her life. Basically she was kicking up her heels after spending a lifetime being overly proper. The perfect example was that at seventy-something she had bought her first pair of jeans and subsequently fallen in love with all things denim. The trip she was returning from spotlighted the change as well: she had gone to Peru alone, though I understood she'd met up with a tour group when she got there.

"I brought you something, Casey," Madeleine said with a happy squeal as she released me from the hug. "What a trip!" She reached down into her carry-on and pulled out a small cloth tote and presented it to me. "It's alpaca yarn. I went to a ranch and saw the actual alpacas whose fleece it's made from."

I was surprised at the gift and thanked her profusely as I looked over the bag of balls of soft yarn in shades of browns and beige before dropping it into the larger tote I had on my shoulder.

"Look at the shoes I bought there," she said, kicking out her foot to show off her espadrilles. "I think they are perfect with these jeans." She gestured toward the shredded knees and I had to restrain a laugh. She seemed years younger than her actual age now. It was partly from her new style of clothes and her swinging bob haircut, but it was mostly from her attitude. It was as if she was doing everything for the first time. Well, actually, it was sort of true.

There was something more that affected our relationship. She and her sister had offered my aunt a discount on the rooms and meeting space for the retreats and had passed it on to me despite the manager of Vista Del Mar wanting to take it away. Without the discount I couldn't continue the retreats. It wasn't that I kissed up to Madeleine, but let's say I felt an extra responsibility to take care of her. It also made me happy to help her have new experiences.

"I owe this all to you. If you hadn't included me in the retreats and your investigations," she said, dropping her voice at the last word, "I never would have had the nerve to take this trip. When I saw how independent you are, I wouldn't even let my sister meet me at the airport. Do you know where they left my golf cart?" She didn't wait for an answer and went on about how freeing it was to take the airport shuttle and then drive herself back home.

Another van pulled up and people started to get off.

"Madeleine, don't leave," someone called, and she looked up. Her gaze stopped on a man who had just gotten out of the other van. He waved and then got stalled as the bags were unloaded.

There was an instant change in her demeanor. She began smoothing her hair and straightening her shirt with a definite expression of interest at the new arrival.

"We met on the plane. Such a nice man. He was so friendly and interested in everything about Cadbury. I suppose it's because of what he does." She turned to look at me. "I couldn't believe the coincidence that he was coming here to Vista Del Mar. His name is Don Porter and he's a travel writer. He's going to be one of the speakers at the writers' conference going on this weekend." She turned to me. "I did a lot of talking up about Vista Del Mar. We want to make sure he has a wonderful time this weekend. He didn't say anything exactly, but I bet he's going to write something about Vista Del Mar while he's here."

"You should tell that to Kevin St. John," I said, referring to the Vista Del Mar manager.

"Of course, I'll talk to him. But wouldn't it be wonderful if Don wrote a piece just about your retreats, too?"

I nodded at the idea and then gave him another look. He was nice looking, in an everyman sort of way. Of course, he was a travel writer, I thought with an inner chuckle. The clothes were a giveaway. His khaki cargo pants were made of that lightweight material that probably dried overnight, his vest had a million pockets and the camp shirt underneath seemed pretty wash-and-wear, too. But all was not right in his world. Through my assorted jobs, I'd become good at reading people, and the way his brow had a slight furrow made it seem like he was worried about something.

"This is the person I was telling you about," Madeleine

said when he finally reached us. I smiled at him, but all his attention was on Madeleine. This was not the time to make a pitch about my yarn retreats. Besides, I saw the three early birds rushing toward me.

"There she is," Bree Meyers said as she threw her arms around me for a hug. I was going to excuse myself from Madeleine and Don Porter, but it wasn't necessary. They'd moved off to the side.

"I'm sorry your pre-retreat is only going to be a couple of hours this time," I said to the three of them.

"It'll be fine," Bree said. She looked the same as she had the first time I'd seen her. She had a frizz of short blond hair and was dressed in what I'd call busy-mommy wear, which was basically comfortable jeans and a gray hoodie. She let out a sigh of relief. "To think that I freaked out when I found out Vista Del Mar had gone unplugged. Now I'm the one who helps others." She had her phone in her hand and then shrugged as she put it in her purse.

Vista Del Mar had gone unplugged recently. There was no cell service, no Wi-Fi and not even television. There were vintage phone booths with landlines and a message board for guests to communicate with one another. I was always clear in the copy for the retreats about the modes of communication, but there was still always someone who had a meltdown. Bree loved to step in and calm them down.

"It's good to be here. There's nothing like spending the weekend with kindred spirits," Scott Lipton said. He'd come to his first retreat so he could knit in public. Even though the first knitters were supposed to have been men, he'd still felt uncomfortable about letting the world know that he knitted. At that time, even his wife didn't know. He had a clean-cut, preppy look—always in khakis and polo shirts. He wore his honey blond hair in a short, businesslike style. The only things that stood out from his conservative appearance were the red knitting needles poking out from under his arm.

His job was to help with any males interested in knitting, whether they were retreaters or guests who joined in one of our sessions. He turned to me. "That being said, I understand we have another of my gender coming this weekend."

"Yes," I said, pulling out my phone. The service didn't work, but my file of photos did. "Jeff Hunter is his name. He signed up online and for some reason thought he had to send a photo with it." I held out my phone so Scott could see it. Jeff did not in any way resemble someone you'd think was a knitter. He had a square, stubborn-looking jaw with several days' worth of stubble. It looked like he was wearing a leather jacket that had seen better days.

"He looks like he'd knock somebody out if they looked askance at his needles," Olivia said. Olivia Golden barely resembled the unhappy-looking woman who'd come to the first retreat. Her almond-shaped face seemed to glow with an inner joy now. "I hope he likes to do squares," she said. She opened the big tote she was carrying. It was filled with small plastic bags. Each had a ball of yarn and a piece of cardboard. She'd channeled all the anger she'd felt toward her ex-husband into getting everyone and anyone to knit or crochet a square the size of the piece of cardboard. Then she put them all together into blankets that were donated to shelters and people in need. She was a perfect example of someone who forgot about her own troubles by helping others.

"I'm glad to see you," Olivia said to me, "but you really didn't have to meet us. We know the drill, and I'm sure you must have a lot to do."

"As retreat leader, it's my job to make sure everything is good for my people." I started to lead the way to help them get registered, but the three of them shooed me away and said they were fine.

I didn't argue but went back across the street and let myself into the converted guest house. One of these days I wasn't going to wait until the last minute to do the final retreat preparations, but that day wasn't here yet. All the supplies for the retreat were on the counter that divided off the small kitchen area from the rest of the guest house and had served as a dining table when I'd lived in the small space.

I set down my shoulder tote, took out Madeleine's gift and put it out of the way. It was thoughtful of her to bring something for me, but I'd have to wait until the weekend was over to really get into it.

I picked up the first scarlet cloth tote with *Yarn2Go* emblazoned on the front and filled it with a schedule, a map of Vista Del Mar, a meal ticket, a pad and pen, a name tag that probably wouldn't get worn past the first workshop and a coupon for Maggie's coffee place that mentioned there was free Wi-Fi. They'd get their yarn at the first workshop. I kept at it until I'd filled all of the totes and loaded them into a bin on wheels. I had to print up the registration list and gather the other sundry articles I needed to check everybody in. The phone rang just as I was heading to the door.

Don't answer it, I told myself. I was sure it was from my mother. No time to talk now. I heard it go to voice mail as I went down the driveway, telling myself that this time, no one was going to die.

2

"WHAT A PERFECT PLACE FOR A MURDER." THE words made me stop in my tracks as I looked at the man who'd said them.

"What?" I said, trying to keep the panic out of my voice.

The man who'd spoken took one look at my expression and laughed. "Fictional, of course. We're here for the writers' conference. He showed off his name tag, explaining it had his name, where he was from and what he wrote. He did a Vanna White move, pointing out that it said *Mystery*. "My friend and I were talking about writing a scenario for a mystery weekend, and this place seemed like the perfect place to hold it." He looked around the large room as if appraising it for his plan and then turned back to me.

"What about you?" he asked. "What do you write?" He and his associate glanced over my black turtleneck for a name tag.

I pointed at the bin I was dragging. "I'm the leader of the yarn group." I gave my name, not that they seemed that interested once they'd heard the word *yarn*. "Hey, Miss Marple was a big knitter," I called after them.

I had been hearing about this writers' conference for weeks. It had been arranged by Kevin St. John, and he'd told me numerous times that it would dwarf my small group. Still, he'd reminded me of the deal that we'd made. If my group was knitting in a public area and any of his writers wanted to join in, I was to make them feel welcome. If those two were any example, I didn't think I'd have to worry.

I continued to wheel my bin of supplies across the cavernous interior of the Lodge. While the buildings with guest rooms were scattered around the grounds, the common buildings were grouped in the center, or what I liked to think of as the heart of Vista Del Mar. A lovely chapel was tucked off to the side near the entrance to the dunes. The Sea Foam dining hall was down the walkway.

But the heart of the heart was the Lodge. A massive wooden counter set off the registration area. On one side, a row of telephone booths awaited customers. On the other side, the door to the Cora and Madeleine Delacorte Café was open, letting out the pungent smell of coffee.

All the way on the other end of the long room, like a mirror image of the café, was a gift shop. The message board was nearby but for now seemed empty. A pool table, along with one for table tennis, was near the back wall. There were also shelves with board games.

The writers' group was set up under the windows that overlooked the driveway where the van had done the drop-off. Their registration had already started, and I couldn't see their table for all the people crowded around it.

My area was under the windows that overlooked the deck beyond. I could see the boardwalk that kept everyone from trampling the fragile plants that covered the soft white sand as I began to set out my supplies.

A fire was going in the large stone fireplace in the center of the seating area. The lamps had amber-colored glass shades that gave off a warm glow and made the barn-like room seem a little cozier.

It was hard to miss Kevin St. John as he circulated among the writers who were waiting to check in. He always wore a white shirt, dark suit and conservative tie, which seemed overly formal for the casual surroundings. The conference was the biggest event he'd ever put on, and I noticed some perspiration on his usually placid moon-shaped face. *Welcome to my world,* I thought. Who knew who was going to show up for the retreat? I always crossed my fingers that there wouldn't be problems, but there always were.

There was nothing in the room to absorb sound, and as more people came in, the din grew louder. I was anxious to finish the setup, put up my sign that registration would begin after lunch and then get out of the Lodge and away from the noise.

Just as I was about to leave, a man and woman approached my table. They looked at the sign and then at me. "Can't she check in now?" the man said. I saw that he had on one of the writers' group name tags and had a computer bag on his shoulder, which seemed almost de rigueur.

There didn't seem to be any reason why not, so I asked

her name. "Lisa Dryer," she said, trying to look over my list. "I'm just a beginning knitter. I hope that's okay."

I assumed she was worried that my people would all be experts and she'd feel out of place.

"Don't worry. You don't even need to know how to knit for this retreat's program. And I have two instructors who can teach you anything you need to know."

She didn't seem completely convinced. "So then, there will be others like me?"

"There's nothing to worry about, really. You'll fit in just fine. I've found that yarn people are very accepting."

"I just thought if there was someone like me, we could kind of be buddies." She looked over the list again.

"It would be better for you to buddy with someone who is more experienced," I said, but she didn't seem interested in the idea. I checked off her name and turned to the man with her. "What about you?"

He laughed and put up his hands in mock horror. "I'm with the other group."

"We're married. This is Derek." She gave his shoulder a pat and I noticed his green jacket. "It is just a perfect weekend for us. I can do your knitting retreat and he gets to go to a writers' workshop." As I glanced back and forth at them, something seemed familiar.

"And in between we get to spend time together," Derek said, shooting her a hot look.

That was more information than I needed or wanted. "I hope the writers aren't upset when they realize there's no Internet," I said, changing the subject.

The grunt he offered in response made me think he

hadn't realized that when he'd signed up. Then I realized why they seemed familiar. They were the couple from Maggie's, with my muffin.

I knew I had supposedly put the new muffins on the back burner, but what harm could there be in asking what he'd thought of it? But I needed to ease into it. "I saw you two in Maggie's coffee place earlier this morning. I couldn't help but overhear you talking about actors. I suppose that means Derek is interested in writing plays," I said in a friendly voice. I expected they might not have realized the name of the place where they'd had coffee, so I described where it was and then waited for some kind of recognition to show in their faces.

"It couldn't have been us," Derek said. He seemed to be trying to cover it, but his expression had darkened. "We just got here. We drove from San Jose." He saw me looking at his green jacket. "You might have noticed I'm not the only one wearing one of these." It was true—when I looked toward the people registering, there seemed to be quite a few wearing the same style green cloth jacket.

I looked at Lisa and Derek again and realized that neither one had any characteristics that stood out. It was almost as if they'd gone out of their way to be so bland they got lost in the crowd. "I guess I must have been mistaken," I said finally.

"No problem," he said. I handed Lisa her tote bag and explained the contents. I didn't have to be concerned about making sure they were checked into their room since the writers' group had already taken care of that, and I didn't have to do the explanation about the meals in the dining hall or that a bell would ring announcing mealtime. That had been covered as well.

"Our first workshop starts at four," I said, and they seemed about to walk away, but then Lisa turned back.

"If there's no Internet or cell reception, how do we get in touch with each other?" Lisa said. I pointed to the message board and explained that there was a pad of paper and a pencil attached.

"Real old-school, huh? It must be a challenge to even see that you have a message," Derek said.

"It's set up to be alphabetical," I said. I watched them walk away, still thinking they certainly looked just like the couple I'd seen at Maggie's. But why would they lie?

All of a sudden, I got it. It was like a case my PI boss had had me work on. Well, *work on* might sound a little grander than it was. My work had all been on the phone, getting information from people who didn't really want to give it. I had a knack for getting them to talk. In this particular case, a man had told his wife he was going out of town for a conference and she didn't believe him. Turns out there was a conference, but it was just a cover for him to meet up with another woman. Maybe it was something like that with them. Like they were married as she said, but just not to each other. Thank heavens that was not my concern.

It figured that they went to check out the message board. They seemed to be actually reading some of the notes. Maybe they were checking to see if they were really alphabetical.

I straightened the sign announcing that registration would start at one p.m., shoved the empty bin under the table and looked toward the Cora and Madeleine Delacorte Café. I'd left them a small batch of the new breakfast muffins, and I was anxious to see how they were moving and if anyone had said anything about them.

The café was a relatively new addition to Vista Del Mar, and it was very busy when I walked in. Just like the gift shop that it mirrored, its walls were almost all windows. The décor was rather plain. A wooden counter offered places to sit and also served as a barrier to the preparation area. Wooden tables and chairs were scattered around the rest of the area. The tables were all full, and from the snippets of conversation I picked up, the patrons were all writers.

I was more interested in talking to the woman behind the counter, though. Her name was Bridget and she hadn't been working there long. She was at the far end of the counter, talking to a customer. A customer I recognized.

Before I could greet him, Sammy was off his stool and coming over, urging me to join him. "Case, you've got to see this. It's going to wow everyone."

"Actually, I wanted to talk to her," I said, turning toward Bridget. She had a cascade of dark blond wavy hair and a smile that seemed like she was trying too hard. I'd checked on my regular muffins with her before and she'd never been particularly friendly. I tried to glance inside the refrigerator case to see what had sold, but Sammy pulled me away.

"You can do that after I show you. C'mon," he said, leading me to the stool next to his. Bridget was staring at me, and there was just the slightest darkening to the expression in her eyes, which seemed strange.

Sammy was Dr. Sammy Glickner, also known as the Amazing Dr. Sammy when he was doing his magic act. He was also my ex-boyfriend. He'd relocated to Cadbury recently, insisting it had nothing to do with me being there or any hopes he had of rekindling our romance, and everything to do with him following his dream to do magic. By day he was a urologist, but he did table magic in the dining hall here at Vista Del Mar two evenings a week and on the weekends.

He had three walnut shells—or at least what looked like walnut shells—sitting on the counter. I figured they were probably some magician's version of the shells.

"So, watch this," he said, holding up what looked like a pea, but I suspected it was plastic. He lifted one of the shells and placed the pea under it. "Keep your eye on the shell with the pea under it," he said, pointing to it before starting to move the shells around.

He kept his patter going while he rearranged the shells. I did my best to keep my eye on the shell despite his talking. Finally he stopped and asked me to pick the shell with the pea under it.

I hated to do it, since it would embarrass him when I was right, but I pointed to the shell I had followed through all his manipulations. His face seemed to fall and I almost wanted to retract my choice and pick another shell, but it was too late.

"Go on and pick it up," he said to me.

"I'm sorry, Sammy," I said as I reached out for the shell. I lifted it and then gasped—it was empty. When I looked at Sammy he was grinning.

"I told you it was great. Want to try again?"

"Oh, Sammy, you really are amazing," Bridget said. She was leaning on her elbows, gazing up at him. When she straightened, I noticed she began to twist a lock of her hair. I might be a flop at flirting, but I still recognized it when I saw someone else doing it. Her grand finale was tilting her head and batting her eyes. Now her behavior toward me made sense. I wasn't sure he realized it, but Sammy had an admirer. And maybe a helper, too. She tried to hand him a deck of cards that had been lying on the counter.

The helper part seemed to be more on her end, though— he pushed the cards away, instead repeating the trick with the shells for a man who had stopped next to him.

I felt protective of Sammy since I felt responsible for his being in Cadbury, no matter what he said to the contrary. I began to evaluate Bridget in a new way. Sammy had no sense about women. Look at the way he wore his heart on his sleeve about me. Would she end up breaking his heart? Or what if there was a happy ending? Visions of a white dress and handfuls of thrown rice fluttered through my mind. Why did I feel such a twinge at the image?

Sammy took a break from the shell game, and Bridget took a napkin and mopped his brow, then gave him a cup of hot water and lemon. "Drink it for your voice," she urged. He seemed oblivious to her moves but took a sip of the hot drink.

I waited until someone came in and ordered an elaborate coffee drink and she had to walk away from us to make it before I said anything. "I think she likes you," I said. "And it's not just the magic."

Sammy seemed dumbfounded. "You really think so?" I nodded in answer and he stared at her as she frothed the milk. We were never, ever going to get back together, so he ought to move on. I should feel happy for him.

It wasn't like we'd had a bitter breakup. If it were up to him, we'd still be together, probably married and living in Highland Park near Chicago. It was all me. If there was a checklist for a good mate, Sammy fit the bill, but there was that special something missing. On my end, there just wasn't chemistry between us.

That didn't mean I didn't care for him. I wanted him to be happy. What if Sammy acted on what I'd just said? He would probably stop calling me Case, his nickname for me, and saying that I was the only one who got him. She'd be the one who got him then.

Suddenly I realized how much I liked the adoring looks he threw my way. The way he was always there, and the way his feelings were so apparent.

"I might have been wrong. I wouldn't rush into anything," I said as she delivered the drink to the customer and then rejoined us. I left without even asking her about the muffins. I was mulling over the whole situation, shocked at my own behavior. It almost seemed like I was jealous.

When I exited the café, I practically bumped into Kevin St. John. "So, there you are," he said. "I have someone who'd like to check in for your retreat." He gestured to the woman with him. The words sounded benign enough, but his tone said volumes. He was implying that I was shirking my duty to my retreat people by not being at the table and not nearly as professional as he was with the writers. Underneath it all was his irritation that I had the special deal courtesy of the Delacorte sisters. I knew if he'd had his druthers, I'd be charged the going rate, which would accomplish his real goal of stopping me from putting on my retreats. Then, just like he'd done with the writers, he'd arrange for the yarn retreat himself.

To counteract his implication, I put on my brightest smile and greeted the woman. "You can go now," I said to Kevin in a dismissive tone.

Of course, none of the subtext of our exchange registered with the woman, and I led the way across the large room. I couldn't even be upset with her for wanting to check in early, because the first thing she did was apologize for being any trouble.

"It's no problem checking you in now. But our first workshop isn't until this afternoon."

"Darlin', I don't care." She had a tremulous voice and an ample build that made me think of an opera singer. Though her hair was gray, she wore it in a long, loose style. Normally, I'd think that the days when that was a flattering look for her seemed long gone, but she somehow pulled it off. Just as she pulled off her face full of makeup, including eye shadow. She wore the makeup; it didn't wear her.

"My table is that one," I said, directing her away from the writers' setup.

"You just lead the way, hon, and I'll follow." She seemed a little breathless as she walked, which I thought might be due to her girth and the large canvas bag she carried, so I slowed my pace. "I don't know what I'd do without these." She pointed down at her light blue Crocs. "What they lose in style, they make up in comfort. I'm just so happy to be here," she said. When we reached the table, I slipped behind it and asked her name.

"Dolly Erickson," she said. She leaned forward and her yellow chiffon scarf brushed the table. She seemed to be trying to read my list upside down. I was surprised when she pointed out her name. She took the Yarn2Go tote bag and pulled out the papers inside.

"You'll see on the schedule that the first workshop starts at four," I said. She looked up with a blank expression until what I said registered. It was then that I saw she'd been look-ing at the map I'd enclosed. I began my spiel about lunch in the dining hall and the activities put on by Vista Del Mar. She had clearly been around long before cell phones and I figured the phone booths would be a fun trip down memory lane, but I went through it all anyway, pointing out the message board.

"How lovely," she said. "It's nice to be invisible for a while." Her comment confused me until she pulled out her cell phone and complained about how tired she was of walk-ing past a store only to have an ad pop up on her phone.

"I suppose you want to know about the program," I said, and she let out a hearty laugh.

"I'm sure it will be fine, whatever it is." She popped the phone back in her bag, and I saw she had a tote bag inside of it filled with yarn.

"What are you making?" I asked, indicating the yarn. She followed my gaze and pulled the bag toward her in a protective manner. "I just started on it. There's nothing to show yet." Then she seemed to realize she'd overreacted. "I might as well tell you. I'm not a very accomplished knitter, and I just started on a scarf. I hope you aren't offended, but it was the idea of a retreat in this lovely spot that appealed to me. And since your brochure said that you didn't need to know how to knit to attend, it sounded perfect for me."

I assured her that it was fine and told her, just as I had Lisa, that there would be plenty of help available during the workshops.

"That's wonderful news," she said with a bright smile. "And now I think I'll go to my room and get ready for lunch." She looked at a cluster of people near the other registration table, and I was about to explain who they were when she beat me to the punch. "So there's a writers' conference here, too."

"Oh, then you must have overheard them talking," I said, indicating the group nearby.

"Yes, I suppose I did, but in my own way. I read lips."

She assured me that she'd already secured her room and could manage just fine on her own. As she walked away, I thought how nice it would be if all my retreaters were as easy as she was.

I was about to leave my table when another woman approached and asked about signing in. It was obvious she'd seen that I'd checked Dolly in, so there was no way to put her off, or any real reason to, either.

I tried not to stare at her appearance, but it was hard. She wore a big hat that threw a shadow over her face, not that I could have seen much of it anyway, with the oversize sunglasses she wore. Her figure was hidden behind a billowy white long-sleeved blouse and a long kelly green skirt.

"Mona Riviera," she said when I asked her name. I wasn't sure if she had a naturally low voice or she was keeping it that way on purpose. I offered her a tote bag and started going through the spiel I'd given the others. Her face was so hidden I couldn't really tell if she was listening or not, particularly since she kept swiveling her head as if she was nervously looking for something or someone.

"If you're wondering," she said, gesturing toward her clothes, "I have a sun allergy."

What were you supposed to say after that? The best I could do was stutter out an "oh." I paused to make a transition and finally said, "Well, lunch is in the dining hall, and then you have free time until the workshop at four." I was easing myself away from the table, but she stopped me.

"I wonder if you could help me with my room," she said in a deep, breathy voice. I glanced toward the registration desk and saw that Kevin St. John was talking to the clerk. I might have still been in the dark about the program for the retreat, but I had made sure all the rooms were ready for my people and that all they had to do was give their names and they'd be given their keys. I considered telling her that, but I was getting the vibe that she was high maintenance and decided to simply do it for her.

"Of course," I said. She hung back and I went to the desk and gave her name to the clerk, glad that Kevin St. John was busy overseeing the rooms for the writers. The less contact I had with him, the better. I returned with her key and started to give her directions to the building her room was in, but then simply offered to escort her.

Was this a portent of things to come?

3

THE LUNCH BELL HAD STARTED TO RING AND A line was forming outside the dining hall when I finally got back to my place. I gladly forfeited the chance for a hot lunch for some time alone. Even though a hot lunch would have been nice. For all my baking, when it came to regular food, I was a dud and lived on frozen meals. Though there was an occasional plate of pasta from my neighbor down the street.

The sky was a brighter shade of white now that the sun above all those clouds was directly overhead. Normally I would have looked at this as the calm before the storm, but it seemed like the storm had already started. At least my kitchen was peaceful. Julius wasn't even hanging around— I figured he was off somewhere sleeping.

My concern about the new muffins was quickly fading

into the background as I focused on the retreat. I had never had so many people insisting on checking in early. It didn't really matter except that it made me feel out of control of my own business. I hoped as the day progressed and registration officially started, things would fall into place.

I made a last-minute decision to bring along a tin of cookies. Somehow that made me feel in control again. While the oven preheated, I lined two cookie sheets with parchment paper and took out several logs of butter cookie dough. I always kept some in the refrigerator so I could get a batch together at just a little more than a moment's notice. In an effort to add a little something extra, I shook on some chocolate sprinkles before I popped the sheets in the oven.

Within minutes the air was filled with the fragrance of buttery sweetness. While the cookies baked, I wolfed down a peanut butter sandwich. I had a tin ready and lined with a checkered napkin by the time the cookies came out of the oven. I'd let them cool on a rack for a few minutes, and then they'd be ready to be packed up.

In the meantime, I did a little freshening of my appearance. I tried to have a professional, put-together look at least for the beginning of the retreats. My clothing didn't vary much—it was more the kind of jeans I wore. Black ones were dressy as far as I was concerned. The constant cool weather made turtlenecks a perfect choice for a top. I let my hair loose from its scrunchie and gave it a good brushing. Makeup was some foundation, eyeliner and lipstick that wasn't too far from my natural lip color. I'd let my boss from the restaurant talk me into a bright red shade once, but when I'd seen my image in the mirror, I'd looked like a vampire.

The final touch was always some embellishment left by my aunt. She'd been an accomplished knitter and crocheter, and there was a basket in the room I used as an office filled with things she'd made for me to choose from. For today, I picked a cowl in shades of turquoise. I was ready to go back and face my crowd.

I had the cookie tin and was heading to the door when the phone rang. I knew who it was before the second ring, as a mechanical sounding voice announced that it was Dr. Feldstein. It could have been either of my parents, but I was sure it was my mother. I'd avoided her earlier call, but if I didn't pick up now, she'd freak and start calling around looking for me.

"Hello, Mother," I said when I grabbed the receiver. To think, not so many years ago, you had to answer the phone with no idea who was calling.

"Casey, I was worried. I called before and you didn't answer. It was too early for you to be busy with your retreat." She left the statement open-ended and clearly wanted me to tell her where I was without her asking.

"I didn't realize you paid such close attention to my schedule," I said. Usually, she conveniently forgot about the time difference between Cadbury and Chicago and called way too early in the morning.

"Of course I do. I was calling to wish you luck on the upcoming weekend. Is everything okay?"

I muttered a yes, not wanting to let on that I had been preoccupied with the new muffins. I hadn't shared that I was trying anything different. She'd launch into her offer for cooking school in Paris and how much more prepared I'd be to create something new if I had a certificate. Not that the offer to go to Paris wasn't tempting. But I had a history of not sticking with professions. Though after putting on a number of retreats and overcoming all the obstacles that came with them, I was beginning to believe that I might have broken the spell.

Maybe because my mother had certificates on her wall proclaiming her an MD—and a cardiologist at that—she believed I needed some kind of certificate to prove my expertise. The jury might be out on the new muffins, but my desserts were such a big hit at the Blue Door that people ordered them set aside before even choosing their main course because they ran out so quickly.

"So then, everything is okay?" she asked.

"Yes, everything is fine," I said in my best impression of a light tone. "I already had some early arrivals."

"Oh," she said with concern. "I hope you made them wait until you were ready for them."

I didn't want to admit the truth. Then she'd give me a lecture about being in control of the situation. It was complicated. I knew she was ultimately on my side, but she also wanted me to do things her way. I also knew it was absurd that at thirty-five, I was still battling with her over the direction of my life. Why couldn't we be two adults having a discussion in a nonemotional manner? I vowed not to react to what she'd said and changed the subject.

"Let me tell you about one of my retreat people. Maybe you can give me your professional opinion." I could picture my mother in one of her countless pants suits, wearing dangling earrings and sitting up straighter as I described what my last arrival was wearing and the reason she'd given. "Is being allergic to the sun a real thing?" I asked.

"I'm not a dermatologist, but you know I believe doctors should know about the whole body and not just their little corner of specialty. So, yes," my mother said, before going into how victims got rashes on exposed skin. "Was she completely covered?" my mother asked. I thought back to the hat, the blouse and the skirt. Just as I pictured the woman's hand as she took the tote bag, my mother asked if she was wearing gloves.

"No. I remember noticing her manicure as she picked up her tote bag."

"Was there a rash on her hand?" my mother asked, and I said no. "Well, then my opinion is that she is not really allergic to the sun. Was she asking for special treatment because of it?"

I thought it over and recalled how she'd asked me to check her in and how I'd escorted her to the building her room was in, things I didn't normally do. "Now that you mention it, she did."

"She could be one of those needy types. You've told me that some of the people who come to your retreats are looking for some kind of transformation. I'd recommend not giving in to her anymore." I was shocked at how this conversation had turned out. We were actually just two adults having a discussion. At least for the moment.

"You listened to what I said about the retreats," I said, unable to keep the surprise out of my voice.

"Of course I did, Casey. Just because I wish you were more settled doesn't mean I don't listen to what you have to say."

Here we go, I thought. *Settled* was code for "married," preferably to Sammy, whom both my parents loved. I should have let it go, but she'd hit my sensitive spot and I couldn't help but react. "I know what you're going to say next," and repeated what she usually said at the end of our phone conversations. "When you were my age, you were a wife, a mother and a doctor, and I'm what?" I shook my head at myself. Was I really saying it for her?

I heard her chuckle. "I guess you listen to me, too." She told me to let her know how things turned out with the woman in the big hat and hung up.

I tried to put the call out of my mind. I hoped my mother was wrong about Mona Riviera. Dealing with a woman with a sun allergy seemed easier than dealing with a woman making a fuss and looking for special treatment. I only hoped the rest of the retreaters would be easier. I grabbed my tin of cookies and went back to Vista Del Mar.

If I had thought the cavernous interior of the Lodge was busy before, it was nothing compared to now. I had to thread my way through the crowd, and the din of conversations seemed magnified by the high, open ceiling. A cluster of people were impatiently hanging around my table, looking down at the sign that said registration would start at one o'clock. Scott, Olivia and Bree came through the crowd and caught up with me.

"Wow," Bree said, looking around before I told her that most of the crowd belonged to the writers' conference.

"It certainly isn't a writers' *retreat*," Olivia said, pointing at her ear. When I'd first started putting on the yarn events, I had looked into what a retreat was supposed to be. It implied stepping away from the hustle and bustle of the everyday world to focus in on learning a skill or spending time reflecting. Basically it seemed to mean spending time someplace quiet.

As soon as we got to the table and were set up, the group formed a line. As I began to check people in, the early birds handed out the tote bags and made sure everyone had gotten their room.

I was besieged by problems. A woman with short knitting needles stuck in the bun on the top of her head had food allergies. A woman with a squeaky voice missed lunch and wanted to know where she could get food. The next two women had come together and they'd just seen their room.

"Are you kidding?" the smaller, dark-haired one said. I saw her name tag had *Rayanne* written in red ink. "There's no TV, no phone and the clock radio is like an antique. It's not even digital. And the beds." She threw up her hands. She had sharp features that reminded me of a ferret.

"More like cots," her friend interjected. Her name tag said *DeeDee*. "There has to be some kind of upgrade we can get." She was taller, with golden highlights in her hair, and appeared softer looking than her friend. When she talked I noticed she had dimples.

"Well, actually, no," I began. "The sparse accommodations are part of the charm of Vista Del Mar." I had a copy of the material I'd sent out describing the retreat, and it was very clear that the rooms were closer to a camp than a posh resort. I held it out to show them, but they ignored me.

"Part of the charm? Says who? This is not what we signed up for," Rayanne said.

"We're going to have rethink our plans." It sounded like

a threat to me, and I hesitated mentioning that Vista Del Mar was unplugged. But when I started to explain, it turned out someone else had told them. Surprisingly they were only mildly upset about that. The two women went off to the side, talking between themselves.

In the meantime, the new male retreater moved up to the table. I'd already seen his picture so I knew who he was—besides, other than Scott, there was only one man registered for the retreat. What a contrast to the mostly older women in the group! Jeff Hunter looked to be somewhere around my age. He wore faded jeans with a dark green pocket T-shirt under a battered-looking black leather jacket that had a bunch of zippers, most of which looked jammed. He didn't in any way resemble someone you'd think would knit. But he certainly wasn't shy about it. He had taken out his needles while he was standing around and was clicking away.

"I heard those two fussing," he said gesturing toward the last pair. "You better hope they leave. If they stay, they'll be nothing but trouble." His needles clicked on. "Not like me. I love the idea of kicking back and chilling with my knitting." Scott came up to him and gave him a high five.

"My sentiments exactly. I don't care about anything but relaxing and knitting," one of the other women said. I wanted to hug her. I was relieved when I checked in the rest of the retreaters without any more problems, though the whole group seemed to be hanging around the table.

Rayanne and DeeDee came back up to me. I'd already nicknamed them the Difficult Duo. "What's this arm knitting and finger crochet?" Rayanne asked in a defiant tone, her hand on her hip.

"Just like what it sounds like. You knit with your arms instead of needles and crochet by using your finger as a hook," I said, repeating what my helpers had told me. "You'll get a good idea of it at the first workshop this afternoon." I went on to explain that I had two experts who led the yarn part of the retreats. "Crystal and Wanda are wonderful. They have different points of view that balance everything out—"

"And we just heard someone saying that in the past not all your retreat people made it through the weekend," Rayanne said, interrupting. She turned to the group, who were now listening with interest. "As in they die before the weekend ends." I heard a collective sucking in of air move through them.

"Who said that?" I asked, wondering if the early birds had said something.

"He did. That man in the dark suit. He ought to know; he looks like an undertaker. Is that what he does? I mean, is he the local undertaker? And if he is, why is he here?" Rayanne demanded. Maybe she thought it was a rhetorical question because she continued without giving me a chance to answer.

"He was talking to that man over there," the dark-haired half of the Difficult Duo said. "Clear as anything I heard him talk about your first retreat and that someone had died during it and that you wouldn't be doing them much longer so there was no reason to include them in anything he wrote about Vista Del Mar."

"He's not an undertaker. He's the manager of Vista Del Mar, and the man he was talking to is a travel writer. They were probably discussing a piece about Vista Del Mar the man was going to write." I tried to leave it at that, but someone asked for details about the death. I was glad when Olivia stepped in.

"The three of us all attended that retreat, and I can assure you that it had nothing to do with Casey, other than she solved the whole thing."

There was another intake of air by the group. "How exciting! How did you know what to do?" asked a woman wearing a long purple T-shirt covered with pictures of cats playing with balls of yarn.

I wanted to downplay it, but I told them about my job working for a PI. I didn't mention that it had been a temp job that lasted only a couple of weeks. "I'm still in contact with the PI I worked for, and he helped me with the investigation." By then Bree had discovered the tin of cookies and was passing them out to the group, mentioning that I was a professional dessert chef as well.

Pretty soon they were all talking among themselves.

My stomach clenched. Maybe Jeff hoped the Difficult Duo would leave, but I didn't. They would insist on a refund, and I'd have to make up the money for their rooms. No way would Kevin St. John agree to give it to them. And it would be another black mark against me with him. No, it was better to deal with them.

"You said the workshop doesn't start until four; what's going on until then?" a woman with a nasally voice asked. She was overdressed in a navy blue suit and had bangs that were too short.

"It's your time to do whatever you want," I began. "There's a boardwalk that winds through the dunes." I pointed toward the window behind me, and they all stepped closer. Beyond the wooden deck and the area called the grass circle—because it was the only spot on Vista Del Mar that had actual green grass between the trees—the beginning of the dunes was visible. "The beach is just past there." I turned toward the other side of the Lodge. The window on the opposite wall overlooked the driveway where the airport van had let most of them off. From where we were standing, the stone pillars that marked the entrance to Vista Del Mar came into view. "If you'd like to leave the grounds, Cadbury has an interesting lighthouse."

I was about to give the directions when the woman wearing the cat T-shirt spoke up. "That lighthouse walk sounds great. When do we leave?"

Apparently, she hadn't understood that they were supposed to be on their own. "Whenever you like. That's the thing about free time."

"What?" one of the Difficult Duo said. "First you tell us the first workshop isn't for hours, and frankly you don't seem to have many details on it, and then you suggest we wander off to some lighthouse and probably not be able to find our way back. We expected planned activities." She left it at that, but it sounded like she was building a case to say I had deceived them about the retreat. I didn't want to give in to her, but I didn't want a problem, either, so I sucked it up.

"Of course I'd be happy to escort you all."

4

"THANK HEAVENS, A FRIENDLY FACE," I SAID. LUCINDA
Thornkill came through the side door of the Lodge as I was
about to lead the group outside.

"What did I miss?" she said in a concerned voice. "How
much trouble could there be already? You just opened registration a little while ago." She dropped her voice quickly,
realizing the group was right behind me. I urged her to drop
off her bag in her room as the rest of them had done and
join us. In the sign of a true friend, she didn't ask where we
were going before she agreed.

Lucinda was my friend and boss. She and her husband,
Tag, owned the Blue Door restaurant. Like the early birds,
she was a regular at my retreats. Even though she lived in
town, she always stayed at Vista Del Mar. It was her chance
to have a short getaway.

"Can you tell me now?" she asked as a few minutes later we led the group up the driveway toward the street. The early birds had seen the lighthouse enough times, so they had stayed behind, glad to sit in front of the fire and knit, which made me even more glad that Lucinda had arrived when she did. Keeping my voice barely above a whisper, I explained why I was leading a walk to the lighthouse.

"I've never had so many strange people come to a retreat. There were people who came too early, and then there's those two." I tried to gesture with my head toward the Difficult Duo, who were not far behind me. "They get the prize. So far they don't like anything."

"But they just got here," Lucinda said. "How much was there for them not to like?"

"My point exactly." I explained my concern about them deciding to leave and expecting a refund.

"I'm sure glad I didn't let Tag talk me out of coming," Lucinda said. "Not that he really had a chance. I can only take so much before I need to get away for a few days. He was nothing like this when we first met in high school." I knew what she was talking about. By the time she and Tag had reconnected, he'd become almost obsessive-compulsive, although he described it as keeping to standards. Countless times, I'd seen him walking around straightening the place settings at the Blue Door. As far as I was concerned, he should thank his lucky stars daily that he'd met up with Lucinda when he was a middle-aged widower and she was divorced. She kept him from going over the edge into full-blown obsessive-compulsive.

We'd reached the open area surrounding the lighthouse,

and the group spread out. The Cadbury lighthouse was different from the typical cylinder-shaped structures placed on the edge of the land. It was set back from the water and to me looked like somebody had taken one of those cylindrical lighthouses and stuck it through the roof of a regular house. But no matter how it looked, it apparently served its purpose very well. It was the oldest continuously operating lighthouse on the West Coast and had been placed on the northern tip, though not quite the edge, of the Monterey peninsula. Its job was to protect sailors who thought they'd reached Monterey Bay. The actual edge of the land was across the street. A bench sat there, near the cliff. Below, the waves crashed on the rocks.

The area around the lighthouse was parklike and a popular stop for both tourists and locals. The ground here was covered in short grass, and several Monterey cypress trees stood guard near the white wood-sided structure. The horizontal shape of the trees' foliage was even more extreme here than on the Vista Del Mar grounds, but then it was the wind that shaped them, and it was stronger here. I was at a loss as to what to do now that we'd gotten here. The retreaters were all adults and should be able to retrace their steps, but after the comment about getting lost, I figured I'd better hang out for a while.

I chose one of the benches along the edge of the grassy space that had a good view of the whole area, so my people could find me. I invited Lucinda to sit, but she was already pulling out her cell phone. I noticed she wasn't the only one. I think my group had started out with the idea of taking pictures and then noticed that they had a signal now that they were away from the dead zone around Vista Del Mar.

"This will just take a minute," she said. "I want to tell Tag where I went on the off chance he comes to Vista Del Mar looking for me." She put the phone to her ear and walked away.

With no sun to warm the air and the constant breeze, it was chilly, and I zipped up my aqua fleece jacket, glad that I'd added the cowl. As I looked over the area, I realized that I didn't know exactly who had come along. I recognized the travel writer by his khaki cargo pants and Windbreaker, which looked straight out of a catalog for easy-to-pack clothing, as he walked toward the lighthouse. He was definitely there on his own, no doubt getting information to include in an article.

I strained my eyes to make out the faces of Lisa and Derek on the bench on the other side of the grass. I was sure they'd come on their own, too. I watched them for a moment and noticed that Derek had binoculars around his neck. Dolly, the woman who reminded me of an opera singer, came across the grass. I waved to her, but she had her head down, probably because of the wind, and didn't see me. I would have remembered if she'd come with the group. She stood out as being the least problematic of the bunch.

The Difficult Duo was hanging out near the lighthouse with a small group around them. I was pretty sure that included everyone who'd been following me. It made me uneasy to see them clumped together that way. Was the Difficult Duo plotting some kind of mutiny?

I shivered as the wind ruffled my hair. How long did I have to stay there? My gaze went back to the bench at the cliff, which I always thought of as sitting at the end of the earth. The bench had a special meaning for me. Now there was something on the ground next to it, and I felt annoyed, thinking someone had been too lazy to throw their trash away. I considered getting up and doing it myself, but then I got distracted. Someone had come up behind the bench and put their hands on my shoulders.

"Thinking about that night, aren't you?" a male voice said. I recognized it as Dane Mangano's and blushed deeply, embarrassed that my thoughts were that transparent. All that had really happened was that I'd gotten lost in the moment and ended up in a very hot make-out session.

"I don't know what you're talking about," I said, trying to cover.

"I'm available for a repeat anytime you want," he said in his usual teasing tone. By now he'd walked around to the front of the bench and I saw that he was in his Cadbury PD uniform and therefore on duty. But his teasing smile was all after-hours. "What brings you to our illustrious landmark?" he asked.

Trying not to react too much to his presence, I told him about the latest group of retreaters, who were already giving me trouble. It was best that I looked away. Something happened when I looked at his face too long. The background fuzzed out and I felt some kind of magnetic pull toward him. So far, he didn't know about my reaction, and I wanted to keep it that way. He lived down the street from me and we'd been dancing around a relationship. He was all gung ho about going forward, but I was holding back. I still wasn't sure why, other than being concerned that it would be like a firework that burned hot—really hot—and then fizzled. Because of me, not him. And then we'd still live in the same small town where everybody loved him. And I could just imagine what everybody would think of me.

It didn't matter that I kept trying to keep him at arm's length, though—he never gave up. To steer the conversation away from romance, I mentioned the bag I'd noticed by the bench. "Maybe you could find out who did it and give them a ticket for littering."

"Huh? You're not exactly making any sense," he said. I realized it was a rather awkward segue and he didn't know what I was looking at.

"The bag of trash somebody left," I said. "Beside *the bench*." Shoot. I was upset with myself about how I'd said *the bench*. My voice had warbled. I didn't want to give away the heat I felt just thinking about that night.

The sound of barking interrupted us, and when I looked toward it, I saw a golden retriever had come out of nowhere and was jumping all over the couple on the bench across the grass.

"What trash?" he said, and I finally looked across the street. There was nothing.

"I guess somebody came and picked it up," I said.

"I got one of the new muffins this morning at Maggie's," Dane said.

"And?" I said, sitting up straighter. He was trying to get on my good side, but when it came to anything I made, I knew he would tell the truth.

"It was delicious, but . . ." He hesitated. "I know you're known around town for muffins, but I think you have to come up with something else to call them. How about Omelet in a Cup?" He saw my mouth slip into disappointment. "Aw, geez," he said, sounding frustrated. "Remember I said it was delicious?" He gave my shoulder a surreptitious squeeze. "C'mon, don't be mad at me."

"Of course not," I said. He had only given me his honest opinion, which was what I'd said I wanted. I chanced a glance up at his face, and he gave me that look: a little teasing wiggle of his eyebrows and a cocky smile. I felt myself getting sucked in and quickly turned my gaze to my group as they walked toward me.

"So that's them," he said. "You want me to go over there and arrest them for giving you a rough time?"

"Ha-ha," I said, getting up. "Thanks for the offer, but I'll manage."

"Well, then it's back to patrolling the mean streets of Cadbury. Look out, jaywalkers." He blew me a kiss and jogged back to the street.

"Boy, has he got it bad for you," Lucinda said when she returned from her phone call. I didn't have to comment because by then all my people had rejoined us and we started walking back.

Lucinda and I kept to the front again, and she told me about her phone call with her husband. "Tag is really getting nuts. You should have heard him," she said. "He kept saying that you don't know what's going to happen anywhere anymore. He's convinced there are things going on right in front

47

of us that we don't see because we don't know what we're looking at." She shook her head, as if to trying to make the words make sense.

I took a last look around the lighthouse. What if Tag was right and I had missed something? But what?

5

I HAD HOPED FOR SOME FREE TIME TO GO INTO the café and find out the fate of my muffins, but when we got back to Vista Del Mar, I had to go right to the meeting room I'd arranged for our workshops.

The buildings with guest rooms were spread all over the sloping grounds of Vista Del Mar, and the smaller single-story buildings with meeting rooms were sprinkled in between. The Cypress building had two meeting rooms. There was the one we were using and a much larger room on the other side. I read the sign on the door of the larger room and saw there was a travel-writing workshop starting earlier than ours.

A number of seats in the first couple of rows in the larger room were already full. The writers didn't realize I was there and were talking among themselves. All I heard were the words *kill* and *perfect crime*. Then I remembered they were all writers and shrugged it off.

As I backed away, I almost tripped over Madeleine Delacorte, who was reading the sign on the door.

"I didn't expect you after such a long trip," I said. "Jet lag and all."

"That's what Cora said. She's still in a snit that I went off on a trip alone. It's disturbing to her that I have a whole new life going. She can sit around the house and go to committee meetings, but I want to be where the action is." She did stifle a yawn before she continued. "I timed my trip so I'd be back for the retreat."

"Good." I hoped it sounded more enthusiastic than I felt. I had hoped she might skip the first workshop. Between my not being that familiar with the program and the few troublemaking retreaters, there were bound to be some kinks. I would have preferred to straighten things out before Madeleine joined us.

"Oh, there's Don," she said, seeing the travel writer coming up the path. He was surrounded by men and women with computer bags on their shoulders. They seemed anxious to get his attention. Most of them were carrying muslin totes that had been given out when they registered. I was surprised that Kevin St. John had left them plain instead of putting something about the writers' conference on them.

As the group filed past us, Don nodded in greeting to Madeleine and me. "So we meet again," he said with a friendly smile.

"It looks like we're workshop neighbors," I said, gesturing toward my half of the small building. Madeleine followed him as he stepped into our room and glanced around. Baskets of yarn were spread around the circle of chairs. But he seemed more interested in the fireplace, the window and the coffee and tea service, along with the tin of cookies I set on the counter.

"I think I like your room better than ours." He seemed to be joking, but Madeleine's face clouded and I knew she was thinking of what she'd said about making sure he was happy with Vista Del Mar. "I'm just kidding," he said when he saw Madeleine's expression. "This room is too cheerful and cozy. They'd be too busy looking out the window, helping themselves to drinks and admiring the fireplace. I need them all looking at me." He checked Madeleine's expression to make sure she got that he was being facetious. I'd grabbed the tin of cookies and offered it to him, saying they were my special recipe. He took two and immediately began to nibble on them. "Too bad you can't see it when my group is here. My yarn retreats are always filled with learning, friendship and fun." Had I really just said that? It sounded a little forced.

"Maybe later in the weekend. Particularly if there are more of these." He held up what was left of the cookies as he headed to the door. "My group awaits. I need to get in there. There's always lots of tension when they're going to share their work and get critiqued."

Madeleine hesitated for just a moment before following him. "Maybe I should see what a writers' workshop is like."

I couldn't have been more relieved at her decision. It wasn't that I didn't like Madeleine; it was just that she required extra care. I always worried that she wouldn't be pleased.

The room had been set up differently than usual. My yarn helpers had suggested that instead of the table we typically had, we'd just have a circle of chairs with tablet arms.

I walked around looking at the baskets of yarn. I picked up a skein of purple yarn. The label said *superbulky*. It was thicker than anything I'd ever used, but that was what Crystal had said we needed. There were balls of cotton yarn as well. I always felt keyed up at the beginning of a retreat, but this time it was even worse. I checked my watch and looked out the door to see if anyone was coming up the path leading to the building. Some late arrivals to the writers' workshop were rushing in, but that was it.

I glanced at my watch nervously. My two helpers, Crystal Smith and Wanda Krug, were supposed to meet me before the start of the workshop so we could go over the program before the workshop began, but I was the only one there. I looked out the window toward the path again, hoping I wouldn't see my people already on their way. I hadn't realized I was holding my breath until I let it out when I saw Crystal and Wanda approaching. It figured—they looked like they were arguing. At least none of the retreaters were around to hear them.

If I had deliberately tried to pick two more different people to work together as a team, I couldn't have come close to Crystal and Wanda. Crystal was all about bright colors and things that didn't match. As she approached I saw that she had layered a bunch of shirts in yellow, aqua and orange. The only pants she wore were jeans. She let her short black hair fall naturally into tight ringlets. I couldn't see her earrings or her socks, but I was betting neither were a matched pair. She was not into symmetry. She and her two kids had moved in with her mother when her rock-god husband had taken off with a younger woman. They ran Cadbury Yarn, though really it was her mother's store.

It still made me feel weird that I knew a secret about Crystal I couldn't tell her. I wondered how she would react if she knew that Madeleine and Cora Delacorte were really her great-aunts. But it was not my secret to reveal.

Wanda was close to her in age, but light-years away in style. When she wasn't helping with my yarn workshops, she was a golf pro at one of the posh Pebble Beach resorts. The blue slacks and floral print top she wore were a standard outfit for her when she was co-leading one of my workshops.

Their disagreement continued as they came into the room. "Maybe your plan will make for a memorable retreat, but you do realize there is good memorable and disaster memorable," Wanda said. She had one hand on her hip and the other one outstretched. Whenever she did that, all I could think of was the teapot song. She turned to me. "I want you to know that I will do whatever I can to help, but I'm going on record to say I was against the idea from the start."

"It'll be fine," Crystal said, sounding a little harried. "It's something different, and you said you wanted to broaden the appeal of the retreats. I'm telling you it will be a novelty to the people who already know how to knit and crochet and it will be a fun way to learn for the others."

Lucinda poked her head in. "Is it okay for people to come in?" I gathered she had heard a little of the exchange and was acting as a buffer. All I could think was how glad I was that Madeleine had chosen to go next door. Wanda's comments were making me very nervous. It wasn't the first time they hadn't agreed on the plan for the retreat program, but this sounded more serious. The last thing I wanted was for Madeleine to be there if there were problems.

"Sure, bring them in," I said with an air of confidence that I didn't feel. Lucinda started waving the group in. The Difficult Duo seemed subdued as they entered. Mona was still wearing her big hat and sunglasses. Dolly came after, with Lisa on her tail. Then the rest of the group trooped in, with Scott and Jeff at the end.

Lucinda took one look at my face and leaned close. "Don't worry. Everything will turn out okay, and one thing is for sure—the weekend will eventually end," she added with a chuckle. I wished I felt more comforted by her remark.

When they had all found seats and settled, I went to the front of the room. "I want to welcome you all to the yarn retreat. It's going to be a great weekend. You'll learn new skills and make new friends. And now let me turn things over to Crystal and Wanda. They are both wonders with yarn, and professional teachers." I just didn't mention that in Wanda's case the subject was golf.

Wanda stayed in the front only long enough to introduce herself before moving off to the side. "This is all Crystal's baby. I'm just here to help," she said. The subtext was clear to me. Doom was impending and it wasn't her fault.

Crystal seemed unconcerned with the comment and took over with confidence. Generally, the first workshop was all about everyone getting to know one another and talking about the plan for the weekend, but Crystal had a different idea. "Let's just dive right in," she said. "Everybody come and pick out your yarn." She indicated the bins of superbulky-weight yarn in assorted colors in the bins behind her.

When the retreaters all had their yarn and were seated again, Crystal started her demonstration of arm knitting. She walked around the group so everyone could watch. It looked a little odd at the beginning, when she put a slipknot on her right wrist and then did a long-tail cast on with the yarn draped over the fingers of her left hand. She was skilled at it, and in no time she had a bunch of stitches on her wrist. Then she showed the group how to actually knit, using her hand to make a loop and pull it through the stitches on her arm. She took her work apart and urged them to work along with her as she started all over again from the slipknot. But of course, they weren't as accomplished as she was and it was awkward. I kept retrieving errant skeins of yarn as they fell from the retreaters' laps, and there was a lot of grumbling. Loops were falling off arms and it seemed everyone was asking for help.

And then it got worse. I glanced toward the window and saw Kevin St. John drive up in his golf cart. He often made the rounds, checking in on the first meeting of group events to welcome everyone to Vista Del Mar. I dreaded having him walk in with yarn rolling all over and the participants looking like they were wearing yarn handcuffs.

But just as he stepped into the doorway, the woman in the big hat let out a shriek, got up and headed to the door. As she did, her feet caught on some of the yarn that had fallen on the floor and she pulled some of the skeins behind her as she ran out.

There was chaos as everyone tried to restrain his or her yarn. In the midst of it, Dolly yelled that her bag was missing. Maybe it was in the context of what was going on around her, but she sounded almost panicky.

"Is this it?" Lisa asked, pointing to a big canvas bag under one of the chairs. Dolly grabbed it and took it back to her seat. Did she honestly think somebody had tried to steal it?

"With everyone getting up and down and the yarn rolling around, someone probably kicked it there by mistake," I said, trying to smooth things over.

Kevin St. John stood near the doorway, rolling his eyes at everything going on, and then he turned to me before he left. "I see you have everything under control."

"WHAT AM I GOING TO DO?" I SAID, FLOPPING IN one of the empty chairs. It was just Lucinda and me in the meeting room now. Even with all the errant skeins caught and Dolly calmed down, Crystal couldn't get the group back on track. She'd tried to move things along by going right to a demonstration of finger crochet, but she'd lost control and it was like the inmates had taken over the asylum. The comments from the group were still resounding in my head. No one was impressed when Crystal explained that once they got the hang of it, they could turn out a scarf in one workshop. She'd held up a sample, and it looked loopy and ungainly.

"It seems stupid to use your finger when a crochet hook works so much better," Rayanne had said. Crystal's answer that it was different and fun had fallen on deaf ears.

"I don't see the point of either finger crochet or knitting with your arms," the woman with the knitting needles stuck in her hair had said. There had been some *yeah*s from the crowd. Crystal was tough, but she was beginning to crack. Wanda had seemed at a loss for what to say.

But then Lisa had made a remark that almost turned things around.

"I think arm knitting and finger crochet could be very useful," Lisa said. "What if you were on a desert island with no knitting needles and a bunch of yarn? You could make a canopy or a blanket and maybe save your life."

That's when I'd stepped in and suggested they all help themselves to refreshments. The workshop had ended with Crystal promising to show them how to use finger crochet to make friendship bracelets.

"What am I going to do?" I said, coming back to the present. "I'm sure everyone will remember this retreat. Crystal was at least right about that." Then I apologized to Lucinda for burdening her with my problems. "You're supposed to be enjoying the retreat like the rest of them." I found another skein of yarn that had come unraveled and started to rewind it. "I forgot about Mona. I wonder if I should go and look for her to make sure she's all right."

"I'll look in on her. Her room is next to mine." Lucinda got up. "And I have every confidence you will figure out how to fix things and make the retreat memorable in a good way." She gave me a quick hug and went out the door.

The room was very quiet after that, and I heard voices coming from outside.

"This would be the perfect place to set a murder," a man said. "It could take place at a writers' retreat. Fifty people check in and forty-nine check out." He said it in an Alfred Hitchcock impression.

"Yeah," his companion said. "The weather here is practically a character. I'd start it out with a line like, 'The fog slipped in and wrapped around the weather-beaten buildings, shrouding them in mist.'"

Writers, I thought, grabbing my bag and heading out the door.

THE GROUP CAME BACK TOGETHER FOR DINNER IN the Sea Foam dining hall. Lucinda and I grabbed three tables near the entrance. Crystal and Wanda had long since gone home, and no one brought up the workshop. Mona Riviera grabbed a seat in the shadows. When Lucinda had checked on her, she'd insisted she ran out because she was concerned that the sun was breaking through the clouds and might shine on her. It made no sense, but I had too many other things to worry about and let it go.

Kevin St. John made the rounds of all the tables. He had a smug smile when he got to ours. "I want to remind you all that for any of you looking for something to do this evening, there are games in the Lodge, a star hike through the dunes and we'll all be gathering around the fire circle for the Roast and Toast." Then, with a gesture toward the door, he said the Amazing Dr. Sammy would entertain them with his close-up magic.

Lucinda nudged me so hard that I almost fell out of my chair as Sammy came into the dining hall. At first I didn't get it. He was wearing his performance outfit—a tuxedo—and waving a greeting at the crowd. But then I saw Bridget come up next to him. She was wearing fishnet hose with spike heels and a very short glittery black dress. She didn't wait for Sammy to say anything but took a bow and said she was his assistant. All this since I'd seen them in the morning?

Normally, I would have made sure my people were okay with their evening activities, whether it be social knitting in the Lodge or the living room of the Sand and Sea building, where they were all staying, or any of the things that Kevin St. John had mentioned, and gone off to the Blue Door to make the desserts for the restaurant and bake muffins for the coffee spots. But this time I'd premade extra cheesecakes with cherry topping for the restaurant and had declared Friday a no-muffin day, so after a stop home to check on Julius and to call my helpers to set up a meeting first thing in the morning to do something about the program, I went back to Vista Del Mar to experience the Roast and Toast.

The plan was that after all the evening activities, everyone would gather outside at the fire circle to mark the beginning of the weekend's programs.

When I got back to Vista Del Mar, I joined the throng of people walking to the Roast and Toast. The outdoor lighting was minimal, making the whole area seem dark and mysterious. The fire circle was located on the edge of the grounds, near the dining hall. A low stone wall with glass on top ringed part of it to define the space and keep the constant breeze out. The actual fire pit was sunken in the center of the circle and surrounded by benches. The crowd was filling in quickly. It was hard to see who was who, but by the sheer number it seemed that everyone was there. By some miracle Lucinda found me and we sat together.

Although it was called the Roast and Toast, it appeared the toast was going to come first. Staff from the kitchen had brought out urns of hot chocolate, and the drinks were passed out.

Kevin St. John seemed to appear out of nowhere and stood near the fire pit. Between the darkness and his dark suit, it almost looked like he was just a floating head as he began to speak. His words were all about the writers' conference as he patted himself on the back for organizing it. "This ceremony is to mark the beginning of events at Vista Del Mar. First we toast; then you can roast marshmallows." He smiled and held up his cup of cocoa. "I know that we've actually already begun. I went around to the workshops today and I could see you writers were already having a wonderful experience."

As Kevin went on, I heard some sniggering behind me. "Obviously he missed the action at Don Porter's workshop," a man said.

"Yeah, I'd hardly call having someone storm out a 'wonderful experience,'" a woman said.

Lucinda nudged me and we traded glances—so our workshop wasn't the only one with problems. I hoped they'd say more, but then Kevin's toast ended and the two people behind us along with everyone else said, "Hear! Hear!" and then began to drink their hot chocolate.

I didn't stay for the marshmallow roast and wished Lucinda a good night. It was only as I walked away that I realized Kevin St. John hadn't even mentioned the yarn retreat.

6

IT WAS LIKE WALKING INTO A CLOUD WHEN I crossed the street to Vista Del Mar the next morning. White mist veiled everything, which made it look as if someone was trying to erase the dark brown buildings. Some stragglers passed me on their way to breakfast, but other than that the grounds were quiet. I caught a whiff of pancakes, bacon and coffee coming from the dining hall and I regretted that I was on my way to meet Crystal and Wanda instead of joining my group for a meal. But I was determined to fix the program before the next workshop.

How had I dropped the ball, or in this case the ball of yarn? I should have put off the muffin test, particularly since it had turned out the way it had. Then I would have realized Crystal's program had disaster written all over it.

The grounds were so empty that it was eerie as I walked to the meeting room, though the fog was beginning to melt. When I got to the Cypress building, the door to the larger room was shut. Crystal and Wanda were already in our part of the building, which I hoped was a good sign.

"I brought you a cappuccino from Maggie's," Crystal said when I walked in.

"Kiss up," Wanda said, rolling her eyes. Crystal ignored the comment and handed me the drink. I thanked her profusely since it was just what I needed.

"I'm sorry that the group didn't seem happy with arm knitting and finger crochet," she said. She had topped her jeans with a gauzy purple top and an orange shirt under it. She had a chunky black shawl wrapped around her to ward off the chilly morning. Her earrings almost matched—they were both hoops, though one was tiny and the other very large. I was still jealous of how she pulled off the heavy eye makeup. Whenever I tried it, I was always shocked at my reflection, sure that I looked like something out of a Tim Burton movie.

Wanda stood next to her, looking all the golf pro in navy slacks and a pale blue polo shirt.

"I could have told you that it wasn't going to work," Wanda said. She had her hand on her hip, and I know she didn't mean to be funny, but I couldn't help smiling as I thought of the teapot song again.

"Let's not waste time placing blame. Anyway, it's really my fault. I should have been paying more attention. The point is we need to figure out something different," I said.

"Lucky for you, I'm quick on the draw," Wanda said. "Right after I got off the phone with you last night, I came up with something."

Crystal tried to defend her plan. "I thought it would be neat that they could finish a number of projects while they were here, since some of them are newbie knitters and crocheters. I didn't expect they'd be so difficult."

I could tell by Wanda's expression that she was about to add a comment, and I was looking to fix the situation, not start a fuss. "Let's hear what Wanda came up with," I said.

Wanda stood up with her tote bag and took some finished knitted pieces out. "I call this Four for One," she said. "We'll have to make a few adjustments." When she explained the projects, I could see that they were all workable, and I felt the clench in my stomach start to relax, particularly when Crystal was agreeable. It also had the benefit that each person's project would be unique. Crystal always got upset at the idea of everyone making the same thing out of the same yarn.

"We can't use the yarn we have," Wanda said, pointing out that all we had was a bin of superbulky yarn and one of off-white cotton yarn. Crystal came up with a plan. We'd take the group to her family's yarn shop for the afternoon workshop. They could pick out the yarn they wanted and start on their projects.

"And this morning, I can hand out instruction sheets and show them their options," Wanda said.

"We'll have to let my mother know," Crystal said. The way she said it surprised me. She didn't say that *she* would tell her mother. Maybe because I didn't react right away, she figured I'd noticed something. "Do you think you could call her?" Crystal chewed on her lip. "The thing is, she wasn't so hot on the idea of the arm knitting and finger crochet, and I just can't face another 'I told you so.'" It was obvious the last part of what she said was aimed at Wanda.

"Fine," I said. "I have to go arrange for a bus anyway. I'll give Gwen a call at the same time." I got ready to leave the pair. "You two won't kill each other while I'm gone, will you?"

Wanda did her teapot pose. "Don't be ridiculous. We might disagree, but we're still friends."

Really? They could have fooled me. I took a last slug of the cappuccino and headed outside. The fog had gone completely now, and the air felt refreshing. Just as I passed the Sand and Sea building, a woman in a housekeeper's uniform came running out. As soon as she saw me, she started yelling.

"I have to get help." Her voice sounded panicky. "There's somebody in Sand and Sea . . ." Whatever she said after that, the wind carried away as she ran past me and down the path to the Lodge.

Sand and Sea was the building all my people were staying in, and I felt an immediate sense of worry as I dashed to the entrance. I rushed through the living room and into the hall where the guest rooms were. The housekeeper's cart was at the end, blocking one of the rooms. I pushed past it and went inside the open door.

My first impression was of a swirl of feathers. Then I saw the body crumpled on the floor. A pillow was nearby with a black hole in the middle of it. There was blood on the floor and on the person's hands, along with streaks of it on the wall and light switch. I stepped closer to see the face. I felt embarrassed at my relief when I saw it was a man and he was neither of my two male retreaters. And then I was horrified when I recognized Don Porter, the travel writer and Madeleine's newfound friend.

I knelt next to him and felt for a pulse on his neck, and then I shrank back. He felt cold and stiff.

"Casey?" Dane said in surprise as he came into the room. I barely noticed that he wasn't in uniform, but he had his gun drawn. "I was on my way in when I got the call. What's going on?" He looked down at the body. "One of your people?"

He didn't wait for an answer, but knelt down beside me and felt for a pulse. "I already did that," I said, the words sounding like a croak because my mouth was so dry. He had to have felt the same cold stiffness that I did, but he showed no reaction.

"He felt cold and stiff to you, right? Like he'd been gone for a while," I said in a slightly clearer voice.

"Yup," he said, looking away, and I realized it wasn't that he had no reaction—he just hid it well. "The paramedics are coming anyway."

Dane was helping me up when Kevin St. John and the housekeeper stopped in the doorway. The manager took one look at me. "Ms. Feldstein, what have you done now?"

Dane was all serious cop now. He ordered us out of there and told us to wait in the living room. As soon as we'd cleared the hall, he moved the housekeeper's cart so that it blocked the whole length of it.

The housekeeper flopped in one of the easy chairs and

seemed to be staring off into space. I was getting back to my usual self and wasted no time in setting Kevin St. John straight. "I haven't done anything," I said in reference to his comment. "Other than go in there to see if I could help." I looked him in the eye. "In case you're wondering, it looks like he was shot and somebody used a pillow to muffle the sound." There was a moment as he absorbed what I'd said. "That's all I have to say. This is all on you. Don Porter was part of your conference."

Two dark uniformed paramedics arrived at the door and I pointed them down the hall, but refrained from making any comment about the condition of Don.

Kevin's moon-shaped face wasn't placid now. In fact, he looked like he was crumbling as the identity of the victim sunk in. "What am I going to do? This is terrible." He was beginning to ramble now. "How am I going to fix the conference? He was supposed to do more workshops. What if they all demand refunds?" Then the manager crumpled even more. "This must sound terrible. Me going on about business when a man is lying in a pool of blood." He took a few quick glances around him to see who might be listening and seemed relieved it was still just the three of us and the housekeeper seemed zoned out, probably trying to process what she'd seen.

I still felt a little shaky, but I was definitely in better shape than he was. I'd never seen Kevin St. John like this. He went on about how this was the first conference he'd put together and it couldn't be a flop. "You seem to know how to take lemons and make lemonade, as that phrase goes," he said. "What should I do?"

Hmm, this was an interesting turn of events. I could have been a jerk and given him the cold shoulder. He certainly deserved it after the all the hassles he'd given me. But I saw no virtue in stooping to his level. It wasn't my style. And I was a little flattered that he thought I could save him.

"The first thing we have to do is take care of now." I looked at my watch. "People are going to start leaving the dining hall soon. Anybody staying in Sand and Sea is not going to be able to come into the building before the morning workshops. I would suggest that we keep everyone from going to their rooms, because it would be complicated to figure out who was staying where. Someone should stand outside the dining hall and make them take the path that doesn't go past the Sand and Sea building. Say something like there's been an incident." I paused for a moment to think. "And say that someone will come around to all the workshops and explain." I nodded at him and he got the message that the someone should be him.

He was listening attentively.

"About anyone asking for refunds. Figure out a way to make them happy." I thought of my retreat. "Think of an outing or some extra activities to make up for it."

Talking to him made me remember what I'd been on my way to do. He agreed to funnel everyone directly to the meeting rooms, and then I said I had to take care of something. We were both heading to the door when a bunch of uniforms came in. I was surprised because I hadn't heard any sirens. We pointed them back to the room where Don Porter's body had been found.

Dane caught up with us. Even out of uniform, he was

clearly acting like he was on duty. He threw me an apologetic glance. "Sorry to say this, but I need you all to stay put until Lieutenant Borgnine gets here."

Both Kevin and I reacted by shaking our heads. "I have this whole place to run and the writers' conference to worry about. The lieutenant will have to find me," Kevin said.

"And I've got my retreaters." Kevin St. John was out the door before I'd finished the sentence.

"Don't tell me you're going to pull the same thing," Dane said with a worried expression. Lieutenant Borgnine would probably be okay with looking for Kevin St. John. But having to find me was another story. The lieutenant and I had a history. I had solved a few murders and he'd never gotten over the fact that I'd been right and he'd been wrong.

I felt bad for Dane, knowing the lieutenant would blame him for my exit. The least I could do was explain. Once he heard that I was trying to save my retreat, he told me to go on and that he'd handle Borgnine.

"What's the worst he can do? Stick me on nights again? If he does, I'll be stopping by the Blue Door when you're baking again. Not the worst thing to happen." He gave my arm a squeeze.

Once I was outside, I jogged down the path, slipping past the two police cruisers and the paramedics rig. The heart of Vista Del Mar still seemed untouched by what had happened, and I was surprised to see a cab had pulled up next to the Lodge.

Gill was working behind the registration counter and looked up as the door opened. He was tall and lanky and wore wire-rimmed glasses that made him seem old-timey, though he was probably about my age. The cabbie was leaning on the counter and seemed irritated. "I have the order right here to pick somebody up for an airport run." The cabbie continued to grumble under his breath about losing business to Uber and Lyft.

"That's fine, but as you can see, there is no one here," the clerk said, gesturing toward the large empty room. "Do you have a name?"

The cabbie was getting incensed and held out his clipboard, tapping on the listing. "It says pickup, nine thirty. The order was put in yesterday afternoon." Gill repeated his request for a name, and the cabbie took out his cell phone and then started cursing under his breath about the lack of cell service. Gill pointed him toward the phone booths.

Gill turned to me. "Hey, Casey, what can I help you with?" He glanced toward the angry cabbie. "Sorry for making you wait." When the cabbie was all the way in the booth, Gill leaned closer and mentioned that the housekeeper had rushed in saying someone was sick.

"It's worse than that." I gave him the rundown.

"That explains why I saw our illustrious manager running down to Sea Foam." He shook his head with concern. "And I thought dealing with that cabbie was going to be the worst problem of the day."

"But no matter what the show must go on," I said. "Or in this case the retreats." I got to the point and told him what I needed. He offered to arrange for the bus and pushed the phone on the counter toward me so I could call Gwen about coming into Cadbury Yarn.

The cabbie came out of the phone booth and tried to slam the folding door, with no success. His mouth was an angry slash when he saw me using the house phone.

"You couldn't have offered me that courtesy?" he said, scowling at Gill. "The passenger's name is Don Porter."

7

"PLEASE, EVERYONE GO DIRECTLY TO YOUR MORNING workshops," Kevin St. John said as he came out of the Sea Foam dining hall, practically in slow motion. I could feel the crowd's impatience as they tried to get around him. I was watching the action from the deck on the side of the Lodge while I figured out my next move.

"I want to stop in my room first," a man in a gray sweatshirt said as he tried to squeeze around Kevin. The manager stuck out an arm to thwart his move.

"No," Kevin said, too quickly—it sounded panicky. He took a breath and tried to compose himself, then turned so he was speaking to everyone. "That's just not possible right now. There will be no stopping in any guest rooms before the workshops." His voice was slow and steady now and I could see that his smile was fake. A real smile was mouth and eyes—his was all mouth, and his eyes had a frantic expression.

"What's going on?" a woman carrying a computer bag asked. She had actually managed to get around Kevin. He sped up and got in front of her.

"Everything will be explained shortly. Now, if you will all stick to this path and go to your meeting rooms." He stepped aside and let the crowd begin to pass. He'd positioned himself so they couldn't divert to the path on the other side of the Lodge that passed directly in front of the Sand and Sea building.

I backtracked through the Lodge and came out on the driveway side, noting that the cab was gone. I took the path that Kevin St. John had ordered the guests not to use, hoping to get to our meeting room in time to give Wanda and Crystal a heads-up before the group arrived.

I had turned my jog into a run when an obstacle appeared in my way and I screeched to a halt. The obstacle was in the form of a man who looked like a bulldog and had the disposition to go with it. His salt-and-pepper hair was getting sparse, and it appeared he'd taken his clothing advice from Columbo. Only he wore a rumpled herringbone tweed sport jacket instead of a raincoat.

"Ms. Feldstein. I see you decided it was okay to leave the scene of a crime."

"Please don't blame Dane—I mean Officer Mangano. He did his best to keep us there."

There was a glint in the lieutenant's eye. "He's been duly dealt with." Borgnine put his hand on my arm, apparently thinking I might sprint off. He began to rub his temple with his free hand. Inwardly, I groaned. More than once I'd heard that dealing with me gave him an instant headache.

"If you could talk to me first, I really have to get somewhere."

He gave me a displeased look. "Justice is never in a hurry." He glanced around the area, and I noticed that there was yellow tape across the door of the Sand and Sea building. "I guess we can talk over here." He led me onto the small porch by the entrance.

I paid no attention to the surroundings—I was more concerned that he was still holding my arm.

"So tell me about your relationship with the victim," he said.

"Relationship with Don Porter?" I said, surprised. "I didn't know him. I barely even met him." I was measuring my words. My goal was to tell him as little as possible. "I just encountered the housekeeper calling for help. While she went to the Lodge to call 911, I went to the victim to see if I could do anything, and then Officer Mangano arrived."

"I know that you seem to have a talent for noticing things," he said. "What can you tell me about Don Porter?"

He had definitely caught me off guard. Had he almost given me a compliment on my investigative talents, or was this some kind of trick? Whatever. I didn't really care. I just wanted to be done with this conversation and get back to trying to salvage my retreat.

"He's a— I mean, he was a travel writer. He was in Peru just before he came here." I almost bit my tongue, afraid he'd ask how I knew that.

"What about your group of retreat people? Any of them know Mr. Porter?"

Oh, no, I thought, *he's going to want to question them all.* "I don't think any of them do," I said, "but how about you let me ask around. They'd be more likely to say something in passing to me, rather than feeling like they're being interrogated by one of your people."

He shook his head. "I don't think so. And no investigating on your own. We're done with that, right?"

"Believe me, I have enough stuff going on. I don't have any time to be doing your job." The words were out before I could stop them, and he glared at me.

"Doing my job? Ha! It was just beginner's luck that you found the killers a few times."

"How about five times, but who's counting?" I said.

"Didn't anyone tell you that it isn't good to gloat?" He scribbled something on his pad. "By the way, where were you last night?"

"Here. I went to the Roast and Toast." He seemed almost disappointed with my answer.

"So, then you're not claiming you were at the Blue Door baking?" I shook my head, and he made a *tsk* sound. I asked him what the problem was. "I didn't see any of your muffins at Maggie's this morning."

"I get it. You were hoping to catch me in a lie." I examined his face and saw that I was right. "I didn't know you were a fan. But actually there were some. My new Breakfast Delight muffins." The new name was impromptu, but I liked it. "You probably didn't see them because they were in the refrigerated section and they look a little different." And then as an afterthought I added, "And they aren't sweet."

"Oh, those," he said. "The wife had one. She said it was like breakfast in a paper cup. You're calling those muffins?"

"But did she like it?" I asked.

He waved his hands around, trying to make his comment vague. "Yeah, she did. I might have had one, too. Her idea."

"And?" I said, sounding more concerned than I would have liked.

"It was okay." He seemed to be avoiding talking about something and yet wanted to talk about it at the same time. "The wife has put the kibosh on me having apple fritters at the doughnut shop. She said those breakfast things of yours were what I should be eating instead. Too bad you can't make one with apples, and maybe a little brown sugar. My mornings get off on the wrong foot without that sweet apple taste." Then he put up his hands. "We're getting off the subject here. Anything else you want to tell me about the victim?"

I tried to think of something to add so he'd think I gave him something and let me go. All of a sudden it registered what had happened in the Lodge with the cabbie. Why would Don Porter have ordered a cab to take him to the airport when he had more workshops to do? Not only that, but it had been ordered in advance. I decided not to share that with Lieutenant Borgnine since it might seem like I was playing detective.

"Well, I did hear some people talking, saying this was a perfect spot for a murder," I said.

"Really, Ms. Feldstein? That's supposed to be helpful? They're a bunch of writers."

Kevin St. John rushed by on the path, and his gaze fell on me first. "I got them all to go to their workshops. Including your people. Now it's up to you to deal with them. Don't let them get hysterical and make a problem. There is still so much to take care of." He turned to the cop in the rumpled jacket. "Can you please move your vehicles so they're out of sight."

Lieutenant Borgnine had started massaging both temples now. "I give the orders around here."

WHEN I FINALLY GOT TO OUR MEETING ROOM, THE retreaters were already there. Wanda and Crystal were at the front of the room and had begun the workshop. I tried to stay in the background as Wanda talked. But even so I saw Lucinda look at me and put up her hands as if to say, "What's going on?"

"I know we have all different skill levels of knitters here. And there are some of you who have never picked up a pair of needles or a hook before you came here, so we came up with something that would work for all of you." Wanda started to take the finished pieces out of her tote and set them on the tablet arms of a couple of empty chairs, draping the rest over the backs of the chairs. "I call this Four for One." She held up two small squares. "This one is knit and this one is crochet," she said. "All four of the projects are based on the same idea. They aren't very glamorous, but they're great first projects when you're just learning and fun projects when you already know the ropes."

She took out a pair of knitting needles, demonstrated

casting on four stitches and then knit the first row. "This is where it gets interesting." She knit two stitches and looped the yarn over the needle before knitting the other two stitches. She quickly did a few more rows, repeating the pattern of stitches, and then held the sample up. It was a tiny triangle. "If you want to make a square project, at a certain point you start decreasing a stitch per row." She grabbed a small blue square off the adjacent chair and held it up, explaining that it was a knitted washcloth and a bigger version could be a baby blanket. Then she showed off two triangles and modeled the smaller one as a head scarf and the larger one as a small shawl. "This is the same pattern as the square but you only increase the stitches."

"And now for the crochet version," Crystal said, stepping in. She took out a crochet hook and another skein of the cotton yarn. The technique was a little different, but the idea was the same—the triangle was made by increasing stitches, and it was turned into a square by decreasing stitches.

Crystal couldn't contain herself and added, "In case you're concerned, you won't end up with cookie-cutter projects. You'll pick out what you want to make, the yarn you want to use and the size hook or needles. So whatever you choose to make, it will be unique. For the more advanced, we can show you how to add edging or beads. Of course, we'll help anyone who needs it."

This was where I stepped in. "This afternoon I've arranged for us to go into the main part of Cadbury for an event at Cadbury Yarn." I was going to talk the outing up more, but it seemed as if once I was in front of the group, everyone remembered they'd been herded to the meeting room with no explanation. Questions about what was going on came from all over the room.

"They were all asking about it when they came in," Wanda said, dropping her voice to keep it just between the two of us. "We didn't know what to say or how to explain why the room wasn't set up." There had been so much to deal with that I hadn't noticed that the fireplace hadn't been lit and the coffee and tea service hadn't been brought in.

I saw Madeleine peeking in the door. I didn't want her to hear about Don in the group. "I'll explain everything in a minute," I said to the retreaters. "In the meantime, Crystal can tell you about everything that will be happening at Cadbury Yarn." I stepped aside quickly and Crystal launched into a pitch about what would be available at the yarn shop.

Madeleine was still in the doorway, and I looped my arm with hers and took her outside. I saw that her golf cart was parked on the path and realized that if Lieutenant Borgnine had done as Kevin St. John had asked and moved the police cars so that they were hidden from sight, she probably had no inkling that anything had happened. The paramedics had no doubt left a long time ago when they realized their services couldn't help the victim.

"I'm so sorry for being late," she said. "I hope you can fill me in on what I missed. I never did see what the program was this time," she said, prattling on. I waited for her to finish. It wasn't just my being polite—I was stalling, not knowing how to tell her about her new friend.

"Maybe you better sit down," I said, indicating a bench

outside the Cypress building. My expression must have revealed that I wasn't just trying to make her comfortable, because suddenly her face clouded.

"Oh, dear. That's not a good sign." She sat and gripped the armrest.

"There's been an incident. The police are here investigating it now," I began. I wanted to somehow soften the blow, but I wasn't sure how to do it, and I had a room full of people waiting for an explanation. "It's Don Porter," I said, and she gasped.

"What? Did he get hurt? He's not—" She stopped as if she couldn't bear to say the word *dead*.

I nodded sadly. "I'm sorry to say he is."

"A heart attack?" she said, almost hopefully.

"No. It appears that he was shot." It was a little blunt, but no matter how I tried to sugarcoat it, we were still going to end up at the same place. Her immediate thought was suicide, but I shook my head. I explained that he'd been shot in the chest.

"But who would do that?" Then she began to get unraveled. "Have you talked to the police?"

"Yes, I spoke with Lieutenant Borgnine a little while ago." I heard her suck in her breath with such force it made an eerie sound in her throat.

"You didn't tell him that I knew Don Porter, did you?"

"I didn't tell him much of anything, and I didn't mention you at all."

"Thank heavens," she said, slumping forward. "You can't say anything to any of the police. They can't know I have any connection with him. Then there will be no reason for them to want to speak to me or think of me as a suspect."

Her response surprised me, to say the least. "Why all the secrecy?" I asked.

"No one can know that I took up with him on the plane. I'd never hear the end of it from my sister if she knew I'd been talking to a stranger on a plane and then he ended up dead. She's already saying she thinks I've lost it. If she thought I was a suspect or even being questioned by Lieutenant Borgnine, who knows what she would do."

Madeleine seemed to have forgotten that she was the older sister, and besides, at seventy-something she shouldn't have to be answering to anybody, anyway. But I didn't feel it was my place to bring it up.

She grabbed my arm. "Please, Casey, you have to do something. This has to be wrapped up quickly. The longer the investigation goes on, the more chance somebody will put me together with him. Can't you use your detective skills to figure it out?"

I promised I would do the best I could, which seemed to cheer her up. Even so, she was worried about staying at the workshop. I told her about the afternoon trip, and she said she would catch up with the group there. Then she headed back to her golf cart and I went inside to face the group.

"I'm sure you all noticed that you might have not been able to get back to your rooms after breakfast."

"Might not be able to," Rayanne said, repeating my words. "That's an understatement. We were told we could not go to our rooms. Not that I was that anxious to go back to our little cell," she said, "but we did pay to have access to it for the entire weekend. What happened, some kind of plumbing issue?"

There was more grumbling as I tried to continue. Lucinda

and the early birds tried to calm the group, now that Rayanne had managed to stir everyone up. It didn't help that DeeDee kept nodding along with what her friend said. They really did deserve the moniker of Difficult Duo. That was it—I wasn't going to skirt around the issue or soften it. I would do it like taking off an adhesive bandage—quick, to get it over with.

"There's been an incident. One of the workshop leaders from the writers' conference here this weekend died. Well, more accurately, he appears to have been killed." As I was talking I was trying to think of something reassuring to say. The best I could do was to tell them that most murders happened between people who knew each other. "So, I really don't think you need to be concerned that there is a killer on the loose."

"Where did it happen?" Rayanne demanded.

I tried to ignore her interruption and spoke to all of them. "Don Porter's room was on the first floor of the Sand and Sea building." When I finished, a roar erupted as it became clear that the crime scene was near where they were all staying. The atmosphere was an odd mixture of excitement at being close to where something happened and dread about the same thing.

I saw the Difficult Duo talking to each other. They seemed to have come to some kind of decision, and I was pretty sure I knew what it was, since they'd been threatening it since they'd arrived. This, they would say, was the final straw.

I looked over the crowd, as if not speaking to anyone in particular. "Just a little reminder if all this has spooked you and you want to leave. The cops will probably insist everyone stay put. But even if they don't, I'm sure they would view it with a suspicious eye if anyone was in a hurry to leave."

"Then we're stuck here," the woman in the cat T-shirt said. She'd changed shirts, and this one had a big cat face on the front of it and the cat's backside on the back of the shirt. "And no cell service. We can't even call for help. Was he just the first? Are we going to start disappearing one at a time?" she said.

"Don't be silly. That's the plot from an Agatha Christie novel," Dolly said. "We're not stuck on an island the way they were." She looked around at the group. "Did anyone else but me notice that while the bodies stacked up in that book and were left to stay where they died, Agatha never brought up the stench they would have created?"

Crystal came up next to me and got their attention. "We can't start on the Four for One until this afternoon, but we can make the finger crochet friendship bracelets I promised." She was smiling, but I could tell she was upset that her plan for the weekend was getting dumped.

"Sure," I said, glad to step aside. She quickly circulated around the room, handing out small skeins of the off-white cotton yarn. She did a bit of a pep talk, assuring the retreaters that finger crochet was easier than arm knitting. "I had planned to demonstrate a number of different crochet stitches using your finger as a hook, but I understand that we need to move on, so I settled on just the one needed for the friendship bracelet." She put a handful of wooden beads in piles on the counter where the coffee and tea would have been and told them all to choose two and hang on to them. Next to the beads, she put out a bunch of small pieces of wire folded in half, explaining that the wire would be used to put the beads on the yarn.

There were no grumbles this time, probably because the retreaters were happier working with yarn than dealing with the fact that there'd been a murder. Trying to show solidarity, I joined in and pulled out a length of the yarn as Crystal told the group to make a slipknot, leaving a long tail. Wanda demonstrated Crystal's instructions and then moved around the group so everyone could get a closer look.

No one had a problem this time, and I heard several people exclaim how much less clumsy it was than the arm knitting. Crystal showed the group how to fasten off the yarn, leaving a long tail. She had them tie the ends together and use a piece of wire to slip on the beads. They added a couple of knots on each strand and they were done. Then they all slipped the finished project on their arms.

"That was great, hon," Dolly said as she admired the bracelet on her arm. The others all agreed, including Scott and Jeff, and Crystal's face blossomed into a smile before she turned to me.

"At least the finger crochet wasn't a total disaster," she said.

I smiled and nodded. Best of all, it had gotten their minds off of murder—for a moment at least.

8

I'D MANAGED TO KEEP THE WORKSHOP GOING ALL
the way to noon. When the bell for lunch started to ring, I
guided the group back to the Sea Foam dining hall on the
path that didn't go past the Sand and Sea building.

Lucinda caught up with me. First she whispered that I'd
done a good job breaking the news to the group, and then
she complimented me on the new plan for the retreat. "I'm
looking forward to the outing to Cadbury Yarn, and I live
in Cadbury," she said with a laugh.

The dining hall was built in the Arts and Crafts style, and
the dark wood might have looked forbidding, but there were
many large windows that brightened the space. I stopped
when we got to the entrance. "Aren't you joining us?" Lucinda asked. I would have loved a hot lunch since my breakfast had been just the cappuccino that Crystal had brought

me as a peace offering, but I had things to take care of. As soon as I told her I wasn't, she offered to act as host.

"Between the early birds and me, we'll make sure Rayanne doesn't stir up any more trouble. You really shut her down before. I think she was all set to announce that she and DeeDee were going to leave until you mentioned how the cops would feel about it."

"I hope she dropped any plans of asking for a refund at the same time." I looked back at the pair we were talking about and saw they had their heads together.

"I'm sure they're just talking about lunch," Lucinda said. I gave her a thank-you hug and let her lead the group inside.

As I went across the street, I couldn't believe how much had happened since I'd traveled in the other direction that morning. I would have been celebrating the saving of the retreat, if only Don Porter hadn't been found dead in his room. I thought of the promise I'd made Madeleine. Well, it wasn't exactly a promise. I think I'd said I would do the best I could, but it didn't matter. I knew she was depending on me to come through.

And all because she was worried about what her sister would say if Cora found out she had talked to a fellow traveler. I was certainly glad no one had that kind of hold on me. Okay, maybe I did still care what my mother said, but I hadn't let it stop me from living as I chose.

Julius met me at the beginning of the driveway and followed me all the way into the kitchen. I really wished he could talk, so I could find out what he'd been up to while I was gone. It made me nervous to let him come and go as he pleased, but he'd taught me from the start that he had to have his freedom.

He was busy checking out a fly that had come in with us, and I doled out a dab of stink fish before he could even let out a meow to let me know he wanted some. All that unwrapping and wrapping up again was a two-handed job, and I waited until the package was stowed in the refrigerator before I grabbed my cordless phone and punched in a number. The ringing seemed to go on forever, and I expected the call to go to voice mail. I had my mouth open to leave a message when someone finally answered.

"Feldstein," Frank said. There was no way his voice mail was so sophisticated that it would know who the caller was, so I realized I'd reached my former PI boss in person. I couldn't see him, but I knew by his tone of voice that he was probably shaking his head. "I told you, you got to make it so your name doesn't show up when you call. Be anonymous whenever you can." It sounded like he took a sip of something. "I haven't heard from you in a while. What's up?"

"Before you say anything, I'm not asking for help. I just want to discuss something with you," I said. I really did want his help, or his advice, anyway, but saying I wanted to discuss something sounded better and more like we were on an equal footing.

"Feldstein, do I take that to mean there's been another death? I'm telling you, one of these days those people are going to realize there's a connection between your arrival in that town and the uptick in people dying. You better give me the details before we *discuss*."

I should have known he would see right through me. I could just picture him in his office chair. It was one of those big leather things that moved back when you pushed on it. I could hear the chair complaining as Frank no doubt tried to push farther than the chair was meant to go. I always thought one day the chair would revolt and somehow catapult him out of it. Of course, I kept that thought to myself.

"It wasn't one of my people," I said. I proceeded to explain who Don Porter was and that I really didn't know him.

"If he's not one of your people and you barely know him, why would you get yourself in the middle of the investigation?" he said. "I'm telling you, Feldstein, you have to stop looking for trouble."

"I'm trying to keep myself out of it," I began. Even though I'd mentioned that Madeleine Delacorte was like the local royalty and along with her sister owned Vista Del Mar and a lot of Cadbury, I explained it again anyway. Frank always hammered me with the fact that he wasn't involved enough with my life to remember who all the players were. "She asked me to look into it and hopefully take care of it quickly. She met the guy on the plane, while both of them were coming back from Peru. She's trying to keep herself from being questioned by the cops."

"I suppose you're going to tell me why," he said. I heard the rustle of paper and a chewing noise and I figured he was having a late lunch. Frank loved his sub sandwiches.

It sounded so silly when I said it now. "She's afraid her sister will find out that she was talking to strange men on the plane. I don't know why Madeleine should care. She's the older of the two. Anyway, she pleaded with me not to mention to the cops that she knew the dead guy. And she asked me to find out who killed him, quickly, so there was no chance she'd get connected to him."

"That sounds suspicious to me."

"If you ever came for a visit and met her, you'd realize it wasn't so strange."

"Okay, then. How was the guy offed?"

"I'm pretty sure he was shot and somebody tried to keep it quiet by shooting through a pillow." I mentioned that I'd seen it firsthand.

"It must have been a mess. That pillow business doesn't work. It just makes an explosion of feathers. Did anybody report hearing the noise?"

"Not that I know of. He'd been gone for a while when I saw him." I explained that he'd felt cold and stiff.

"It sounds like he bought it sometime the night before. The cops will close in on that. As for what you can do—I'm assuming you know the first order of business is to figure out what you know about the guy and who would have it in for him. Then you gather your suspects and figure out who has an alibi and who doesn't. That should be simple enough."

"Easy for you to say," I said with a sigh. "Right now, I know that he was a travel writer and traveled all over the world."

"I get it. He's been everywhere. So what brought him to the edge of the Monterey peninsula and a town that makes me think of chocolate?"

"Oh, I forgot to mention there's another retreat going on here, much bigger than mine, for writers. He was one of the presenters. He was supposed to do several workshops, though he only did the first one."

"Any idea what happened during it?"

I shook my head even though he couldn't see me doing it. "I was having enough trouble with my workshop. The only thing I remember was that some people coming out were talking about writing something for a mystery weekend at Vista Del Mar. You've heard about those. They usually take place in the past and everyone dresses up in costumes and is given a part to play. There's a murder and the group has to figure out which one was cast as the killer. It's kind of like an interactive game of Clue." I paused for a moment, realizing I'd gotten the writers mixed up. "Wrong writers. I think the ones coming out of the workshop were just talking about setting a murder at Vista Del Mar."

I heard Frank chortle. "It sounds like a bunch of crazy writers."

"Yeah, but aren't writers always saying that they should write about what they know? Maybe they took it too far."

"An interesting idea," he said. "My advice is to talk to the writers and find out what they have to say about him. And ask them what went on during that workshop." There was more squeaking of the chair, and by the change in his voice I could tell he was sitting up straight. "Got to go. Client just walked in."

So I was left to try to figure out how to get the writers to talk to me. I thought over what connections I had. There was Lisa. Her husband was signed up for the writers' conference. I could ask her if he was interested in travel writing and go from there. But then I remembered that I had my own retreat to keep going. I called Gwen to reconfirm everything and then went to get ready for the afternoon.

9

"I HOPE YOU DON'T MIND, BUT I DID A LITTLE detecting on my own at lunch," Lucinda said. It was just the two of us, standing in the driveway by the Lodge, waiting for the bus I'd ordered for the outing. She said she'd told the group to wait inside.

"You didn't have to do that, but since you did, what did you find out?" I said.

Lucinda straightened the Burberry plaid scarf she had around her neck. "Usually at the beginning of your retreat everybody introduces themselves and tells something about who they are, but this time with all the fuss with the yarn rolling around, it never happened. So, I sort of did it with the people at my table." She leaned in closer to keep what she said just between the two of us. "There's something up with Lisa. You know how she's here with her husband, even though they're going to separate activities?" Lucinda waited until I acknowledged that before she continued. "He sat with us at lunch, but when Dolly wanted to take a photo of everyone at the table with her phone, both Lisa and Derek started acting kind of weird. Like maybe they didn't want to be seen together."

"I can't believe you said that," I began. Then I told her my theory that they might be married, but just not to each other.

"And maybe they come here every year and take part in whatever is going on here as an excuse to their spouses, kind of like that movie *Same Time, Next Year.*" Lucinda checked that we were still alone. "I found out that Jeff is a long-distance trucker, divorced with a daughter that lives with his wife, and that he started knitting as a way to keep his hands busy on the road when he was quitting smoking."

"What about our friend with the big hat, Mona?" I suddenly remembered that Lucinda had said she was going to see if anything was wrong with our overly clothed retreater after she'd run out of the room during our first workshop.

"She claimed she'd left in a hurry because she remembered she had to make a phone call." Lucinda considered it for a moment. "I suppose it could be true; it just doesn't feel like it is." The bus was just coming down the street and Lucinda glanced over my outfit. "You might want to do a little straightening."

I looked down at my outfit and understood what she meant. There was no way I would ever look as put together as she did, with the Burberry plaid scarf that blended perfectly with the red in her sweater and the khaki in her Ralph

Lauren slacks. Her lipstick was perfectly applied in a red that was just bright enough. In contrast, the taupe turtleneck I'd thrown on in the morning had gotten untucked from my black jeans. The lighter taupe cowl I'd gotten from my aunt's collection was askew. And I could only imagine what the breeze had done to my hair. I'd been too intent on talking to Frank and thinking how I was going to find out what happened to Don to remember to check my appearance.

I must have seemed at a loss for what to do because Lucinda asked if I wanted her help. She was amazing. I did the tucking of my shirt and the unskewing of the cowl, while she fixed my hair and produced a mirror for me to look at while I put on some lipstick.

Her final touch was to turn up the collar on my black fleece jacket that looked like a shirt. By the time I sent her to retrieve the group, I felt like I'd had a makeover.

I waved to the driver and he opened the door. "They're all just coming," I said.

Lucinda returned and, before she got on the bus, said she'd save the seat in the front for us. Scott and Jeff were right behind her. They seemed to have bonded, which made sense since they were the only two men at the retreat.

"The others are right behind us," Scott said. They got on the bus as more of my group came outside. Since I didn't trust my memory, I had a clipboard with the registration list and checked the names as everyone got on.

"That's it," I said to the driver as I boarded and she shut the door behind me. "We're off to a great afternoon," I said, speaking to the group before I slid onto the seat next to Lucinda. The bus went forward a couple of yards and then screeched to a stop. I looked up and saw Lieutenant Borgnine standing in front of the bus with his hand up in the universal signal for *stop*.

The driver opened the door as I stood up, and I motioned for her to close it as soon as I stepped on the ground. "What's going on?" I demanded when I reached the rumpled cop. His mouth was set with annoyance, and I did my best to block the retreaters' view of him.

"I could ask you the same thing. Who said you could leave? I need to get statements from everyone."

It had taken a while for me to understand what my responsibility was in putting on the retreats. I'd put only one foot in at first, not sure if I was going to split and run, but now my feelings had changed. These were my people and I was going to take care of them. I had gotten Wanda and Crystal to handle the yarn part. Vista Del Mar provided the rooms, meals and some activities. But it was up to me to take care of the group. It was up to me to get the program changed when it turned out to be a mess, and it was up to me to make it all right when they were being kept from their rooms while a murder investigation went on. I glared at Lieutenant Borgnine. "I am simply taking my group into town so they can continue with their retreat activities. I will bring all of them back later and you can talk to them then."

He didn't look happy. "You know I could take you all into custody," he said, trying to hang on to his authority.

"But you're not going to do that, are you? They're just a bunch of people who want to spend the afternoon working with yarn. Can you imagine how they'd react if I told them you canceled our trip and you were going to keep them locked up somewhere until you talked to them? How helpful do you think they would be, anyway? Do you think there's a chance they would be cooperative?"

I watched as his eyes went skyward and his head rocked from side to side in distress. He knew what I said was right. He didn't say anything for a few moments, and I was sure he was trying to come up with a way to save face. "I suppose it is a way to keep you from mucking around in my investigation for a few hours." I was still holding the clipboard, and he stepped forward and counted the names. "I am holding you personally responsible to come back with the same number you left with," he said finally.

"Deal." I put out my hand to shake on it, but he was having none of that and turned to walk back to the Lodge. When he was inside the building, I got back on the bus and the driver shut the door behind me. Lucinda looked up at me, giving me a tiny round of applause.

"Well done." She patted the seat next to her. I was about to sit down when I recognized Dolly's tremulous voice.

"What was that about?" Dolly asked. I turned toward the group, realizing I ought to explain. Maybe it wasn't the worst thing to let them know that the cops would want to talk to them. I could do kind of a cat's-on-the-roof thing, so it wouldn't come as a complete shock.

"As I mentioned before, after what happened, the police are going to want to get a statement from each of you. It's not that they think you are suspects, but they'll want to know if you saw or heard anything."

It sounded like all of them sucked in their breath at once, and I tried to reassure them that no one was going to take them into a locked room, like they did on some TV shows.

"That happened to me once," Jeff Hunter said. I was still getting used to him as a knitter. Scott, with his preppy look, had been a little easier to accept. Jeff just seemed so rough around the edges, but now that I understood there was a purpose to why he'd learned to knit, it made more sense. "There was a robbery at a truck stop. I was in the john doing a cleanup on myself when it went down. The cops were all over me, asking what I saw. And Casey is right. They didn't take me in a room and shine a light in my face."

I thanked him for his input and was about to tell the driver we were good to go when Madeleine's golf cart roared into the small parking lot adjacent to the driveway, as much as a golf cart could roar. She quickly saw that we were all on the bus and as soon as she'd parked the golf cart rushed up and knocked on the door before I had a chance to tell the driver to open it.

"That's it. Next stop, downtown Cadbury," I said as soon as Madeleine had sat down in the seat next to Dolly.

The group erupted into upbeat-sounding chatter and I didn't think they noticed the cop cars partially hidden by the bushes. The ride to downtown Cadbury took less time than the fuss to get going had taken. The bus pulled into a spot on Grand Street, which was the main thoroughfare in Cadbury. Before everyone got off, I told them the plan. We'd go to Cadbury Yarn first, and then they'd have time to look around town. I'd promised to bring them all back to Vista Del Mar, but I hadn't said when. And since they were still locked out of their rooms, the longer we stayed away, the better.

"This way," I said, feeling very much in charge for once as I led the way to the side street that sloped down to the water.

Cadbury Yarn was located in a bungalow-style house. A rainbow-colored windsock hung on the front porch and flapped in the constant breeze. I brought everyone into what had once been used as a living room. When I looked back, I saw that Mona had stayed on the front porch. It was easy to know it was her, since there was no one else in the group wearing a big hat. I slipped outside to bring her in. She seemed to be just standing, gazing at the street. It wasn't like she was looking for something in particular, more like she was taking it all in. I noticed her shoulders rise and then fall, like she was sighing.

"Is something wrong?" I said. Mona turned to face me, but it was impossible to read her expression with the big shadow the hat made. Sunglasses covered any feelings that might have shown in her eyes. She shook her head, or at least I thought she did, because the hat shimmied a few times. Then she turned and followed me inside.

Gwen Selwyn, owner of Cadbury Yarn and Crystal's mother, was in the process of greeting the group. I noticed that Mona had moved to the far corner. All I could do was shrug it off. I'd tried to see if she had a problem. What else could I do?

I don't think anyone would have picked Gwen out as Crystal's mother. There were none of the wild outfits and unmatched everything. I was sure she'd made the nubby toast-colored cardigan she wore over pants in a darker shade of brown. Her hair was cut short in what I called a shower-and-shake-in-place style, and any color in her complexion was completely natural. She caught my eye and gave me a friendly smile.

I mouthed a thank-you and, holding my palms together, made a minibow with my head in gratitude to her for pulling this event together so quickly.

It was so strange that only the two of us knew the truth of who Gwen really was. Well, unless you counted Frank. I'd discussed the situation with him a number of times, asking his advice. It had always been the same: stay out of it.

I hadn't followed his suggestion. Once I'd come across the evidence that Gwen Selwyn was really the love child of Madeleine and Cora Delacorte's long-deceased brother Edmund, I had told her. All she needed to do was have a DNA test to prove hers matched with his using the samples of his hair I'd found. She'd balked at first but had finally gotten the test, and the results had proved it was true.

Now the problem was, what to do with that information? Edmund had been very clear in his will that he wanted Vista Del Mar to go to his children, and Gwen was his only surviving offspring. It should mean she was entitled to the hotel and conference center and a share of the family inheritance. Gwen had been clear that if it was just about her she would leave everything as is, but she'd thought about her family and particularly Crystal's son who had a strong feeling for Visa Del Mar.

It was all in her court now to decide when she was going to go public. It certainly would shake up the town.

"Wanda and Crystal will be taking over from here," Gwen said. "I have a yarn tasting set up in the room at the back." She went on to explain that the retreaters could try the different samples to decide which yarn they wanted to use for their project. There were assorted needles and hooks to choose from as well. It all fuzzed into the background for me as I went back to thinking about Don Porter's death. Something Frank had said stuck in my mind: I should find out what had happened at the workshop Don had presided over. Maybe there was a clue there.

I was trying to think how I could track down which of the writers had been there, when the obvious hit me. Madeleine had been there, and she had a reason to be helpful because she wanted me to wrap up the case. I eased over to where she was standing, and when Gwen led the group to the former dining room, which had been set up for the tasting, I stuck with her.

The long table looked colorful with the spread of projects, yarns and tools. "Any of these yarns can be used for your projects with a few adjustments," Gwen said.

Wanda let out a sigh and stepped in. "You will notice that I have put out a yarn and the needle size or hook size next to each of the sample squares and triangles. You can try the other yarns and tools, but I'd suggest you stick with my selection."

Crystal screwed her mouth up in annoyance. She was all for everything being unique, but Wanda was right. Too many choices would spell chaos. As the group surged into the dining room, I touched Madeleine's arm.

"Can I talk to you first?" I said when Madeleine turned to me.

"Is it about Don?" she said in a whisper. When I nodded, she looked around and pointed to a small alcove that was set up with baby yarn. "Let's go in there. I don't want anyone to hear what we're talking about. I can't be connected with him. I simply cannot be questioned by the police." She said the last part with a frantic tone.

I don't know what she thought I was going to say, but she seemed disappointed when I asked about the workshop she'd attended.

"I was hoping you had a lead," she said. She took a moment to collect her thoughts. "He started off by talking about travel writing in general and how great it was. It was travel with a purpose and it was a write-off, whatever that means." She stopped for a moment. "Oh, and he said that it was important to be efficient. That you could write a number of different kinds of articles from one trip. He even knew people who brought back things from their travels and then sold them. Then he talked about markets and how to submit things, which I didn't quite understand." Lucinda walked by the alcove and started to come in when she saw me. I stopped her with a shake of my head, which Madeleine didn't see as she prattled on.

"I kept thinking that now that I'm into traveling, travel writing would be just the thing for me. I could tell Cora that I'm working when I go on my next trip." She started to look around the shop with new interest. "I could even start before then. I could write the article about Vista Del Mar and the yarn retreats that we talked about."

"You certainly could do that. But if we could get back to the workshop," I said, gently trying to prod her. "What else happened?"

"I wish I had thought about becoming a travel writer when

I was in there. I could have taken notes," she said. "Let me see." She stared off into space before continuing. "He said there were two kinds of travel writing. One of them was about places to stay and things to see. The other was more like an essay of impressions." She considered what she'd said for a moment. "That's the kind for me. I certainly wouldn't write something like the first man who read aloud wrote. He called it jazz writing before he read it. Whatever it was, Don didn't like it."

"Really," I said. "How could you tell?"

"Don said so, of course. That was the second part of the workshop. People read things and Don used them to demonstrate dos and don'ts. That man's stuff was full of don'ts."

"How did he take it?" I asked.

"Not at all well. He got up and yelled at Don, saying that he didn't understand and that he was trying to knock other writers to make himself seem more important. The man stormed out after that." Madeleine adjusted the tote bag she was carrying. "Oh, dear," she said suddenly. "He was so angry. I didn't think about it then, but you know you hear about all these crazy people going off about something. Maybe he's the one who killed Don."

"What happened after the man left?"

"Don tried to calm everything down. He gave a little speech about needing a thick skin if you were going to be a writer. Then he kind of laughed and said you needed a thick skin if you were going to be a workshop leader, too." Madeleine stopped and looked down at the skin on her arm, and I realized she had taken him literally. It was hard doing catch-up on a whole life when the first seventy-something years had been so sheltered.

I explained to her what it really meant. "Oh, now it makes sense."

"Did anybody else read their piece after that?"

"Oh, yes. And Don pointed out mistakes in all of them."

"How did the people take it?"

"I guess okay," she said with a shrug. "Nobody else yelled and rushed out." I could tell she was thinking again. "After I left, though, I passed some of the writers on the path and they seemed pretty angry."

"Could you be a little more specific about the guy who stormed out?" It stirred something in my memory. Hadn't I overheard someone talking about a storming out of the workshop? I wished now I had paid more attention, but then I had no idea Don was going to die.

"What are you going to do? Find him and question him?" she said.

"Not exactly. I'm not the cops. I'll have to figure out a way to ease into talking to him. But first I have to find him."

"You know that I've gotten into contemporary fashion lately. He was wearing a green jacket—I would say there was something military looking about the style. I don't know all the names for shades of green, but it seemed to me to be what I've heard referred to as olive green. If I'm going to be a travel writer, I better study up on colors. Don said giving details so they seemed real was important."

My hopes sagged as she continued. It seemed like half the men at the writers' conference wore similar jackets. After seeing so many of them, I had asked Lucinda for details since she was a fashion expert. "It's called an army field jacket. It must be the writer look," I said.

"I think he had a decal on it," she said.

"Did you notice what it looked like?"

She shook her head in response, and her mouth looked sad. "It's still sinking in that he's gone. Oh, dear, it's a dark day for Vista Del Mar."

"We better join the others before they think something is up."

10

WHEN EVERYONE HAD PICKED OUT THEIR PROJECT and the yarn for it, we gathered on the porch. I laughed when they all took out their phones, almost in unison, and proceeded to stare at them. They looked like a bunch of zombies, and suddenly I appreciated that Vista Del Mar was unplugged.

Lucinda came up to me. "I'm just going to pop over and see Tag." She looked sheepish. "I know, I know. I'm always saying how glad I am to be away from him, but as long as I'm here, I want to tell him what happened and make sure he knows I'm okay." I told her when to be back and she took off.

Crystal and Wanda came out and I thanked them for what seemed like the success of the new plan. It took me a few moments to wrench the group's attention away from their screens, and I reminded them that they now had some time to explore downtown Cadbury. I gave them some suggestions and told them when and where to meet the return bus. They took off in a flash. Now I had a chance to stop into Maggie's coffee place to check on any developments with the new muffins and get another one of her fabulous cappuccinos, which I sorely needed after the morning I'd had.

Maggie's place was just a short walk down Grand Street. I drank in the pungent smell of coffee as I walked in. It came from the burlap coffee bags she used as wall covering and years of brewing beans, and it totally permeated the place. With all its cloudy days, Cadbury was a big coffee town, but Maggie's was the most popular café. The coffee was great and she had a way of interacting with the guests, as she called them, that made them feel special and noticed.

Maggie waved me to a table and I heard her call out my order to one of her assistants working the espresso machine. I knew she'd join me when she had a chance. In the meantime I looked over the crowd. I'll admit it—I was looking to see if anyone had one of the breakfast muffins in front of them. True, it was afternoon, but part of my pitch had been that breakfast items being available all day was all the rage. I hadn't been able to see the refrigerated display case, but I was pretty sure there were muffins left. One of the good things about this new concoction was that since they were heated before being served, they would stay fresh through the weekend. Of course, I'd thought that would be unimportant because I figured they would disappear from the shelf the first day they were available, just like my regular muffins did.

I didn't see any of the breakfast muffins on any of the

tables, but I did notice three men and a woman at the table next to me. They had backpacks slung on the backs of their chairs and were all hovering over their laptops. I had a feeling they were from the writers' conference, which was confirmed when I saw one of the cloth bags Kevin St. John had given out.

One of them mentioned Don Porter and my ears perked up. I used the small-town-friendly card and inserted myself into their conversation.

"It's just terrible what happened to him," I said, turning my chair around so I was almost sitting with them. They seemed a little surprised by my interjection. "I'm Casey Feldstein. I'm running the other event going on at Vista Del Mar this weekend."

Now they seemed more friendly, and one of them moved his chair over so I could fit closer to the table. "We were just looking over all the pieces that Don wrote," one of the men said. "He really was a big-time writer. Actually a lot more big-time than the other workshop leaders. We were just saying it's kind of surprising that he came to the conference." He stopped and then stuck out his hand. "I'm Dennis, that's Jennifer in the Vista Del Mar T-shirt, the ginger head over there is Miller, and Lewis is the guy in the black-rimmed glasses that he thinks make him look smart. We're from San Jose."

"I was going to go to the program he was supposed to do today. Now I wish I'd gone to the workshop yesterday," Jennifer said.

"Then none of you went to the workshop he did yesterday?" I asked. Miller looked up from his computer. He had the fair skin that usually went with his hair color. It struck me as funny that it was called red hair when in actuality it was more burnt orange.

"I went to the night-owl session after dinner last night. It was more informal than the workshop and turned out to be really just people reading their pieces and then getting critiques from Don and the group, but mostly Don."

"How'd that go?" I asked, thinking about the man who had left the first workshop in a huff because of Don's comments.

Miller rolled his eyes. "You get some high-strung people at these conferences. They bring a piece they've been working on for years and that they think is the best thing since sliced cheese. And the workshop leaders can be brusque. There isn't a lot of time to pat egos, so they just give their opinion. That's pretty much what Don did. He really reamed one guy." Miller emphasized it with a shake of his head. He started addressing the whole group. "You should have seen him. The dude has a tattoo of some kind of bird on his chest. You could just see the eyes staring out at you."

"Then he didn't take Don's comments well?" I said.

"It's not so much that he said anything. It was how he looked. Kind of like he was going to explode, but somehow kept himself together."

"Miller, you dunce, he could be the one who killed Porter. Did you tell the cops about him?" Dennis asked.

Miller swallowed hard. "No way. I'm not getting involved. The guy didn't say anything. I don't know how he really felt." He pushed back his chair. "We better get back. The next set of workshops begins soon."

"Nice meeting you," Dennis said as he shut his computer and put it in his backpack. The three others muttered something similar before they all headed to the door.

Maggie appeared just then with my cappuccino. She watched the foursome as they went outside. "Was it something I said?" she joked.

"They're from the writers' conference at Vista Del Mar. Also known as Kevin St. John's shot at a big event."

Maggie pulled out a chair and set her coffee on the table. "I always use your coming in as an excuse to take a break." She took a tentative sip of her coffee. "Excellent, if I say so myself." She glanced at the empty table. "Kevin St. John must be having a fit. All the conference people keep coming in here instead of going to the Cora and Madeleine Delacorte Café on the grounds." She laughed. "I wish I could say it was our coffee that was bringing them here, but it's all about the Wi-Fi."

"So they haven't been the only ones to come in?"

"No," she said. "I take it back; it isn't just about the Wi-Fi; it's about the cell signal, too." She pushed my cappuccino toward me until I tasted it and gave my approval. "This guy came in yesterday afternoon," she continued. "He at least commented on the coffee. He said it deserved five stars. He had a computer, but he didn't want to use our Wi-Fi. Something about it not being very secure. He had some black thing with him. It was about the size of a credit card and he said it worked off a cell phone signal and it gave him his own superprivate hot spot. I say, whatever floats your boat."

She had piqued my interest and I asked her what he looked like. "Nice looking in a boring sort of way." She seemed about to leave it at that. "Well, there was one thing I did notice. His clothes reminded me of things I've seen in one of those travel catalogs." She was almost finished with her coffee and was looking at the counter like she wanted to get back.

"I'm pretty sure I know who you mean." I hesitated, unsure if I should say more. Obviously word hadn't spread about Don's death. She was going to find out anyway, so I told her what had happened.

"How terrible. Any idea who did it?" she asked. Then she muttered to herself how strange it felt that he'd been in there and now he was gone. "Now that I think about it, he seemed tense when he came in, and after he'd done whatever he had to online, he seemed relieved."

With that, she got up and went back to work, and I left to find my group. I couldn't help but wonder what it was that had made Don so tense.

The group was waiting when I got back to our appointed spot. I considered offering them more time in town, but I could stall the inevitable only so long, so I called the bus and told the driver to pick us up.

The outing seemed to have done them all a lot of good, and they were talking among themselves as they climbed onto the small bus. I thought it was funny how they all took the exact same seats as before, but then so did I. I was standing next to the front seat, about to make sure everyone was on board, when Lucinda rushed up and got on.

With all accounted for, I gave the order to leave and we both sat down in the front seat. "Sorry if I held you up," my friend said. She seemed a little breathless and took a moment to readjust her Burberry scarf and pat her hair back in place.

"How did it go?" I asked, remembering that she'd said she was going to stop in and see her husband.

"Tag went nuts when he heard about Don Porter. I kept telling him it had nothing to do with me, but he tried to talk me out of going back with you all." She leaned back into the seat as if she was relieved to be there. "You should have heard him. He's got it in his head that no place is safe, and spies and secret agents are all coming to Cadbury to carry out their plots." She let out a sigh. "I thought the OCD stuff was bad enough, but now he's getting paranoid."

The bus left downtown Cadbury and we passed through a residential area of apartments and small homes. "What about you? Where'd you go?" she asked.

"You know me. I went to Maggie's for a cappuccino." I conveniently left out the rest.

LIEUTENANT BORGNINE WAS NOT STANDING BY TO do a head count as the bus let us off in the driveway next to the Lodge. I wasn't sure where the investigation stood and if my people could go to their rooms, so I had them wait outside while I went into the Lodge to find out.

Gill was behind the registration counter and he glanced up when I came in. He seemed to know what I was going to ask. "Sorry, not yet. But we have your meeting room all set up. We brought in a long table as you requested. There's a fire going. Coffee and tea service is waiting."

When I came back out, I announced that we'd be going

to our meeting room without mentioning that the retreaters' rooms were still off-limits. I took them around the Lodge building and up the path that didn't pass Sand and Sea.

They were all anxious to work on their projects, so no one objected. The room was set up as Gill had said and the retreaters arranged themselves around the long table. It was a much better setup. All the tote bags still stayed on the floor, but there was more room to lay out yarn and tools. It was a peaceful transition, and I was about to pat myself on the back for handling it when I saw Lieutenant Borgnine coming up the path. Madeleine saw him as well. The next moment, she'd gathered her things and was out the door, going the other way. I knew she'd said she didn't want to talk to him, but I was still surprised to see her take off like a rabbit.

The lieutenant seemed to have such a short neck that it appeared his head sat directly on his shoulders, and his herringbone tweed jacket seemed more rumpled than usual. I chuckled to myself when the first thing he did when he came in was count heads. I think he was disappointed that everyone was there. He had no way of knowing that Madeleine had taken off since she had missed his original head count.

He forced his mouth into what he probably thought was a friendly smile when he turned to the group. "Due to the unfortunate incident this morning, I will need to speak to each of you individually." I could tell he was waiting for some kind of uproar, but the group accepted what he said without comment. Again, he seemed almost disappointed.

"You see, it's just like Casey told you," Lucinda said to the group. Now the lieutenant looked more annoyed than disappointed when he realized I had talked to them.

"We're set up in the next room," he said. "We'll come get you one at a time."

Olivia volunteered to be the first one, but the uniformed officer who came in insisted we go in order around the table. He pointed at Lisa, who was seated at the end.

The group watched in tense silence as she followed the cop without seeming at all intimidated. All the interest in working on projects seemed to have dried up as everyone waited for Lisa's return.

Lisa seemed as unperturbed upon her return as she'd been when she'd left. She pointed to the woman in the next seat. "Your turn."

The woman wasn't wearing her name tag, and to me she had become the woman with the knitting needles stuck in her hair. That sounded crazier than it looked. They were short knitting needles and I think she thought of them as decoration in the bun sitting on top of her head. Her reaction was a lot different than Lisa's. She walked to the door like a calf being led to slaughter.

"So, what happened?" Rayanne asked Lisa. DeeDee was leaning close to her friend, nodding in agreement with the question.

Lisa took her seat. "We're not supposed to say anything." She glanced around the table. "There's nothing unusual in that," she added quickly. "They don't want you to be influenced by what someone else said." She took out the green cotton yarn she'd gotten at Cadbury Yarn along with the circular needles she'd bought as well. She'd managed to cast on the four stitches for the small shawl she wanted to make, but when she looked at them sitting on the cable that joined the metal needles, I realized she had no idea what to do.

Because this was an impromptu workshop, neither Crystal nor Wanda was there. I momentarily froze, but then Olivia stood up with a glow on her almond-shaped face and offered her help. I wanted to hug my early bird.

"This is just the most basic of patterns," she said, picking up the needles. She demonstrated knitting the first two stitches and then sliding the yarn over the needle. "That's called a yarn over and is what adds a stitch to your work." She held it up for everyone to see and pointed out the small triangle shape of the work. "Now you just knit the rest of the stiches in the row. You just keep on doing that, row after row, and you'll see it will keep getting to be a bigger and bigger triangle."

"Thanks for the refresher course. I can certainly manage that," Lisa said, taking back the needles and yarn.

"As long as I have everyone's attention, I might as well do a pitch on my squares." Olivia went back to her place and rummaged around in her canvas tote. She chuckled as she looked up. "Oops, wrong bag." She turned to her neighbor and apologized and then found the right one. "There are so many tote bags around here, and they all look the same."

At first I thought she meant the red totes with *Yarn2Go* on the front, but as I looked around the table, I realized most of the retreaters had brought bags of their own with their works in progress and simply put my bags inside of them. Some of the bags stood out, but most were natural-colored canvas.

Olivia laid out a sample of the squares. They were made

in different yarns and were knitted and crocheted, but all were the same size. Then she held up a plastic bag with a small ball of yarn and some folded instructions. "I collect squares and then put them together into blankets, which in turn are given away to shelters. They provide warmth and that special something that comes with something hand-made. I have these kits available for anyone who wants to make one or more. I'll be in the Lodge this evening if any of you want to join in."

She had an aura of joy as she looked over the group. "I don't want to sound preachy, but this project of making blankets has changed my life. Thinking about helping others got me to stop dwelling on my own problems. The funny thing was that when I stopped thinking about myself all the time, everything sorted itself out."

There were a lot of supportive nods. I added mine, glad that she'd also managed to get their attention off the questioning. The woman with the knitting needles in her hair returned almost unnoticed, and Jeff Hunter got up for his turn with the police.

He didn't return unnoticed. He came back into the room, gave the group a big thumbs-up, and then held up his hands, showing off how they weren't in handcuffs. The group didn't seem to know what to make of him, and he laughed. "Just kidding. It was fine. They don't ask trick questions or any-thing."

Even with his comment, when Dolly got up for her turn, she walked hesitantly to the door. "I'm afraid I'll be so ner-vous, I won't remember my name."

"Don't worry. They're asking for ID anyway," Jeff blurted

out, then seemed to regret it. "I probably wasn't supposed to say that."

As the retreaters continued to go and come back, the others went back to work on their projects—either something they'd brought with them or the one from Wanda's new plan.

"I think DeeDee and I should go together," Rayanne said. DeeDee sat blinking her eyes and nodding her head. It seemed to be a combination of her agreeing with what her friend was saying and a nervous habit.

When I nixed the plan, the speed of DeeDee's movements picked up and Rayanne finally went off on her own.

To further distract everyone, I urged them to help themselves to the coffee and tea along with the cookies still left from the first workshop. With all the movement around the room, it made it less obvious when someone returned and the next person left.

Mona made her way to the door without comment. I wondered if Lieutenant Borgnine would make her take off her hat and sunglasses so they could check her appearance against her ID. She came back the way she went in, quiet and hidden.

Bree was the last to go in. When she returned, her blond frizz of curls bobbed as she held up her arms in a triumphant gesture and danced around. "We're done!"

Lieutenant Borgnine came in and gave her an odd look. Bree dropped her arms and went to help herself to a drink.

"Thank you," he said to the group. "I appreciate your cooperation, and we may be getting in touch with you again during the investigation." A look of discomfort passed through the group, and it was clear they hadn't taken his last comment too well. I was afraid he was going to say more that would upset them, so I decided to try to distract him. By now I knew he had a sweet tooth, so I grabbed the tin of cookies and offered it to him.

He looked over the selection of butter cookies with chocolate on top and hesitated. "They're homemade," I said, trying to entice him.

I could see he was weakening, and he finally took one. "I just promised the wife no apple fritters."

11

THE DINNER BELL BEGAN TO RING AND I WANTED
to give myself a high five. Somehow I had managed to distract my retreaters, though I suppose Lieutenant Borgnine's
questioning helped, too, and no one had said anything about
not being able to go to their rooms.

Lucinda joined me at the front as I hustled the retreaters
to the dining hall on the back path that didn't pass by the
Sand and Sea building. The bell had just stopped ringing
and the line was beginning to move inside.

"Can you keep an eye on things for a while?" I asked
Lucinda. I explained wanting to go across the street and she
understood.

"No problem," Lucinda said. It really was no problem
for her. She was so accustomed to acting as the hostess at
the Blue Door that she always made the rounds with the iced

tea pitcher and made sure everyone had what they needed, even when I was there.

Now that it was getting dark, I could just see Julius pacing in front of my back door as I came up my driveway. I was glad that Lucinda hadn't asked why I needed to go home. The truth was I needed a sounding board, and since I felt constricted by what I could say to her, it had to be somebody else. I had promised Madeleine not to tell anyone of her involvement with Don and that included Lucinda.

The black cat followed me inside and then walked in a circle around my legs with his tail held high and switching back and forth, like he was protesting how long I'd been gone.

I glanced down at Julius and was going to bring up that he hadn't suffered in my absence. He could come and go as he pleased. His bowl was filled with cat crunchies and there was a full bowl of water. But then I just threw up my hands and cut to the chase. "Okay. Stink fish coming up."

I went through the ritual of unwrapping it with my nose closed. Julius swirled around my feet, doing a victory dance, thinking he'd won. But actually he hadn't. I'd merely taken his stink fish allotment for the day and fed it to him in tiny dabs. Chalk one up for the human.

I glanced at my watch and considered the time difference. It was late, but not that late. I punched in the number and it began to ring. I knew my name showed on the phone, so if Frank didn't want to talk to me, he could just not answer.

I heard the click as he picked up. "Okay, Feldstein, this better be some kind of emergency. You do know it is Friday night and some of us have plans."

"Hello to you, too," I said with a laugh. "I wouldn't call it an emergency, but I wanted to talk some things over with you."

"No one else has died, have they? We're talking about the same victim you called about before? The travel writer, right?"

"Yes, Frank, I'm calling about the same guy. I'm sorry to bother you, but I can't really talk things over with anyone here." I knew I had his attention for only a short time, so I launched right into it. "I found out that he was a pretty big deal in the travel-writing business. Such a big deal that some of the people who came for the writers' conference wondered why he came to such a small conference."

"That might not be such a big mystery. Maybe he had another reason to come to the area. You're always saying how beautiful it is. And it was a way to get his trip paid for."

I mentioned seeing him around the lighthouse.

"There you go; he was probably gathering information for something he was going to write. If that's it . . . ," Frank said in a tone like he was going to sign off.

"No, there's more, absolutely. I did what you said." Nothing got people's attention more than when you said they were right about something. Frank was no different.

"Good girl, Feldstein. What exactly did I tell you to do again?" He'd lost the sound of someone trying to end the call.

"You said I should find out what happened during the workshop Don Porter led. I found out about that and that he also had a small group session. Both of them involved him critiquing people's work."

"I bet I know," Frank said. "That hotshot writer probably stepped on a few toes, hard. You don't know this about me, but there was a time when I was going to write a book based on my exploits and I went to one of those writers' conferences. And I went to a workshop. I planned to just watch to see how it all went down. One guy read a few pages of science fiction. Not my thing, by the way. I like what's real and right in front of me, like having a client come in and ask if you can arrange to off his wife."

"What?" I said incredulously. "Did that really happen?"

"Sort of," Frank said. "And believe me, I turned him in. But back to what happened." Julius had finished his stink fish now and was cleaning his paws. "When the guy finished reading, the whole group gave their opinion. Geez, the comments were pretty raw, and it wasn't just from the leader. The guy got all defensive, saying that they didn't understand or something. I thought he was going to cry. Needless to say, I kept my pages to myself."

"Wow, Frank, I had no idea you wanted to write a book."

"Hey, there's lots you don't know about me," he said. "So, anyway, you were saying."

"You're right again," I said. The chair made a sudden squawk and I knew he had sat up with a start. It was obviously a shock to keep hearing that he was right. "Don did step on a few toes, as you put it. A man threw a hissy fit at the workshop and stormed out. And then at a small gathering, another man got reamed but appeared okay with it."

"Did you talk to the actual people whose work got trashed?" Frank asked.

"Not exactly." I told him that both stories had come secondhand.

"You've got to get it from the horse's mouth," Frank said.

"One of them is going to be a little hard to track down," I said. "The only description I have of him is that he was wearing one of those army surplus jackets."

"A field jacket? They're great. I had one myself." I was having a hard time not chuckling. I never had considered Frank caring about clothes. He seemed to be strictly the kind who blindly reached in his closet and wore whatever he touched first.

"The other guy should be easier to find." I told him about talking to the three men and the woman at Maggie's and how one of them had been at the small gathering and remembered that the guy who had gotten his work pulled apart had an unusual tattoo. "He said it looked like a bird or something and the two eyes seemed to be peering out from the guy's open collar."

Frank chortled. "Sounds like a weird tat." He paused for a moment. "Did the guy who told you about it mention if his work had been critiqued?"

"No," I said.

"Just a thought, but sometimes when people point a finger, it's a way to keep it from being pointed at them."

"Frank, you're amazing. I never would have thought of that," I said. The chair made another sound and I gathered he'd had a positive response to what I said.

"There's something else to consider. The crime scene. I don't suppose that cop with no neck let you anywhere near it."

"Remember, I said I saw it. That's how I knew he'd been dead for a while—because he felt cold and stiff. And the pillow, I thought, was used to absorb the sound."

"It's coming back to me. Right, I did say that pillows don't do much of a job. I have a few cases of my own to think about. I can't remember everything." There was a moment of silence. "I'm waiting, Feldstein. Tell me what you saw again."

I closed my eyes and tried to imagine looking around the room. "There were feathers all over the place and a pillow on the ground with a black hole in it. Don was crumpled on the ground. I could see the twin bed under the windows. I saw colors." I strained to remember what they were. "They were folders. I saw a blue, a yellow and a red one." When I said red, the image of blood appeared in my mind's eye. "There was blood on his shirt and I think his hand, too." I mentally scanned the room. "And on the wall."

"You mean blood spatter?" Frank asked.

"No, it was like streaks of it on the light switch and then down the wall. Like he'd reached out and his hand dragged against the wall as he fell."

"You tell me what you think happened," Frank prompted.

"He could have been trying to turn on the lights," I said.

"Yeah, maybe, but under the circumstances it doesn't seem that he'd be thinking about turning on the lights. More likely he was trying to say something, like write something on the wall, but he couldn't finish."

"You mean like write who killed him?" I said. Frank grunted an *uh-huh*, and I was about to give him another compliment and tell him how useful it was to talk to him, but I heard a voice in the background.

Frank's demeanor instantly changed, and he seemed distracted. "Sounds good, Feldstein. You should be able to take it from here." He spoke to the other person. I heard something about pouring a glass of wine.

"Frank, do you have a date?" I asked, suddenly putting the pieces together.

"Don't sound so surprised, Feldstein. Underneath this hard exterior beats the heart of a romantic." Before I could comment, he hung up. Frank was full of surprises.

Julius had jumped up on the table and was rubbing against my shoulder, a sign he wanted some cuddle time. Cats! It was always on their schedule. I set the phone down and picked him up. He closed his eyes with pleasure and began to purr as I held him close and stroked his head.

If he'd been a little Yorkie, he would have stayed in that position and pawed me if I stopped with the pets. But cats had their limits. A few minutes of cuddles and Julius pushed away, as if I was forcing the affection on him. He gave me a look before jumping down, and then with a flick of his tail he went down the hall, probably for a nap.

No nap for me. I looked at my watch and realized the call had taken longer than I'd expected and dinner was almost over. I wasn't worried about my people—Lucinda would make sure they all were taken care of. It was me. I thought back over the day and couldn't remember having had anything more than the cappuccinos from Maggie's. My stomach rumbled, reminding me that I still had a long night ahead of me.

While I excelled at making desserts, I wasn't much good at cooking meals. I totally relied on frozen dinners, plates of pasta Dane left for me and, when I did retreats, the meals provided by Vista Del Mar.

I did a quick pick-me-up to my appearance, pulled on an ivory-colored fleece jacket and headed outside. The air felt fresh. Even though it was dark, the temperature was just a little lower than it had been at noon. I never got tired of the weather, even if it seemed to have only subtle differences. I crossed the dark ribbon of the street and rushed past the two lighted stone posts that marked the entrance to Vista Del Mar. As I got closer, the smell of hot food urged me to move faster.

The Sea Foam dining hall was almost empty when I walked in. I went directly to the cafeteria line, hoping they were still serving. I had to settle for what was left and ended up with a plate that looked like it had come from a buffet of small bites. A dab of macaroni and cheese sat next to a spoonful of scalloped potatoes. An end sliver of meat loaf abutted two fried chicken fingers. The rest of the plate was filled with broccoli sautéed in garlic. Apparently there was a lot of that left.

My mouth was watering from the smells as I looked over the tables, trying to decide where to sit. Sammy waved at me from across the room. He and Bridget, wearing their magic-show garb, had one of the large round tables to themselves.

I watched her smile fade as I walked to their table. It was pretty obvious that she didn't want me to sit with them. I left a seat between us and sat down next to Sammy. He saw my plate of food and the sad-looking piece of meat loaf and offered me some of his. Bridget muttered something that I took to indicate displeasure. I accepted his meat loaf anyway, and the three of us made conversation about Don Porter's death and the investigation.

It hadn't occurred to me before, but Bridget seemed to have been in the middle of things since she'd been working in the café all day. She not so subtly wrapped one of her arms around Sammy's. I absolutely had her number. She was going to simply claim him as hers.

She wore the glittery black dress as she had the night before, and close up I could tell it was less revealing than it seemed. It appeared to be a one-piece thing that was mostly a body stocking. I wondered if she knew that holding on to him so tightly made her look needy.

I was sure she knew my history with Sammy, which could have been why there were daggers in her eyes when our gazes met. I was okay about letting Sammy go—to the right person. And I didn't think it was her. Even so, I wasn't going to be rude. I had to deal with her all the time because of the café.

"It must have been a tough day in the café after what happened," I said to her in a friendly voice.

"The writers spent the day in there, mostly crabbing about not having Internet," she said. "Some of the cops came in. And some of your people, too. Or maybe it was just one of your people. That one with the big hat hung out at the counter asking me questions."

"Really," I said. "What did she ask about?"

Bridget made a face like she thought what she'd been asked about was strange. "You won't believe this. She kept wanting to know about Mr. St. John."

"Like what?"

"Was he married, did he have kids? Where did he live? Stuff like that," she said. "It was all personal."

"What did you tell her?"

"Nothing. I really don't know anything about him anyway. Does he even have a life outside this place?" she said.

"That's a good question. He's very secretive about his

life. I do know that he grew up in Cadbury and that he was brought up by his grandmother, who died under suspicious circumstances."

"I know something about him, too," Sammy said. "When he heard that Don Porter was a travel writer, he was all over him. He didn't say it in so many words, but it was obvious that he expected him to write a glowing piece about Vista Del Mar."

"Then Don was definitely writing something about the place?" I asked.

Bridget suddenly straightened. "I know about that. The guy in the travel clothes asked me about Mr. St. John, too. He wanted to know if he was always so . . . Let me think of the word he used. It was a long one. *Obsequious*, I think. I thought it was a compliment, so I said yes."

Sammy's head swiveled toward her, a surprised look on his face. "Ah, that's not really a compliment. It means too anxious to please. It makes sense, though—Kevin would want him to write a good piece about the place. But maybe he was pushing too hard. It sounds like it might have backfired."

Sammy looked at my plate of food, which was still virtually untouched. "Case, you're not eating." He unhooked his arm from Bridget's and pushed the plate a little closer and gestured for me to dig in.

"It's been a long day," Bridget said, giving her chair a little push away. She turned toward Sammy, who was watching me eat. "It's time to go," she said to him, apparently deciding to skip being subtle.

It seemed to take a moment for him to process what she'd

said, and then he turned toward her. "Sure, go on. And thanks for your help."

Her face clouded with irritation. "I thought we could both go now."

He didn't say anything, and she finally stood up and left.

"You do realize that she likes you," I said, and he sort of shrugged and nodded. "What? Maybe she's coming on too strong?" I said.

He looked down at the table and muttered, "Yes"; then he looked up at me. "I knew you would understand. Like I always say, you're the only one who gets me."

Sammy waited until I'd finished. The staff was wiping down the table and refilling the condiments when we walked to the exit. When we got to the Lodge I pointed toward the door. "I want to make sure all is well with my people before I leave."

He gave me a quick hug and headed off into the darkness.

12

THE INTERIOR OF THE LODGE SEEMED NOISY AND bright after the darkness outside. There seemed to be clusters of people everywhere, and it took me a moment to get it all in focus. I stopped at the registration desk, relieved that Gill was manning it. He was so much easier to deal with than Kevin St. John. He assured me that my retreaters all had access to their rooms now. I almost bumped into a big sign near the registration desk. "What's this about?" I asked, reading over the announcement that there was a movie in Hummingbird Hall at eight o'clock.

"Kevin wanted to add a special activity tonight. He thought it might smooth things over after today." He always called him Mr. St. John to his face but referred to him as Kevin when he wasn't around. "He had me drag out the popcorn cart and spend my break making batch after batch of popcorn."

"What's the movie?" I asked, and Gill tried to repress a laugh.

"*Around the World in 80 Days*. Somehow he thought that would pacify all the writers who came to learn about travel writing." We both shook our heads at the same time.

My goal was to check on my people and make sure all was well before I headed off to the Blue Door. I was glad to see that Olivia had set up shop in the seating area. She had spread a selection of her square-making kits on the coffee table. I recognized a number of our group seated on the couches around her. Some of the writers had joined in as well.

The deal I had with Kevin St. John was that anytime my group gathered in a public area to knit, other guests were welcome to join in. Lucinda was seated in the middle of the group, and when she looked up, I waved. She knew what I was doing and gave me a thumbs-up in answer.

My next stop was the Sand and Sea building. Even though the clerk had said the building was open to my retreaters, I wanted to see the exact situation and check out what was going on in the area around it.

I walked up the small hill that led to the building. It wasn't until I was at the door that I saw that only a leftover piece of yellow tape was stuck to the handle. The building was definitely open again. Inside, the living room area appeared normal. There was a fire going in the fireplace, and a number of comfortable chairs were spread around it, though all were empty. I walked to the corridor that led to the guest rooms. It was lined in dark wood and the lights along the ceiling didn't do much to brighten it up. Don Porter's room was at the end. The only hint that anything had happened was the sign on the door that said NO ADMITTANCE.

I went all the way down the corridor on the other side of the living room, which ended in the back entrance, and saw that it was open as well. I went out through there and onto a small patio. The door to the Sandpiper building was across the patio, and I decided to walk through the building instead of returning to the path.

The living room of Sandpiper was much larger and cozier than the one in Sand and Sea. A fire glowed in the fireplace. There were couches and chairs surrounding it, and I thought the area was empty until I noticed a man sitting in one of the wing chairs reading.

When I got closer, he looked up, and as he did, I saw what seemed like two beady eyes and a beak showing through the opening in his plaid shirt. As it registered that he was the one the writers at Maggie's had mentioned, I fumbled for a way to start a conversation, until the obvious hit me.

"That must be a really good book." I stopped in front of him.

"It is," he said, holding it up to show me the cover. *The Year's Best in Travel Writing* was emblazoned above a drawing of a globe with a plane flying around it. It seemed he was going to go back to reading without any more comments.

"Impressive tattoo," I said, pointing at his chest. Now I could see more of the bird's head. The beak appeared viciously sharp, and an inked drop of blood clung to the tip. The man's face seemed a sharp contrast to the violent image of what I was now sure was a hawk. His features were mild mannered. He smiled at the compliment and looked me over.

"Where's yours?"

"My what?" I asked, perplexed.

"Your tat." He unbuttoned his shirt to display more of the bird. There appeared to be a lot of detail with the feathers.

"Don't have any." I slipped off my jacket and pulled up the sleeves of my shirt as further proof. He was clearly surprised.

"Really? I thought everybody our age had at least one," he said.

"I guess being ink-free makes me a rebel now," I said with smile. The tattoo had broken the ice with him, but now I wanted to talk about Don Porter. "So, you like travel writing," I said, trying to direct the conversation.

It was like popping the cork off a bottle of sparkling wine. He instantly became animated and bubbled over with comments. "You do know there are different kinds of travel writing. This book is all essays. There's one by Don Porter." It seemed to occur to him that I might not know who he was, so he digressed by explaining that he was a famous travel writer. "He's the one who died." His voice cracked as he pointed in the direction of the Sand and Sea building.

"I was just rereading his essay. It's on Santa Fe and all the colors and tastes, along with how spectacular the light is." He shook his head solemnly. "It's so sad to think there won't be any more essays from him."

"You must be with the writers' group," I said, holding out my hand. "I'm Casey Feldstein. The yarn group is mine."

He took my hand and nodded. "T. Lance Baroni at your service."

"Interesting name," I said, thinking it was a touch pretentious. "What do people call you?"

"Mostly, 'Hey, you,'" he said with a chuckle. "But really the T. Lance is just for my writing. My friends all call me 'T Dot.'" I must have looked confused, and he seemed disconcerted at my reaction. "Don't you get it? It's like *T* with a period after it. Get it? T Dot."

I smiled, but I was thinking he'd gone from pretentious to trying too hard to be memorable. "So, T Dot, it must have been exciting for you that he was here. Did you get a chance to talk to him?" I had an innocent expression, which I hoped didn't let on that I knew he had spoken to Don and more.

He stared off into the distance as he began to speak. "I went to his night-owl session last night. I don't know why it was called that. We met right after dinner." His lips pressed together, as if the memory wasn't pleasant. "People got to read their work, and then the group and Don commented on it."

"Including you?" I asked.

He nodded. "I wrote up a descriptive essay on Vista Del Mar. I described how you could taste the fog and that the dark buildings seemed to be hiding secrets. Don didn't like it. Not at all."

"I'm sorry," I said. "It must have upset you."

He appeared hesitant but then let out a sigh. Obviously there was something on his mind, and just as I'd hoped, he saw me as a sympathetic ear. "I didn't tell the cops any of this. You have to keep it to yourself, okay?"

I nodded my agreement and he continued. "I just told them that the last time I saw him was at the session. I didn't mention anything about him critiquing my work or what came after." I was trying to keep my breathing even and a placid expression on my face so he would keep talking. I wondered if he was going to confess.

"I was pretty pissed at Don and thought he was probably just jealous because my piece was so good. But then I read it over and read one of Don's pieces and I realized he was right—it needed some tweaking. I rewrote the piece really quickly and stuck it in a blue folder. I was going to slip it under his door. I wrongly figured he was at that Roast and Toast thing and wasn't in there. I guess he heard me fumbling around, because he opened the door."

"And . . . ," I said, trying to keep him going.

"He acted kind of weird and stood blocking the way, as if he didn't want me to see in."

"Maybe he had someone in there with him."

"You mean like a woman?" T Dot laughed. "Good luck if he was expecting to get any action. Have you seen the beds? They're barely as wide as a twin." His lips slipped back into a straight line. "The thing is, I'm taller than him, so I could see over his shoulder. If there was anyone in there, he must have hidden them in the bathroom. All I saw were two folders, a red one and a yellow one, on the bed, and a tote bag."

"What color was the tote bag?" I froze, suddenly thinking it might have been one of the red ones I gave out.

He was befuddled by the question. "It was no color." He thought for a moment. "You know the color of the beach here? It was that color." I was very familiar with the sand at the Vista Del Mar beach. It came from some special kind of rock and was silky soft and a pale shade that was almost white. "I think that color is called natural or neutral," I said.

He hit his forehead with the heel of his hand. "Damn, I should have known that. Travel essays are all about description. Don described the rocky cliffs outside of Santa Fe as 'a pale shade of bubble gum with holes like Swiss cheese.'"

I tried to steer him back to talking about the previous night.

"Do you know what time it was when you saw Don in his room?"

"I don't know." All of a sudden he got why I was asking. "Nobody saw me, and I went to the Roast and Toast afterwards. So nobody knew I was there." He looked hard at me. "I shouldn't have told you." His eyes were hard for moment before they flickered with panic. "There was that woman . . ."

"Woman?" I repeated. "What did she look like?" She could be his alibi if she saw him talking to Don and then leave. Or she could place him at the scene.

He shrugged. "I don't know. I think she was wearing a scarf."

I didn't want to say anything, but I didn't think T Dot had a future in writing that depended on observation and description.

After I bid him a good evening, I went back toward the Lodge. Light spilled out from the wall of windows that surrounded the gift shop. I slowed and glanced in. But when I saw the Difficult Duo were inside and seemed to be having a moment, I stopped. Rayanne's face was squeezed into annoyance and DeeDee's head was jerking in a nervous gesture. *Now what?*

I prepared myself for battle but put on my best smile as I headed inside. They were standing near a display with baskets of yarn. Whenever I put on a retreat, Gwen always stocked the gift shop with a supply of basic yarn as well as knitting and crochet tools from Cadbury Yarn. It was for my group's needs, but also for the other guests. Seeing my group working with yarn seemed to inspire other guests to want to do the same.

Rayanne latched onto me as soon as she saw me. "Good, you're here. I've changed my mind and I don't want to crochet a stupid washcloth. I want to make something grander, like the shawl. And I want to knit it." She poked through one of the baskets of yarn. "I don't have the instructions and I didn't understand them anyway. What kind of yarn should I use?" I was trying to absorb what she'd said and think of how to handle the situation. The small woman seemed so uptight that I bet the waves in her dark hair were afraid to move when she gave me a disparaging shake of her head. "What kind of retreat is this anyway? The program was a complete disaster. And then we're rushed out of here and rushed into making a decision of what to make because nobody wants us to know that we can't get into our rooms because the whole building is a crime scene." She paused to suck in some air. "We should have left when we had the chance. We can't even do that now because the police lieutenant said that everyone had to stay put and anyone trying to leave could be detained."

She picked up that I was surprised at her comment. "Yes, when he questioned me, I mentioned wanting to leave. There is still a matter of a refund. I could complain to my credit card company."

DeeDee had a nervous smile that showed off her dimples.

"Can you help her? Can you help her?" I nodded to stop her before she repeated it a third time.

Inwardly, I was panicking. Neither Wanda nor Crystal was there to take over. I considered going out into the main room and rounding up one of the early birds, who were more proficient than I was. But an inner voice ordered me to pull myself together and deal with the situation.

This was my fifth retreat, and even though I had started out as a complete novice on all fronts, I had picked up more about yarn and knitting than I'd realized. While I had to agree there was some truth to Rayanne's complaints, I also wasn't going to be bullied by her and her threats of demanding a refund.

I took a deep breath and went through the basket of yarn as I remembered what Wanda had said about the different yarns for different projects. It came back to me that Wanda had kept it simple by suggesting a worsted-weight blend and had given a large size for the needles. I picked up a skein of dark red yarn and read over the label. It was covered with lots of numbers, including the weight, length, percentage of the different fibers, dye lot and code for the color. Finally I found the words *worsted weight*. "This should work," I said, handing it to her.

I added that the cranberry color would look good with her dark hair. I grabbed a pair of circular needles and cast on four stitches and then knit across as we stood there. I did a row with the increase, showing her what I'd done. "Now just continue on with that, row after row, until it's big enough," I said, handing her the yarn and needles. I'm not sure who was more surprised—me or her. It seemed I was paying attention even when I didn't know it. I wished somebody had been filming the encounter so I could send it to my mother. I let her put the yarn she'd gotten that afternoon in the basket as an even exchange. I told the clerk to put the needles on my tab.

Rayanne took over the knitting, but I could tell she was looking for something to fuss about. She knitted a few rows while we stood there, managing the increase with ease.

I watched her as the rows added up. There were so few stitches at the beginning that she had a number of rows done in no time. As she leaned forward to look at her work, the pale blue scarf around her neck slipped forward and I thought about what T Dot had said.

"You better tell her. You better tell her," DeeDee said to Rayanne with a shake of her head, which made her hair swing forward. DeeDee had said very little before, but now I was beginning to get that she repeated everything.

Rayanne gave her a sour look and made a *shush* noise, then turned to me. "I'm sure you have someplace to be." She actually gave my shoulder a little push as encouragement.

"If you don't tell her, I will," DeeDee said. I waited, expecting her to repeat it, but she said it only once. "Rayanne didn't tell the police she talked to that man who died. That man who died."

Rayanne started to speak at the end of DeeDee's repeat. "DeeDee, I don't know why you brought it up."

DeeDee seemed more nervous than usual. "I don't want to have to call my husband from jail and tell him I got arrested because you withheld evidence."

Rayanne appeared disgruntled. "Will you calm down? I simply didn't see any reason to admit to any contact with him." She turned her attention to me. "She's making a big deal out of nothing."

"You said the man wasn't nice to you," DeeDee said.

"You have to understand the circumstance," Rayanne said to me. "I heard he wrote about travel and I figured he'd probably back me up about how terrible the rooms are. I saw him looking around the lighthouse on that lame outing of yours. So I asked him how he'd rate the accommodations at Vista Del Mar. He snapped at me and told me not to bother him. He walked toward that bench that overlooked the water. I figured he was going to meditate or something. But even so, there was no reason to be so unpleasant."

It was a relief to be able to smooth something over for Rayanne. Hopefully, it would give me some points to outweigh all her complaints. "Unless you were planning to confess to his murder after that, I don't think Lieutenant Borgnine would care that you left it out." I meant it as sort of a joke, but she glared at me and I realized she didn't have a sense of humor. I told them about the movie and made sure they understood it was for all the guests of Vista Del Mar before I gladly moved on.

I found Dolly outside the Lodge. "There's a movie in Hummingbird Hall," I said, pointing down the path.

"That's just where I'm going." She seemed a little breathless and I noticed she was carrying a large canvas bag.

"You can leave that at the desk in the Lodge if you'd like." I even offered to take it in for her, but she refused. "I carry around way too much stuff, but when I don't have it, I feel lost." With a wave, she moved on.

I was ready to head for my place and get my car just as Lisa passed.

"On your way to the movie?" I asked, and she nodded. Then it struck me that she was alone. "Is your husband meeting you there?" She had said that the whole point of the weekend was that when they weren't going to their respective workshops, they could spend time together.

"No, Derek is staying in our room, slaving over something to bring to the flash-fiction workshop."

"I didn't think to ask you before. Did he go to any of the sessions with Don Porter?"

Her brow furrowed. "I didn't think it was a good idea, but he told the cops he hadn't gone to any of them. But someone took a picture during the session and Derek was plainly visible. So now since they know he lied, that cop in the tweed jacket keeps asking him questions."

For a moment I felt some sympathy for Lieutenant Borgnine. Was anybody telling him the truth? But then I thought about Madeleine. If Derek was being harassed by the cops for lying, I could just imagine how Lieutenant Borgnine would react if he found out about Madeleine's deliberate plan to mislead him.

13

THE STREETS WERE ALREADY QUIETING WHEN I finally headed to downtown Cadbury. The stores had long since closed and the restaurants were in the process of shutting for the night. The Blue Door was located on the main drag in town, Grand Street. The building had once been a residence and from the outside still looked like a house. I went up the stairs to the long porch that ran along the side of it, where the entrance was. As the name suggested, the restaurant's door was blue—or at least half of it was. The top part was glass.

The last patrons were paying their check as I walked in. Tag was handling the transaction and gave me a nod. It didn't matter that I'd seen him countless times; I still always did a double take at his head of hair. Tag was well into his fifties, and his hair was so thick, it looked like a wig. But I knew for a fact it wasn't. I was glad that he was occupied, as I hoped it would keep him from grilling me about Lucinda.

But he caught up with me as I crossed what had been the home's living room and now was the main dining area. "Let me help you," he said, taking one of the recycled grocery bags that held the supplies for the muffins. A server was moving around the room, setting the tables for the next day. Tag and I continued on through the adjacent room, which probably had been the real dining room at one time, and on into the kitchen. I was relieved to see that the chef was already gone. We had territory issues about the room, and it was best when we didn't see each other.

"Give me an update. Have they caught the killer? Is Lucinda all right?" He didn't wait for an answer and went into a diatribe about how unsafe the world had become. "It's not the Cadburians I worry about. It's all the people from all over the country and world who come here."

"Don Porter was most likely killed by someone who knew him, and I doubt it was a random act," I said. "Whoever it was had a reason. Lucinda is fine and having a great time." The news didn't seem to calm him much, and I didn't want to start going in circles.

The best strategy with Tag was to get his mind on something else. I gestured toward the living room. "I think I saw the server putting the knives down so they were crooked." Tag instantly forgot what we were talking about and charged out of the room. I heard the clank of silverware and chuckled to myself. It was too easy to distract him. And in all honesty, I *had* noticed the server had been a little haphazard with the place settings.

I pulled the bags of muffin supplies off to the side and started taking out the ingredients for the pound cakes I was going to make for the Blue Door. I was very appreciative of their letting me use the kitchen for my muffins, so I always worked on the desserts for the restaurant first.

I was going to bake extra pound cakes so I could spend Saturday night with the retreaters without worrying about baking. They were my old standby because they could be served a lot of ways and stayed fresh for several days. I would put buttercream icing on a couple of them and leave the rest plain. The plain ones could be turned into strawberry shortcake by adding the berries and whipped cream, or a slice of the cake could be topped with a scoop of ice cream and a drizzle of caramel sauce. The cake could even be served naked with a garnish.

I set the butter and eggs on the counter to get them to room temperature while I measured the sugar and cake flour.

Tag came in a few minutes later to announce that he was leaving. Apparently he'd worked everything out with the place settings. I waited until I heard the outer door shut and let out a relieved sigh that the place was finally mine. I put on some soft jazz and got into my baking mode.

I'd just started creaming the butter when a knock on the door startled me. *What now?* I was about to arm myself with a frying pan, but I took a peek from the kitchen.

I could just make out Dane's face as he leaned close to the glass. I left the frying pan behind and opened the door. "What up?" I said.

"Guess who's back working nights, thanks to a certain

cop who is pissed that I let you and Kevin St. John go? Well, it's really more about letting you go. I thought I'd start getting used to the schedule by stopping by here the way I did when I had a break."

"I'm sorry," I said, and stepped aside to let him come in.

"It's okay. And once he gets over it, I'll get better hours." He hadn't started the bad hours yet, so he was dressed in street clothes. Nobody could wear an old pair of jeans and a T-shirt better than he could. All the karate and jogging had left him with a great body, and he knew it. He was cocky, but in a teasing way, so he didn't come across as a jerk.

He looked around the empty place. "So nobody's here. I thought you might have company. I saw Sammy and the woman from the café at Vista Del Mar walking down the street before." He didn't give anything away in his expression, but I knew he wanted to get that information to me. "She grabbed his hand," Dane added, checking my reaction.

"Sammy is free to hold hands with whoever he chooses." I tried to keep my voice sounding light, but inside I was wondering how that had come about. Had she just showed up at the B and B down the street where Sammy lived? Probably. And I guessed she would just keep doing things like that until he gave in.

I could hear the smooth sound of the mixer and knew that the butter was creamed sufficiently and it was time to add the sugar. "Let's move this into the kitchen." I led the way and he followed. He leaned against the counter and I began to pour in the sugar. When I opened the bottle of vanilla, the delicious scent filled the air.

143

Dane poked through the bags of muffin-making ingredients. "What's on the menu tonight?" There was something wary in his tone, like he was holding something back.

"I'm not making more of those," I said. He winced, realizing I knew that he knew they'd been a flop.

"I tasted one of them and they're great—almost like the real food you say you don't make. You just have to come up with another name. Maybe Breakfast in a Cup," he said. I didn't take failure well, and it must have showed in my face. He put his arms around me and gave me a reassuring hug.

The hug was going on a little long and I pulled away. It wasn't like I didn't like the hug; it was more that I liked it too much. "I'm working on something else," I said. I told him about Lieutenant Borgnine's apparent love of apple fritters, which his wife had forbidden him to eat.

"He told you that? He admitted that his wife bosses him around? Wow."

"Yes, he did. It gave me an idea for a new kind of muffin that would almost be like an apple fritter, but one that his wife wouldn't object to. He kind of doesn't like me and I thought that might make things better between us."

"I'm sure it would get you points, but if you really want to make things better between you, don't go solving his cases for him." Dane's eyes danced with good humor.

"Speaking of that," I said, cracking the eggs and mixing them in a bowl before I added them to the batter. "Any inside info on what's going on?"

"Aha—do I suspect that you have launched your own investigation?" he teased, and I pretended to swat him.

"No comment," I said.

"Okay, I get it." He grinned. "I bet you already have a whole list of suspects."

"No comment," I said. "But tell me what you know anyway."

"That's all I am to you—just an information source." He turned away in mock hurt and I rolled my eyes. He gave it a moment, then shrugged. "Okay, here goes. I'm just going to give it to you in plain language instead of cop talk. He was shot with a small gun, which we haven't found. Believe me, we looked. Borgnine got it in his head it was in the kitchen trash. You can guess who got stuck sorting through it." He wrinkled his nose as if remembering the job. "We don't know what kind of gun it was yet. No one reported hearing a gunshot, which probably means it happened during the Roast and Toast." I'd begun adding the flour mixed with baking powder. "What exactly is the Roast and Toast?" Dane asked.

"Roasting marshmallows and toasting with hot chocolate. Very G-rated. I think those writers would have preferred wine." I had the tube pans lined up, and Dane helped me fill them with the batter. The instant they went in the oven, the air was filled with their sweet buttery scent. "What about motive?"

"So far, not so good. All Borgnine has heard is that Don was a well-known writer and an excellent teacher. He's trying to see if he has some kind of history with anyone here."

"What about the crime scene? Your people must have seen the blood on the wall."

"Aha. You are into this one," Dane said. "Since it was dark, Lieutenant Borgnine thought he might have been turning on the lights. I hope you realize that all the forensic stuff is going to take a while and you won't hold it against me that I don't know anything about fibers or fingerprints."

"But your people must have at least looked inside the tote bag on the bed. What was in it?" I asked, remembering what T Dot had said he'd seen.

"Tote bag? I don't recall any bag on the bed, just some colored folders."

Again I thought of what T Dot had said about what was there when he saw Don and what he left with him. "Do you recall how many or what color?"

He narrowed his eyes. "Are you on to something? You know, it's only fair that you share since I did."

"Okay. Someone I talked to said he'd gone to Don's room during the Roast and Toast and he'd seen a tote bag on the bed and two folders, a yellow and a red one. I just thought if there were more it would mean someone else came to the room after the person I was talking to."

"I'll have to check. Very quietly. If Lieutenant Borgnine thinks I'm feeding you information, he'll figure out something worse than the night shift. It's lucky he doesn't know about me taking my breaks here." I had begun to take out the supplies for the muffins. Dane stood by, watching. "Why are you involved, anyway? It's not like the travel writer has anything to do with your group."

I hesitated. I was in the same bind with him. I couldn't tell him it was Madeleine who'd gotten me involved or why. "Oh, you know me. Miss Nosy."

"That's the truth," he said, teasing. "And I get that you're not going to share."

"I would if I really knew something, but for now I'm still just checking things out."

"Okay by me. I'm off duty and I'd much rather talk about other things. Like when are you going to admit that you're crazy about me?"

HOURS LATER, WHEN THE STREETS WERE completely quiet, Dane accompanied me as I left a supply of plain vanilla nut muffins at all the usual spots. He nibbled on one of the sample apple fritter muffins as he helped carry the containers. "I think you should have had me be the taster on those breakfast muffins. I could have saved you some grief." He held up what was left of the sample muffin. "This is really good. It's different than your usual muffins, but enough like a muffin so that no one should object."

"A few more tweaks and it should be ready for the real test: Lieutenant Borgnine," I said.

When we'd delivered them all, Dane walked me to my car before going to his red Ford F-150 truck. Although I got a head start, he was on my tail in no time. I pulled into my driveway and he stopped the truck. "I could help you with the delivery to Vista Del Mar," he offered. "Maybe followed by a romantic walk on the beach."

"Are you kidding? Once I drop them off, all I'm going to want is bed."

"That could be arranged," he said. He saw the little shake of my head at the comment. "C'mon. You have to admit that you threw me the perfect setup." I rolled my eyes and he laughed. I waved him on and said I could manage taking the muffins across the street on my own.

"Fine. Have it your way. I just hope nothing jumps out of the bushes." His eyes were dancing, and he waited for a moment to see if I'd relent. When I didn't, he hit the gas and drove down the street.

Whew, if only he knew how close I was to taking him up on his offer.

I unloaded the container of muffins and walked them across the street. The lights on the stone pillars that marked the entrance to Vista Del Mar were like dots in the darkness. I didn't have my flashlight and had to feel my way down the driveway, but I'd walked it so many times, I knew every crack and bump in the asphalt. It felt like the whole place was asleep, and the sound of the ocean seemed louder with nothing to compete with it. The constant breeze felt refreshing after being inside.

Light spilled out of the window from the Lodge. It was open 24/7 but was completely deserted at this hour. I was surprised to see Gill behind the registration desk. He had a stack of magazines.

"What are you still doing here?" I asked as I crossed the large empty room.

"The night clerk has a stomach bug." He eyed the container of muffins. "But my stomach is just fine."

I had some more of the samples of Lieutenant Borgnine's apple fritter muffins and figured I might as well get another opinion. I'd barely opened the bag when he took one hungrily.

I went to set down the container outside the Cora and Madeleine Delacorte Café and then returned for the verdict.

"Different, but very good," he said. I offered him seconds. "I was hoping you'd say that." He took another one from the bag. "I've got some tea back here. Want a cup?"

He handed me a mug of tea that smelled of orange and spices. "So, anything happen after I left?"

"No, I'm pleased to report." He finished off the muffin. "What a day. And having to fuss around with that cabbie on top of everything else." I must have given him a blank look. "You were here, remember? He had an order to pick up the guy who died."

"That's right. How strange."

"What's even stranger is that he must have put in the order shortly after he got here. I saw that the time was yesterday afternoon."

"That is really weird," I said. "I understood Don Porter was scheduled to lead workshops all weekend. Why would he plan to leave? I don't imagine Kevin St. John knew."

"No way did Kevin know anything about it. He was convinced that Don was going to write something about Vista Del Mar and Kevin kept telling me that we had all weekend to wow him." Every time Gill referred to him as Kevin he got this naughty-boy look. "Kevin wanted him to write something like this about Vista Del Mar." Gill pulled out one of the magazines and opened it to a two-page spread. I saw that the byline read *Don Porter* and the article was about a resort on an obscure part of Maui. I read over the beginning, and it went on about the rustic quality of the place and related that the guest quarters were in tree houses. It sounded wonderful.

"Kevin was under the impression that Don was the kind

who wouldn't write anything unless it was good—until he saw this piece." Gill pulled out another magazine and opened it to a spread about some cabins by Lake Michigan in Indiana. I read lines like *overrun with field mice* and *if you're going there, be prepared to battle mosquitoes when you use the outdoor plumbing.*

"Oh," I said, imagining Kevin's expression when he saw it.

"Kevin is so bonkers about this place, I actually heard him tell someone that now that Don was dead he didn't have to worry what he would write about Vista Del Mar."

I drained my mug of tea and set it on the counter, left Gill another muffin and headed for home.

14

IT WOULD HAVE BEEN EASY TO SLEEP IN SATURDAY morning. After a night of not enough sleep, and the murky light coming in the window, snuggling under my comforter felt like the perfect idea. But my alarm went off and kept on making its grating noise. I had deliberately placed it across the room so that I had to get up to shut it off.

Julius was snuggled in the crook of my arm and gave me a dirty look when I pulled back the flower-print comforter. The air was cold and the floor was colder, but at the same time not cold enough to turn on the heat. My feet found their way to my fuzzy slippers and I went across the room to end the annoying noise of the alarm clock.

I looked out the window and saw that the clouds were so low that the tops of the Monterey pines disappeared into a white mist. I had pulled on a warm robe and made it to the kitchen when I heard the banging on the door.

"Madeleine?" I said as I opened the door and saw her. "Is something wrong?"

She rushed inside and told me to shut the door quickly. My eyes were barely open, but they were open enough to take in her continued love affair with jeans. She had turned into quite the fashion plate and wore ankle boots with her skinny jeans and oversize burgundy-colored sweater. The contrast with the Chanel suits and green eye shadow that she used to wear and her sister still did was mind-boggling. Madeleine might be the older one, but with her new look she seemed decades younger than her sister. I would have told her how cute she looked, but she seemed too agitated to care.

"I was just going to have some coffee," I said and offered her a cup. I think she got it that whatever she had to say ought to wait until I'd had a hit of caffeine. I took the easy way out and boiled some water for instant, and we sat down at my table together.

After a few sips, I felt my mind clear, and my eyes opened wider. "Okay, what is it?" I asked, preparing for some new disaster.

"I'm worried that someone may have seen me talking to Don when we got to Vista Del Mar. What if they remember and mention it to Lieutenant Borgnine?" Her face took on a look of determination. "I really need this case closed."

I wanted to tell her she was overreacting and not to worry, but then she reminded me how she had helped me. "You know that Cora wasn't so sure about letting you keep the arrangement we gave your aunt. I fought for you. I told my sister that your retreats were life changing for people and it was a public service to have you putting them on."

"I have some suspects," I said, and she brightened.

"Good. How many? Who are they? I need some hope that this will be resolved soon."

I had to give her something to calm her down. "There's the man you said threw a fit at the first workshop Don led, but I haven't been able to locate him. You said he was wearing one of those army jackets and it had something on the front. I think you said it was a decal. It would help if you had any more details."

Madeleine thought about it for a moment. "Did I tell you there were letters on it?" I shook my head in answer. "I'm sure they were letters, and something about them made me think of you. I just can't remember why."

"Let me know if you figure it out," I said before moving on. "I did talk to someone else who went to a smaller critique group that night. I'm not sure he was telling me the truth, though. But he definitely could be a suspect." By now I was half talking to myself as I remembered that Dane had said there was no tote bag found in the room. "It sounds silly, but it has to do with whether there was a tote bag in Don's room or not."

Madeleine seemed troubled. "How could I have forgotten what he said." She looked at me. "I was sitting by the door and just before he went outside he said something like 'I'll show you.' That sounds like a threat, doesn't it?"

"It certainly could have been. I'll get it figured out. I promise," I said, hoping to calm her down.

"Do your best," she said, getting up. "Please do your very best, quickly."

I sat at the table for a few minutes as I finished my coffee. I looked at my watch. It was early here, but the two hours' time difference between here and Chicago made it not too early to call Frank.

I had his number on speed dial by now, and the phone began to ring. And ring. And then it went to voice mail. "Geez, Frank. Where are you? Please call," I said, then realized that was a stupid request. I wasn't going to be at home to answer, and my cell was useless across the street. "Actually, I'll call you." I hung up feeling a little better. At least I had taken some action.

Now I had to hurry. I needed to get across the street in time for breakfast. It was all about the food. Breakfast was my favorite meal at Vista Del Mar. They always had pancakes or waffles, eggs, potatoes, fruit, toast—all the good stuff, and the staff was very nice about my creating my own little buffet and getting a little bit of everything.

The bell had already rung when I approached the Sea Foam dining hall. The smell of hot food and coffee beckoned me. The smell got even better when I opened the door.

Lucinda was acting as hostess to the three tables with my people. I went straight back to the cafeteria line and took a tray. The server recognized me. "I know what you want," she said with a friendly smile. After making her way past all the containers on the steam tray, she handed me a plate piled with eggs and blueberry pancakes, fruit, potatoes and a piece of raisin toast.

Lucinda had saved the seat next to her for me. She looked

put together, as always. It was the touches like the emerald green scarf, the perfectly styled hair and the lipstick that I could never seem to manage. I knew that my hair looked windblown. I was pretty sure I'd forgotten to add lipstick when I'd slapped on a little foundation and eyeliner. And this morning I'd forgotten to add some embellishment from my aunt's stash—I probably looked pretty dull in my usual black jeans and apricot-colored turtleneck topped with a black fleece jacket.

She waited until I set the plate down and then filled my coffee cup. I nodded a greeting to the rest of the table. "Go on and eat something quickly; you're going to need the strength."

"What?" I said. "Is something wrong?" I tried to keep my voice low.

Rayanne was next to me before Lucinda could answer. "Last night while DeeDee and I were at the movie, someone went through all of our rooms."

"What?" I said incredulous. "What was taken?" I added, figuring I was going to have to replace whatever it was.

"Nothing was gone. Nothing was gone," DeeDee said. She seemed very nervous to be speaking and her head jerked so much that her hair kept swinging.

Rayanne took back the position of speaker. "Things were just moved around. I think someone must have poked around my yarn because when I got back it was on the floor and I know I left it sitting on my bed."

Mona stood up from across the table and seemed very upset, or at least I thought so. She was still hidden, with her big hat and sunglasses, but she waved her hands like she

155

was very upset. "It's like I was violated," she said in a low voice. "I suppose I should be grateful they didn't throw things around. You could almost miss that anyone had been in there, but a few things were rearranged. It was as if they didn't want anyone to know someone had been in there."

Rayanne took back the floor. "You don't have to think too hard to figure out who it was. I'm sure it was the police with the help of him." She pointed at Kevin St. John, who was making the rounds of the tables, asking if everyone was enjoying their breakfast.

"It wasn't just us," Lisa said, and I gulped. "Derek said he thinks they may have gone through the writers' rooms, too. One of them mentioned that something had been moved. The rest of them didn't seem to notice."

"Maybe it was housekeeping doing turndown service and they were clumsy," the woman in the cat T-shirt said. The group considered it for a moment, and then they laughed.

"This place? I don't think so. That would be like getting mints on your pillow at camp," the woman with the knitting needles in her hair said.

One by one the rest of the group all said either that they had noticed that things had been moved around or, now that it had been mentioned, that they were sure things had been moved around.

I turned to Lucinda, who shrugged. "I wasn't going to say anything since nothing was missing and the room seemed the same as when I left it."

"Oh, no," Dolly said. "I was so tired after the movie, I didn't notice. I suppose they went through my room, too. Any idea what they were looking for?"

"I bet they were looking for clues to who killed the travel writer," the woman with the knitting needles stuck in her bun said. "They must think one of us did it."

"Why would they look through our stuff?" Bree asked.

"Haven't they heard of warrants?" Rayanne added angrily. "Are you going to do anything, or is this just more dysfunction?" She glared at me and then turned to the group to rally support. "Maybe we should band together and demand a refund."

I put my hands up to stop her. It had been bad enough to think about the Difficult Duo asking for their money back, but all of them? My eyes flew skyward just thinking about it. "Let me get to the bottom of this," I said. I surprised myself by the authoritative sound to my voice, and even more surprising was that I wasn't was faking it. When I'd taken over my aunt's business, I hadn't really been committed. It was like I was just dipping my toe in and could cut and run whenever I wanted. But as I'd put on more retreats, I'd changed and become protective of my people. I was ready to roar when I caught up with Kevin St. John.

He was holding a coffeepot and talking to a table of writers, seeming very much the host.

"I need to speak to you," I said in a terse tone. Had he really given the cops permission to go through the rooms? And what were they looking for?

He threw me a dirty look and told me he was occupied and would talk to me shortly. I stood there, getting more steamed by the moment. He continued to ignore me as he made the rounds with the coffeepot.

"Ms. Feldstein, you need to learn some self-control. You

can't simply interrupt me and expect me to rudely ignore my conference-goers," he said finally when he stepped away.

I ignored the reprimand. "Kevin how could you have given Lieutenant Borgnine carte blanche to go through all the guest rooms? I guess you thought your writers wouldn't notice. What was he looking for, anyway?"

"What are you talking about?" he demanded as his normally placid face went through a cycle of expressions from annoyed to disturbed. I explained what I'd heard from my retreaters and he seemed shocked.

"You should check with your group," I said. "One of my people came with one of your people and she told me her husband said some of the writers said their rooms had been gone through."

He gestured for me to lower my voice and then pulled me all the way to the side of the room. I explained again that just about all the people in my group had reported that it looked like things had been moved around in their rooms, but nothing was missing.

"It wasn't me. I certainly wouldn't give anyone permission to do that or hand over the master key." He instinctively glanced in the direction of the Lodge.

"Who had access to it?" I asked.

"It hangs on the side of the wooden pigeonholes where we keep the regular guest keys." He seemed upset with himself for revealing that information. "That's classified information."

I wanted to laugh at his last comment. The spot he'd talked about was available to anyone who worked behind the registration counter and anyone who came to the side of it and had a long reach. "You might want to find a more secure location."

His lips curled into a snarl. "I don't need you to tell me my business. Now, you better get back to your people and smooth things over."

When I went back to the table, the chairs were all empty except one. Lucinda was sitting next to my plate of food.

"They all wanted to check their rooms, and Rayanne was trying to stir up a rebellion." She saw me looking at my plate. "Do you want me to see if I can get the kitchen to warm it up for you?"

"No time. I'll try to make it up at lunch."

15

AFTER BREAKFAST, THE GROUP STILL HAD SOME
free time before the morning workshop started. I went on
to the meeting room. Everything was set up as usual. The
fire glowed in the fireplace and the coffee and tea setup was
on the counter. I checked the cookie tin and saw that the
supply was dwindling and made a mental note to bake some
more when I went home.

Wanda was sitting at the end of the table, knitting. From
the looks of her work, I decided she was making a soft blue
washcloth. Unlike me, who had to keep my eyes glued to
my work, Wanda could knit while looking out the window,
as she was now. She looked in my direction when I set down
the cookie tin.

"You look a little harried. Did something else happen?"
My hand went right to my head to try to smooth my hair.

"It depends what you mean by 'happen,'" I said in a throw-up-my-hands sort of sarcastic tone. Then I told her about what my group had said.

As I was speaking, Crystal came in, looking like a burst of color. The only thing plain about her appearance was her jeans. Her long sweater was purple and it contrasted with the orange, pink and kelly green scarves she had twisted together. I saw that she had a tote bag brimming with more color. After greeting us, she began to unload the bag and lay things out on the table.

"What's that?" Wanda said in a warning tone.

"I brought some samples of what can be done with the basic pattern." Wanda put her work down and stood up, looking over what Crystal had put out. I was amazed at what she'd done. She'd made the triangle-shaped shawl with stripes of color. She'd added beads to the edging on the head scarf. The baby blanket was done half and half in different shades of lavender and she'd added a pretty border.

I expected some kind of praise to come from Wanda, but she seemed disturbed. "Put it away," Wanda commanded. "We finally have them on track working on projects. They'll see these and want to change everything. It's too many choices and will make chaos." She looked at both of us. "It's Saturday morning and the retreat ends tomorrow. We want them to leave here knowing how to finish what they began, not hysterical when they realize they don't have the beads or know how to add them."

Crystal seemed undaunted. "If anyone wants to add beads, they can get them in the gift shop. My mother always leaves a nice supply. Then I can demonstrate. It's really very easy."

Her corkscrew curls bobbed as she leaned over to place the head scarf in a more prominent place.

"I've had my say," Wanda said, and went back to her knitting. "It's up to Casey, anyway."

The words reverberated in my head. Of course, it was really up to me. I was the one in charge. I had been letting everyone else run the show up until now. Leaders had to be decisive. "I say let them see everything," I said.

Madeleine came into the room with the tote bag she'd gotten at Cadbury Yarn to carry her project. I would have happily given her one of the red Yarn2Go bags, but I think she liked to show that she was somehow separate. Not that her bag stood out. Almost everyone had brought a tote in the same unbleached muslin color as hers and simply put my bag inside.

She took a seat at the table and let out a sigh of pleasure. "It is so nice to spend time being with the group." She reached toward the center and picked up the head scarf with the beads and tried it on. "What do you think?" Madeleine was having so much fun with the new turn in her life, it made me smile. And it looked cute on her.

"I like it on you," I said.

"Then it's settled. I want to add beads to mine." She took it off and put it on the table before holding up the small triangle she'd made so far. "Tell me how to do the beads." She looked from Crystal to Wanda.

Wanda rolled her eyes with displeasure. "Talk to Crystal. She's the one who can't leave well enough alone." She muttered something about this being what she'd thought would happen.

Crystal seemed undaunted by Wanda's comment and showed Madeleine that the beads were actually added in the edging. "You can wait until you're finished with the body of it before you have to pick out the beads."

Madeleine pushed her chair back. "I want to get them now. I'd like your help in choosing them."

"They have some at the gift shop that might work," Crystal said.

I glanced at my watch, trying not to be too obvious. The retreaters would be arriving soon and it was not a good time for Crystal to leave. But I accepted that Madeleine needed special care. Wanda picked up on what was going on and urged Crystal and me to both go with Madeleine. As we rushed out the door, I glanced back. As I'd figured, there was a plan in Wanda's move. She was packing up the pieces that Crystal had arranged around the table. No matter what she'd said about it being my decision, I'm sure she thought I was making a mistake and had found a way to overrule me.

I was in the lead as we went down the path, so I tried to quicken the pace. Madeleine was talking eyeliner with Crystal. My helper did a great job with eye makeup, which I had tried to copy. On her it came off as exotic, and on me—well, I looked like a raccoon with a headache.

I glanced back at their friendly conversation, wondering how they would feel if they knew they were related. If Crystal's mother was the child of Madeleine's late brother, then Crystal would be Madeleine's great-niece. I wondered if Gwen would ever really act on the information I'd given her.

The Lodge was mostly empty as we passed through on the way to the gift shop, which was tucked in the corner of the building. A few of the writers were looking around at journals and books when we walked in. The display of yarn and supplies was toward the back of the store. A small basket in the midst of the yarn held packets of beads and accessory items such as stitch holders.

Generally, Gwen checked the supplies over the weekend, replenishing them if needed. "Your mom must have been out here this morning," I said, noting that the baskets of yarn were overflowing.

Crystal looked over the display and seemed puzzled. "It does look full, but I know she wasn't out here." She picked up several of the skeins of beige yarn and read over the labels. "She never would have brought this yarn. She always sticks to basic worsted-weight blends and a selection of cotton yarns." Crystal's black curls jiggled as she shook her head. "I don't even think we carry this stuff."

Madeleine had found the basket with the assorted supplies and was looking through it for beads.

"How strange," I said. I thought it over for a moment and then remembered that Rayanne had made a change of plan and I'd allowed her to exchange the yarn she'd bought at Cadbury Yarn with the yarn in the gift shop. But that couldn't account for this extra yarn, particularly since Crystal said Cadbury Yarn didn't even carry it.

Finally, Crystal shrugged. "It's kind of like reverse shoplifting. It's shop-leaving."

"What do you think of these?" Madeleine said, holding out a package of small wooden beads."

"I think they're perfect," Crystal said. "And they're on me."

As we walked back, Crystal talked to Madeleine, explaining how to get the small beads on the cotton yarn. "Never mind. You won't get to it until after the retreat. You can just call me and I'll come over and help you," Crystal said. Madeleine's face lit up and she squeezed the younger woman's hand.

The meeting room was full when we returned. As I'd expected, all of Crystal's samples had disappeared from sight and Wanda was walking around the room, checking on everyone's progress. Lucinda caught my gaze with a question in her eyes. I used my head to point toward Madeleine, and Lucinda responded with a knowing nod.

Madeleine reclaimed her seat while Crystal and I went to the head of the table. Crystal might have been able to shrug off the extra yarn in the gift shop, but it troubled me. "Did any of you leave some yarn anywhere?" I glanced around at all the faces for a response, but no one's face lit up with recognition. I went further and brought up the colors, using words like *beige* and *toast*, and still there was no response from the group. I thought if they'd left yarn somewhere in the Lodge, someone might have thought it belonged in the gift shop.

"Ahem." It was a man's voice, clearly trying to get my attention. I turned and felt my shoulders drop as Kevin St. John and Lieutenant Borgnine joined us at at the head of the table. I caught a glimpse of Madeleine shoving her things into her tote bag and slipping out the door behind them.

The two men gave me a look that said they were in charge, and I stepped aside and let them take over.

Kevin St. John tried to smooth things over first. "I know this weekend hasn't gone quite as we all planned. Before

Lieutenant Borgnine speaks to you, I want to let you know that we here at Vista Del Mar want to do what we can to make up for any inconveniences you've had. So tonight, we're going to have a party for all the guests in Hummingbird Hall. We will kick off an open mike session. Anyone can read a short piece of writing. There's a sign-up sheet in the Lodge. After the writers show off their stuff, the Amazing Dr. Sammy will show off his in a full-blown magic show. I understand he is going to be cutting his assistant in half. The evening will be capped off with square dancing."

There were some mutterings about not knowing how to square-dance and not having the right clothes. "No problem," Kevin St. John said with a confident smile. "There will be a lesson first and we'll have an assortment of skirts with crinolines available."

By now, Lieutenant Borgnine was scowling and seemed impatient. He gave Kevin's arm a nudge. "We have had the report of an incident which incorrectly was tied to the police." Kevin was looking directly at me with a piercing stare. "Lieutenant Borgnine wants to set the record straight."

He gave the floor over to the cop. I think the lieutenant was trying to appear friendly, but it also appeared that he had a headache, so his smile came across as pained. Meanwhile, Kevin slipped away.

"I want to make it clear. No one connected with Cadbury PD went through any rooms last night."

There was some whispering throughout the group, and he held his hand up to quiet them. "But apparently someone did. And so, once again, I'd like to talk to each of you separately. I want to thank you for your cooperation," he said.

He was clearly trying to make it sound like it was voluntary, but nobody fell for it, and there was a rumble of grumblings.

He ignored them completely and pointed at Bree, in the first seat. "We'll start with you." He turned to the rest of them. "And like before, when one comes back, the next one should come out." Bree looked back at the group and shrugged as she followed him out.

The room erupted into noise as they left the room. I picked out a few of the comments, including "Not again" and "Now what?" Wanda and Crystal looked to me to handle things.

"I'm sure this is just routine, so they can get a handle on what might have happened last night. In the meantime, why not settle into working on your projects. I'm sure you all know how soothing knitting and crochet are. And now you can look forward to a fun evening of dancing and magic." I think my voice faltered on *magic*. Was Sammy really going to cut Bridget in half? Of course, I knew it was just an illusion, but I was sure it must take practice. So they must be spending time together. I considered the thought of Sammy having a girlfriend. I told myself that it would be a good thing. Then I wouldn't have to feel so responsible for him.

I realized I'd stopped talking as these thoughts were circulating through my brain and the whole group was staring at me. Finally, DeeDee asked if there was something wrong.

"This weekend certainly isn't what I expected when I signed up," Jeff Hunter said, picking up the slack. The sound of a male voice coming from the group still startled all of us. He glanced around at the group, realizing the effect his voice had.

"You and me should talk more so we don't surprise them," Jeff said, turning to Scott, who was sitting beside to him. He directed the next thing he said to me. "You gotta understand. I've never knit in a group before. I heard about them and saw groups in movies . . ." He stood up, and there was no way not to notice that he was a little rough around the edges. Maybe it was the boots that clunked when he walked, or his clothes: the beat-up leather jacket with chains and the cigarette behind his ear. "I realized I probably wouldn't fit in with a group of ladies meeting at a hospital making baby hats."

I pressed my lips together not to laugh at the image of him sitting down at a table with a bunch of women making pink and blue hats. The rest of the group didn't withhold their reaction, and there was a wave of chuckles.

"See, I'm right. You know it, too. Those ladies would never have accepted me." He nodded his head and his fierce look softened as his lips curved in a smile. "But I figured coming away for a weekend might be different." He shifted his weight. "Especially when I heard I wouldn't be the only guy." Scott smiled and made a fake bow and added a flourish with his hand. Yes, they were both guys, but that was about the only thing they had in common.

"You can sit down and still talk," a woman at the back said.

Jeff nodded. "Yeah, you gotta forgive me. I'm still not clear about the etiquette of all this." He sat back down and continued to talk. "I got the feeling that it was okay to open up and kind of bare your soul in groups like this." His gaze moved around the group. "That's not something I've ever had much chance to do. I'm out on the road most of the time. Alone in my rig. When I meet up with other truckers, mostly we talk about sports. They don't know about this." He held up his knitting. "Or how it saved my life when I had to quit smoking. I was a wreck and needed something to calm my nerves and keep my hands busy." He pointed to the cigarette behind his ear. "That's to remind me that I am in charge."

Several of the women clapped their hands. Someone else called out that he must have been a lot of places. He found the woman who'd spoken and directed his comments at her. "I have been a lot of places, but I wouldn't call it traveling. Though there have been moments." His gaze softened and he seemed to be seeing memories. "There's something about dawn in the desert. The way the air is light and brittle cold. The pastel colors of the sky and then the piercing sun as it shows over the horizon. You'd think the surroundings would all be just brown, but there are so many different shades." He caught himself and seemed embarrassed.

I was surprised by how poetic he was, and I thought of the travel essays Don Porter had talked about in the workshop Madeleine had attended. "You could write about your travels," I said.

"I was kind of thinking about that. I've seen a lot of stuff. Not just rain splatting against my windshield on a dark night, either. There are a lot of stories I could tell."

"So, tell us one," DeeDee said.

Jeff shifted his weight again and glanced up at the ceiling, searching his memory. "Okay, here's one. I was doing a run with cargo for a big retailer, and right after I'm loaded up, this woman who works at the place comes up to me and asks me if I'll be passing through Flagstaff. She's got a dog on a leash. There was a story attached. Her daughter moved to Flagstaff and left the dog, but now she misses the pooch. Could I take it to her? We're not supposed to do stuff like that, but it wasn't the first time I'd carried cargo I wasn't supposed to. Someone would say, 'As long as you're going . . .'"

The story went on from there about how he liked having the dog with him so much, after he dropped it off, he went to a shelter and adopted a dog. The group was almost in tears as he described picking a golden retriever mix that was on its last day at the shelter. "We kind of saved each other," he said. Then he apologized. "I didn't mean to hog the floor."

No one seemed to mind, and if anything they were interested in hearing more. I was glad that he seemed to have distracted them from having to talk to Lieutenant Borgnine again. It struck me that just like Don Porter, Jeff traveled for a living.

When the workshop broke up, everyone scattered for their free time before lunch. Lucinda hung back. "I feel like you've been holding something back," she said. "Is it something about Tag that you don't want to tell me? Whatever it is, whatever he's done—just tell me." My friend sounded a little frantic, which was not her usual way. Nothing that went on in the restaurant or her relationship seemed to rattle her.

"I wanted you to enjoy the retreat without any worries," I said, trying to cover up the truth that I had been holding something back.

"If you want me not to have worries, I have to know what's going on," she said, and I realized that what I'd said had only made her more concerned. I had a lot to learn in the how-to-be-a-leader department. I apologized but still suggested that she go off and enjoy the free time until lunch.

She was undaunted. "No. There's something going on, and I want details."

"Okay," I said, already trying to figure out what I could tell her and manage not to say anything regarding Madeleine. I didn't want our conversation overheard, so I suggested we find a bench on the boardwalk that cut through the dunes to the street and the beach.

It was a good place to talk because while there were people passing by, there was no place for anyone to eavesdrop. We claimed the bench and sat, each of us instinctively pulling our jackets a little tighter. Mine was a plain taupe fleece, but she wore a Ralph Lauren one that reminded me of a Native American blanket.

The constant breeze off the ocean was more pronounced here, making it feel colder and sending our hair flying. The white sand was visible around the plants and bushes that grew wild. The way the light reflected off the sand reminded me of how it looked when the snow fell in Chicago. It seemed extra bright, despite the sky, which looked as if it had been spread with an even layer of clouds.

"We're alone and away from prying ears," Lucinda said. "Spill!"

"First, let me tell you there is nothing wrong with Tag, other than he misses you." She seemed instantly relieved. "I'll tell you about my efforts to find out who killed the travel writer, but you can't ask me why I'm looking into it."

171

"A mystery within a mystery," Lucinda said. "Okay, I won't ask. I'm sure you have a very good reason and you'll tell me someday, right?"

I promised I would when it was solved. I was relieved that Lucinda wasn't offended that I was keeping something from her, and I was grateful to have someone to talk with about the crazy stuff going on.

"I gather the guy wasn't much of a diplomat when it came to critiquing people's work," I began, and then went on to tell her what T Dot had said about him. "But in the end, T Dot said he thought the criticism was justified. That's when it gets a little strange. He admitted to me something that he didn't tell the police. That he went to Don's room during the Roast and Toast, which is also when the cops think Don was shot."

"T Dot?" Lucinda said, laughing. "That's not really his name."

"It's *T*, the initial, and dot like a period." I explained his rather pretentious name starting with an initial and how it had become shortened. "You should see the tattoo he has on his chest."

Lucinda's eyes bugged out. "Just how intimate of a conversation did you have?"

"It was nothing like that. You can see the hawk's hooded eyes through his open shirt collar. I just imagined what the rest of it looked like."

"So, do you think he did it?" Lucinda asked.

"It's more like I think he could have. There was something weird, too. He mentioned seeing a tote bag on Don's bed, but Dane said there was no tote bag on the bed when they went in there."

"Dane?" Lucinda said with a twinkle in her eye. "When did you talk to him?"

I brought up my baking, making sure to mention that I'd left a nice supply of pound cakes. "I went with traditional muffins until I can figure out how to make the new ones work. And I might even have another specialty." I mentioned Lieutenant Borgnine being ordered not to eat apple fritters, probably because of all the sugar and fat. "I would probably earn a lot of points with him if I came up with something similar to his favorite, but a version that his wife would let him eat."

Lucinda shook her head to clear her brain. "How have you had time to do all this while the retreat is going on?"

"It helps that you've played host a lot," I said. "By the way, T Dot isn't the only one who Don insulted. I heard there was someone at the workshop he did on Thursday who threw a hissy fit and stormed out with some kind of I'll-show-you-type threat."

"Have you talked to him yet?"

"I would have if I knew who he was. All I got was a vague description that he was wearing what I figured out was one of those green army surplus jackets."

Lucinda got it right away. "That could be a lot of people. Those writer men seem to favor those jackets. Didn't you get anything else that could help identify him?"

I searched my mind for anything else that Madeleine might have said about him. She'd said something about a patch on the jacket with letters on it that reminded her of me. As I said it, something pinged in my mind and I was pretty sure I knew why she'd thought of me. The letters could be *KC*, which sounded like my name. "I think I figured out something that might narrow it down."

As soon as Lucinda heard about the letters, she offered to help. "You know me, always playing hostess. I'll extend it to the writers. That ought to give me a chance to check out a lot of their jackets."

"You're the best," I said. "I'm sorry if you felt left out."

"The retreat was a little flat without me getting to be your sidekick. It's pretty impressive how you got T Dot to tell you so much."

"Speaking of telling stuff, how did it go with Lieutenant Borgnine?" I asked.

"I think he treated me a little different than the others since I live in Cadbury and I said that I hadn't noticed anything moved around in my room. He seemed to think it was some kind of hysterical reaction from the others. You know, one person says they think someone was in their room because things were shifted around, and then everybody imagines that it happened to them, too."

"Talk about things being shifted around," I said, half to myself. Lucinda stopped talking and asked what I meant.

"Someone dropped off yarn in the gift shop. They added it to the display that Gwen left. Crystal was with me, and she said the shop didn't even carry that kind of yarn."

"Why would someone do that?"

"I don't know, but I sure would like to find out."

16

LUCINDA WENT OFF TO FRESHEN UP, AND I CUT through the Lodge. As I passed the café, I remembered the traditional muffins I'd dropped off. I wondered how they were selling. Bridget was behind the counter and I considered changing my mind. It felt uncomfortable now that I knew there was more going on between Sammy and her than I had thought.

I suddenly felt very self-conscious about how to act. She flashed a smile that seemed a tad triumphant, which made me feel even more uncomfortable. But it was too late to back out now. I looked at the counter where the muffins were usually displayed in a basket.

She figured out what I was doing. "The ones you brought in today moved like usual. Though someone came in and got one of those." She indicated the cold display case and the breakfast muffins. "I'm not sure how long we're supposed to keep those."

"They should be fine through the weekend," I said. I couldn't resist asking if she remembered who had bought it.

"That cute cop," she said. "He came in here with the one with a rumpled jacket. I guess they're still investigating. It's funny how they never thought about talking to me," she said. "I see a lot from behind this counter. And I hear a lot, too."

"Really?" I said. I wondered if Sammy had mentioned my investigative abilities and she was trying to compete. "Like what?"

"How about I heard a couple of those writer guys talking about how to commit the perfect crime," she said.

"Like you said, writer guys. They were probably talking about a story." If she was trying to outshine me, she would have to do better than that. I turned to leave.

"You probably don't know yet, but Mr. St. John is having Sammy do a special show tonight." She flashed the triumphant smile again. "He said he'd do it as long as I would be his assistant. We practiced that act until late last night." I didn't know what to say and left with just a wave.

On the way across the main room of the building, I saw that Gill was still behind the registration desk. "You're still here," I said.

He nodded quickly. "It's amazing what a couple of black eyes will do." He realized I didn't know what he was talking about and explained it was a cup of coffee with two shots of espresso. "I'm still wide-awake," he said, sounding a little buzzed. "How's it going? Anything new?" I recognized it as nervous talk. Though Gill asked the questions, he never gave me time to answer, but just went off on a talking tear. I was trying to extricate myself until I heard him mention Don Porter. "I wonder what he had in that bag."

"Bag?" I said, suddenly tuning in.

"The bag he had when he asked me for the directions to the lighthouse. He had a nylon bag, messenger-style, but it looked like it was full of something." Gill continued, "I offered to let him leave it here at the desk, but he pulled it away when I made a reach for it. I was just trying to be helpful."

"So you couldn't see what was in it?" I asked.

"All I saw was, like, the handle of a cloth tote." He glanced around the room; one of the writers was walking through. "Like that," he said, pointing to the man's bag, "but it must have been fuller to make it stick out of the messenger bag."

"He was probably going to the lighthouse to make notes on it so he could write about it," I said, but Gill shook his head.

"I think he was meeting someone." Gill shook his head in a nervous version of dismay. "I tried to give it to him, but he was gone." The desk clerk had gotten cryptic, and he was talking very fast.

"Take a breath," I said.

He followed my order and he seemed to calm a little. "I'm not making sense, am I? It's like my brain is thinking faster than I can talk. What I meant to say was that Don dropped a folded square of paper. I picked it up to give it to him, but he was already out the door." Gill stopped and seemed to have blanked out, so I prompted him, asking why the scrap of paper had made him think that Don was meeting someone.

"I know Kevin is always telling us to mind our own business, and I realized it was from the message board, but I opened it anyway. It said *Snow Drop* on the outside, and inside there was something about the lighthouse and a bench and a time. I think it was around three o'clock."

THOUGHTS WERE SWIRLING AROUND IN MY HEAD as I went across the street to my place. I'd asked if Gill still had the paper, but he said he'd thrown it away. There was no telling what it actually said without seeing it. And what did it mean, anyway? It wasn't as if someone had lured him there and then killed him. I guessed it was from one of the writers wanting to have a private meeting. Maybe *Snow Drop* had some meaning related to his writing.

I flipped on the oven as soon as I got into the kitchen and opened the refrigerator to make sure I had enough logs of cookie dough. Julius appeared from somewhere, reacting to the open refrigerator.

"You've become a stink fish machine," I said to the cat as he stood next to me and looked up at the shelves. "You've already had some. I'll give you more tonight." I hoped I sounded firm when I said it and then laughed at myself—as if the cat would understand. It almost seemed like he did. After making a sharp, plaintive meow, he walked away.

But only for a moment. Did he realize he might have hurt my feelings? When he returned he circled around my ankles a few times and then gave one of them a rub.

I put out the cookie sheets and laid a sheet of parchment paper on each one. I tried to keep the slices of dough even, and then topped each one with some butterscotch chips.

I had just put the cookies in the oven when my phone rang. I grabbed it before it even announced the caller.

"Feldstein, you called?" Frank said after I'd gotten out a hello.

"You really called me back." I couldn't keep the surprise out of my voice.

"Yeah, I'm a polite guy. I return calls. So what's up?"

He'd caught me a little off guard. I had so much more information than when I'd originally called him, I didn't know what to say. "I wanted to use you as a sounding board," I said finally. "I have a lot of disjointed information and I thought if I threw it all at you, the answers might bounce back at me."

"Oh, no," Frank said in a mock distressed voice. "You were just going to use me and then hang up."

"Well, maybe I hoped for some advice from you, too. You're such an expert. I thought you could see something that I missed."

"That's better, Feldstein. If you want help from someone, you have to stroke their ego." I heard his chair squeak, as if he was settling in. "I'm all ears, so shoot."

I was trying to mentally arrange the information so it would make sense. "I think the travel writer was meeting someone, and he was carrying a bag that seemed overfull."

"Okay, if I'm a sounding board, I'm supposed to throw it back at you. What do you think that means?"

"Maybe he was carrying a package he was going to give whoever he was meeting." I paused for a moment to consider.

Frank knew all about Vista Del Mar being unplugged. He thought it was laughable that there was a message board. I was rethinking the note and had a new theory. "He might not have known who he was meeting." I explained the folded note Gill had found. "And they might not have known who he was. Otherwise, why address the message to Snow Drop?"

"So, he could have been meeting someone, but I think it's going to be pretty hard for you to figure out who it is. Maybe you can talk to that rich dame; what's her name?" He stopped and started muttering to himself. "I have this new method for remembering names. I link them to something. The name I'm thinking of has something to do with an angry line dancer."

"Huh," I said, and then he interrupted me in an excited voice. "Madeleine. Get it? Mad line. Didn't you say she met the dead guy on a plane? Maybe they talked about things like if he was going to be meeting someone while he was there. Or maybe it was her and she called him Snow Drop."

"That's a good idea. I'll talk to her," I said.

"Weren't you going to track down some writers?" Frank asked. "Most likely one of them is your killer. Their hurt feelings made them fly into a rage. Did you find out what kind of gun the killer used?"

"Not exactly. I just know it was a small gun and the cops haven't found it."

"Feldstein, if you're going to be any kind of detective, you have to get rid of your squeamishness about guns. You should know a Glock from a Smith and Wesson. You know

I said you ought to be carrying, the way people keep dropping in that town." He chuckled. "A small gun, hah."

The bell went off, letting me know the cookies were done, and I cradled the phone as I took them out of the oven and set them out to cool. "What about your group? Any suspects?"

I was going to laugh it off, but then I thought of Lisa and her husband. "There is one woman whose husband is in the writers' group."

"There you go, Feldstein. Maybe she became a she-wolf when her husband's writing was slammed and she sought revenge in his name."

"That sounds like a plot line on a movie poster," I said. "Wait," I said, suddenly remembering something. "The dead guy, as you call him, ordered a cab to pick him up on Friday morning and take him to the airport, but according to the schedule I saw, he was supposed to do several more workshops over the weekend and lead a couple of critique groups."

"Maybe he changed his mind after he saw the place. You said he was some big-deal writer," Frank said.

"You could be right. The manager was practically jumping out of his skin trying to get Don to write a positive piece about Vista Del Mar. Don could have had enough of Kevin St. John hovering over him and knew he was going to write something unflattering about the place and wanted to get out of there." The cookies were already cool enough to begin packing in the tin. I laid a sheet of wax paper between the layers, but even so, some of the melted butterscotch chips got smooshed on the paper.

"Or," I said, having a flash of inspiration. "The writers I talked to all seemed surprised that someone as well-known as Don Porter would come to an obscure writers' conference. I also heard from more than one person that one of the things about travel writing was it was kind of a two for one. What if he really came there for another reason? And it was just a cover for him so he could meet someone? And then once he met whoever it was, he decided to leave."

I could hear Frank's chair squeaking and squawking, which was a sure sign he was getting impatient. I got ready to sign off. "There's just one more thing I want to ask you about," I said.

"Okay," he said in a tired voice, like he had one finger poised over the off button on the phone.

"I've told you that the cop in charge here doesn't like me. His wife won't let him have apple fritters. Do you think it would make a difference if I came up with a muffin that was sort of like an apple fritter that his wife would let him have?"

"Geez, Feldstein, I don't know. He lets his wife boss him around like that? That's why I'm not married. No woman would keep me from an apple fritter if that's what I wanted."

And then he was gone.

Julius followed me to the door. I didn't think it was a last play for stink fish this time. It seemed more like he was sorry to see me leave.

The clouds seemed to have thinned a bit and the sky had an apricot-colored hue, as if the sun was working its way through the moisture and might even make an appearance.

Even the promise of sun warmed the air, and I left my fleece open as I went back down the driveway.

The lunch bell had just started. I made a detour and went to our meeting room to drop off the tin of cookies.

A line had already formed inside when I reached the Sea Foam dining hall. The sun seemed to have changed its mind and the cloud cover had thickened. The interior seemed bright and welcoming, with the fire going in the massive fireplace and the smell of hot food in the air.

My group was just coming back to their tables, carrying plates of lunch. I looked for Lucinda but didn't see her, at first, anyway. Eventually I spotted her on the other side of the large open space, moving around the tables of writers. Some of them had hung their jackets on the backs of their chairs and some were still wearing them. She was holding a pitcher of iced tea and doing the whole friendly thing as she looked around at the jackets. I was sure none of them had any idea what she was doing.

Just then Kevin St. John came in. He stopped near the entrance and took in the whole room. I saw his gaze stop moving when it landed on Lucinda. Before I could do anything, he'd made a beeline for her, obviously figuring something was going on. She seemed surprised when he took the pitcher from her and pointed her toward our tables.

"Thanks for trying," I said when she was next to me. "What did he say to you?"

She laughed. "He said he didn't know what I was up to, but he was sure that you had put me up to it and would I please mind my own business and eat my lunch."

"He certainly wasn't being the host with the most," I said. "I suppose by now his nerves are a little frayed. He's had to scramble to fix the program and try to make his conference people forget that one of the workshop leaders was killed." Something occurred to me. "I wonder how far he would go to protect the reputation of Vista Del Mar."

Lucinda grabbed my hand. "C'mon, we can talk while we get our food."

There was still a line waiting to move past the cafeteria setup, and we stood at the end.

"You probably guessed I was trying to find the guy you were looking for," Lucinda said. "I would have found him, too, if Kevin hadn't butted in. I can tell you that I checked all but the last three tables. I'm an expert at working a room."

We'd reached the food line and I saw that lunch was a slice of quiche and a salad with tapioca pudding for dessert. I had never managed to eat my breakfast, and the smell of the food reminded me how hungry I was. While I put the plates on our trays, Lucinda looked over the dining room.

"I was giving it a last try. Hoping I could see something from here," she said.

I turned to follow her gaze and gave up. From here it was just a sea of people. "You gave it your best shot."

We picked up our trays and went back to our table. As before, everyone had returned to the seat they'd chosen at the first meal. It was funny how it always seemed to turn out that way. I was glad that Dolly and Mona had ended up next to each other. They were talking as they ate. I was sure that it was thanks to Dolly, since Mona kept to herself so much. I'd have to see what Dolly had found out about her.

I glanced over the rest of my people, and everyone seemed to be talking. "Thank heavens they all look pretty happy. Hopefully they've already forgotten that Lieutenant Borgnine questioned them again." I turned to my friend. "I hate to say it, but I think Lieutenant Borgnine was right and it was just a hysterical reaction. Why would anyone want to go through their rooms, anyway?"

Lucinda shrugged as an answer and poked at the quiche. "They should stick to more basic stuff. This is kind of over-cooked."

"Ahem," a voice behind her said, and she jumped. Kevin St. John was almost touching her chair. "The quiche is not overcooked. You are just not used to our cook's style of making it." He checked the faces at the rest of the table to see if they were listening and seemed relieved that most of them were busy with their own conversations. That was except Mona. There was a shadow on her face from the brim of her hat, but even so it seemed like she was staring right at him. He picked up on it, too, and leaned in close to me.

"What's with that woman? I keep finding her hanging out in the corner, watching something. It seems like she's watching me. Do you have any idea why?"

I felt cornered by his comment. Where did my responsibility for my people end? I had no idea why she was watching him and even if she really was. When all else fails, go for flattery. "Maybe she finds you attractive. She seems a little older, but these days that's no obstacle. I kind of remember her asking about you. If you were married, things like that." I realized this was an opportunity to find out about him. His life was a mystery. Nobody knew if he had a social life or even if he was gay or straight. I pressed on. "So what should I tell her about you? Are you dating anyone? Would you like to go out with a woman?"

"Ms. Feldstein, really." He punctuated it with an angry shake of his head. "That is none of your business. And I certainly don't want you discussing my life with the guests. I am just here to make sure their visit is pleasant." He turned to Lucinda and kept his voice low. "And Mrs. Thornkill, I would appreciate it if you have a complaint about the food that you let me know directly rather than discussing it at the table."

Okay, I got it. I didn't think he wanted me to try to fix him up.

"Will you please get the attention of your people?" he said. I stood up and clapped my hands, something I'd learned when I was a substitute teacher trying to round up the kids. The combo of the standing and the noise got their attention, and I turned the floor over to him.

"I wanted to let you know that the minibuses will be leaving as soon as lunch is over." He went on to remind them of the great activity that he had planned for all the guests of Vista Del Mar. They were going to be taken through the famous 17-Mile Drive, which had some of the most breathtaking scenery in the world, including the famous Lone Cypress. The drive went past impressive mansions, through a forest and up above the clouds. I wondered if he would let them stop at any of the luxurious resorts along the way. Even with all the history and natural beauty connected with Vista Del Mar, if they saw the lawn that rolled to the sea and the fancy shops and classy restaurants at one of them, they might view Vista Del Mar as a lesser place.

Beyond that, they were going to Point Lobos, a natural reserve, where they could watch for whales going by. It was one activity that I regretted missing. No matter how many times I viewed all that scenery, I never got tired of it.

17

I FELT LIKE A MOTHER HEN WALKING MY GROUP TO
the driveway next to the Lodge to wait for the bus. The line
of minibuses arrived just after we did, and my group trooped
onto the first one. Lucinda tried to talk me into going along,
but I begged off.

I waited until the line of buses had pulled onto the street
and disappeared, and then I went back inside the Lodge.
Time was flying by and I was nowhere with the investigation. All I seemed to have was a bunch of disjointed facts.

Frank had suggested that Madeleine might know more
than she thought she did. Who knew how long she and Don
had talked on the plane or about what. Don might have
dropped a comment about meeting someone. Madeleine had
disappeared from the morning workshop when Lieutenant

Borgnine started questioning the group again, and there was no telling when she'd make another appearance.

The easiest option was a phone call, so I picked one of the vintage phone booths that were lined up on the opposite side of the massive registration desk from the café entrance. As I shut the door on the tiny cubicle, it was hard to imagine that these were once common. There was even a seat inside.

The phones were not vintage, but even so, when I read over the directions, they were too complicated, and I left. I was glad Frank couldn't see me. "Feldstein, really? You're flummoxed by a pay phone? What kind of detective are you?"

I had to walk all the way to the guest house before my cell got a signal. I clicked on Madeleine's number. She answered, but as soon as I mentioned Don Porter's name, she talked me into coming over.

With the group gone for a while, going to Madeleine's house was no problem. The Delacorte sisters lived in a beautiful Victorian perched on top of a slope that looked over the town. It was painted a pale shade of lavender and had several porches and a turret on the second floor with curved windows.

Madeleine was waiting by the door and opened it before I could even hit the bell. "I am so glad you came over," she said, taking me inside. She walked ahead purposefully, but I lingered, checking out the details of the interior. There was even a fireplace in the entrance hall.

The living room was spacious and the furniture elegant. "Sit, sit," she said, pointing to a sofa with swans carved into the armrests. "I'll tell Lucy to make us some tea." She went on for a moment, telling me all the different kinds of tea they had. Then she smiled at me. "It's all thanks to you that I found out there was more in the world than orange pekoe." Then she left the room to talk to the housekeeper.

It was hard to believe the restricted life Madeleine had once led. Her mother had taken the idea that they were like the royalty of the small town too seriously and had brought her daughters up with rigid standards for clothes, behavior and even tea. It seemed that Cora, though she was the younger sister, had taken their mother's place and continued to set the tone for both of them.

I wasn't sure I wanted the credit that Madeleine gave me, insisting that it was coming to my retreats and becoming friends with me that had opened a door to a world she hadn't been aware of and now was anxious to explore. She thanked me, and Cora blamed me.

"We're having Earl Grey," Madeleine said proudly when she returned. A few moments later Lucy came in and set a tray down on the mahogany coffee table before pouring the tea. I waited until the uniformed young woman left the room.

Madeleine immediately began telling me how glad she was that I'd called. "Cora is off at one of her ladies' club meetings. She tried to drag me along. I said I'd go, but only if I could wear this." She stood up and showed off her denim pants and long cream-colored sweater. A multicolored cowl added a cheerful accent. "You should have seen her face. I never realized how not fun my sister is. I wish she'd take a lesson from me for a change."

Like that was going to happen. I cringed imagining the

scene if Madeleine suggested it. I wanted to get to the point, but I knew that it was going to take time if I was going to get any new information from Madeleine. When I'd worked for Frank and done phone interviews for him, I had discovered it was all about being friendly and letting people talk rather than hammering them with questions.

As I looked around the lovely room, I thought of the tiny house that Gwen shared with her daughter Crystal and her two teenage kids. Would Gwen ever tell the Delacorte sisters who she was? There was sure to be some upheaval if she did, but maybe the sisters would be glad to have some family, since as it stood now, they were the end of the family line.

"It's such fun to have you come over. Everyone my sister brings over is so dreary." She checked to see that my teacup was still full. "I'm sorry I took off this morning. I was really looking forward to being one of the group. I've barely had time to get to know any of them." She picked up her cup. "When I saw Lieutenant Borgnine come in the room, I had to go. You do understand that I simply can't be questioned by him." Her eyes flew skyward. "I've declared my independence from my sister's ways, but I don't know what she would do if she thought I was going too far."

"You mean picking up with strange men?" I asked, and she nodded.

"You have to understand that our mother left her in control. So if she thinks I'm doing things that are too out there, she can make it so I can't do anything. Please tell me you're here because you have it all figured out."

"I wish," I began. "I wanted to ask you about Don Porter."

At the mention of his name, her eyes opened wider and she seemed nervous.

"Oh, dear, oh, dear. I'm just so worried that someone is going to tell Lieutenant Borgnine that I knew him, and then he's going to show up and ask me a lot of questions, and then Cora is going to wonder why he's asking so many questions. If she finds out the truth . . . She just can't. I won't be pushed around by her anymore." She stood up and modeled her denim outfit. "You don't understand. She already thinks my clothing choices indicate that I'm not in my right mind." She fidgeted with a cloth tote bag and took out her knitting. "Is he still hanging around the resort? I really want to come back this afternoon. I dropped a stitch and I don't know how to pick it up. And I heard about the party tonight. I've never done square dancing."

I told her there was another workshop in the late afternoon and that it seemed Lieutenant Borgnine was finished talking to my retreaters. I even told her that he thought the whole thing about the rooms being gone through was a hysterical reaction. She didn't seem to understand what that meant.

"It means that it wasn't real. Their rooms weren't gone through. One of them started it and then the rest of them imagined that things had been moved around. The real point was that they all agreed that nothing was missing." Madeleine smiled at the news.

"Good. Then he doesn't think our people had anything to do with what happened to Don."

Now that she'd brought him up, it was easy for me to get

to why I was there. "I wanted to ask you. Did he say anything about meeting someone when he came to Vista Del Mar?"

She thought about it for a moment. "No. He did say that he might write about the place, and he made a point of saying that he couldn't guarantee that it would be all positive. Why?"

I wondered how much I should tell her. I decided to go for broke and told her I had reason to believe that he went to the lighthouse to meet somebody.

"Oh, dear," she said, seeming distressed. "I wish I'd never started talking to him on the plane."

When I left, she said she'd be there for the workshop and the square dance. She was particularly excited about the skirts.

All that I'd gotten out of the trip to see Madeleine was that she was bordering on panic over the whole matter with Don Porter. It really did seem she was overreacting, but then she was rather fragile. The discussion had been more tiring than I'd realized, and while it might have been nice to go home and chill out for a while, I felt I had to go to Vista Del Mar to be there when the group returned.

It was almost creepy quiet when I went into the Lodge. But then I heard voices coming from the café. Madeleine's tea had been nice, but I really needed a coffee drink, and it was another chance to see how the regular muffins I'd dropped off the night before were selling. By this time of day, the basket should be empty.

My eye went to the basket on the counter as soon as I walked in, and I was relieved to see that all the muffins were gone. There was something else missing, too, though: Bridget was not behind the counter. Did that mean she was off with Sammy? I grumbled to myself that I needed to get used to thinking of them as a couple, because Bridget was going to make it happen.

I ordered a coffee from Bridget's replacement, an older man whom I'd seen before and who was the opposite of talkative. While I waited for him to fill a mug, I checked the room for the source of the voices I'd heard. The clouds were thinning and the light that poured in from the two walls of windows had a hint of sunshine, making it seem very bright. All the tables were empty except for one in the corner.

Lisa and Derek were huddled over mugs of coffee and seemed unaware that I'd come in. I was surprised that they hadn't gone on the outing. Immediately I thought of how I'd figured they were married to other people and this weekend was some kind of secret meet-up for them. It was none of my business, but I was curious to know if I was right.

As soon as I got my coffee, I went over to their table and, without waiting for an invitation to join them, pulled up a chair.

"I hope you don't mind," I said, putting down my mug. "So, you didn't go on the trip." They had been so deep in conversation that they were startled by my presence and instantly separated.

They fumbled for a moment and then Derek said that Lisa had a headache. He pointed at the mugs of coffee. "Caffeine is supposed to work with aspirin."

"And it worked," Lisa said. "My headache is all gone."

I sensed that they were going to leave, so I launched right

into conversation to keep them there. "I'm sorry you missed the trip, but it's nice to have a chance to talk to you. I barely know anything about you besides your names."

They glanced back and forth at each other as if trying to pass some sort of secret message, which made me only more sure that I was right about their relationship.

"I'm afraid we're pretty dull," Derek said. "This weekend has certainly been the most exciting thing we've ever done. And that was before Don Porter died. I suppose you probably know all about him. He didn't say much about himself at the workshop."

I perked up at the word *workshop*, particularly when I noticed Derek's green jacket stuffed behind him on the chair. Could he be the one who'd caused the scene Madeleine had described?

"So then you were there. Did you bring some writing to share?"

"No, no, I was just there to get an overview of what travel writing was all about," he said. It wasn't the answer I was hoping for, but if he wasn't the one who'd done it, he was at least a witness.

"I can understand it must be unnerving to read your work in front of an expert like Don Porter. How did it go with the people whose work got critiqued?"

"One man stands out. He absolutely came unglued at Porter's comments. It was painful to watch." I noticed that Derek seemed to be relaxing the more we talked about Don Porter. He turned to Lisa. "I'd forgotten all about him."

I took a few sips of my coffee, trying to appear nonchalant. "I suppose you could point out the man."

Derek shrugged. "If I'd known what he was going to do, I would have paid more attention. I was just watching Don Porter, wondering what it was like to live his gypsy lifestyle."

I'd been so busy trying to figure out who might have killed Don, I hadn't thought much about who he was. "Did Don talk much about himself at the workshop?"

"There was a bio in the bag of stuff we got, but it didn't say much beyond that he lived near the airport in Florida with no mention of the town. He said something at the workshop about being a citizen of the world."

"Did he say anything about meeting up with someone while he was here?"

"You know, he did say something about meeting someone. I think at the lighthouse. I figured it was somebody he knew from before. Just curious—do you know who he met?"

"No," I said, slightly annoyed, though I didn't show it. I hated it when the answer to my question was a question. I pressed on anyway.

"Did he say anything about what he thought of Vista Del Mar?" I asked. Derek shrugged as answer. "I was just wondering because he was planning to leave the next morning."

"That's odd," Lisa said, entering the conversation. She quickly added that Derek had mentioned wanting to go to another of Don's workshops later in the weekend.

They both wondered how I knew, and I explained running into the cabbie. "It would seem like the killer would be the one making an unexpected exit," Derek said. "Was there anyone else trying to leave?"

I immediately thought of the Difficult Duo, but it seemed ridiculous to think of Rayanne and DeeDee as killers. I wasn't going to say anything, but Lisa had apparently overheard them and she brought it up. Derek jumped on the idea and suggested telling the police. All I could think of was how Rayanne would react if Lieutenant Borgnine was suddenly all over her with questions. I had to steer him away from it.

"It's more likely it was someone who knew Don. You know, the police always look at spouses or family members first. I wonder about Don. Did he have a wife or children?"

"Children, really?" Lisa said. "Would they really be considered suspects?"

"There is a lot of turbulence in families," I said. "What about you two? Do you have children?" I hadn't even realized what I was doing, but I had brought them full circle to my original question about them. And I'd caught them completely off guard. I looked back and forth as she shook her head and he nodded.

Aha! They had just told me that I was right.

"Well, no time off for me," I said. "I want to check our meeting room for this afternoon's workshop."

As I walked away, I thought over our encounter. Even my short time working for Frank had taught me how to be a student of people. I had known right away there was something off about them as a couple.

18

AS I WALKED UP THE PATH TO THE BUILDING WITH
our meeting room, I saw Lieutenant Borgnine approaching.
He was certainly not a master of the blank cop face I'd heard
about. Even from a distance I saw his mouth contract into
annoyance as he saw me. When we were face-to-face, he
greeted me with a grunting nod.

"So, you're still here," I said. "Your people are certainly
being discreet this time." My gaze moved over the area, and
I finally noted one police cruiser mostly hidden by bushes.
"Have you found any suspects?"

His face registered surprise. "You're not really asking
me that, are you?" He let out a mirthless laugh. "Cadbury
PD has everything under control. We're tracking down some
leads, if you must know." I thought he was going to simply

walk on, but he seemed to have a second thought and turned back to me.

"What about you? I'm sure you've been nosing around. What have you found out?"

"So that means you've got nothing, right?" I said. He grunted an answer, which I was pretty sure meant I'd hit on the truth.

"The problem is that there are too many suspects to sort through," he said. "The logistics of trying to figure who was where are baffling. And they're all a bunch of smarty-pants writers who know too much about interrogation techniques. I just wish someone would confess and get it over with."

His honesty almost knocked me out. He seemed like he was dragging, and I asked him if he felt all right.

"I'm fine," he said, but the tone of his voice didn't go with his words. And I had a thought.

"Is it because you're not getting your apple fritter fix in the morning?" I asked. His face grew stormy and I thought he was going to tell me to butt out, but he finally gave me an acquiescing nod.

"The wife doesn't get it. I need that taste of apple and richness with a cup of black coffee to start things off right."

"So what is it that she objects to?" I asked.

"All the sugar and grease." After he'd spoken, I saw that his expression was changing as he realized how he was opening up to me.

"What if I had something that tasted sort of like an apple fritter?" I said quickly. "Something that had the apple and spice taste, with less sweetness and wasn't fried?"

His eyes suddenly became alert. "Is there such a thing? Where?" He was looking around as if the treat would somehow drop out of the air.

"I haven't perfected it yet, but I made something last night that might just tide you over."

I couldn't believe I was doing this, but I asked him to follow me to my house. As we came up the driveway, I looked for Julius, but he wasn't in his usual position on the stoop outside my back door.

I saw Borgnine glance from side to side, as if checking to see if anyone was watching, before he followed me inside.

I was taking a chance. The apple fritter muffins were still in the experimental stage, but he looked pretty desperate. I had them setting on the table with a napkin over them. Whenever I made something new, I tasted it when it was freshly made and then one day and two days afterward to see how the taste changed.

He stared at the muffins as if they were gold. I knew he was reacting to the scent of cinnamon, which I hoped would give them the fritter-like taste.

"May I?" he asked.

"Wait. Didn't you mention coffee? All I have is instant, if that's okay."

"As long as it isn't decaf. The wife has been pushing that, but that's farther than I'm willing to go."

I couldn't believe I was actually doing this, but I put the water on to boil and invited him to sit down. I wished that Julius was there as some kind of distraction. It felt so strange to have the cop sitting at my kitchen table.

I was about to pour hot water over the dark crystals in a couple of mugs when I looked up. Dane was standing at the door, peering in. He could see only the back of the lieutenant, but there was no mistaking his shape and his trademark jacket. Dane's mouth was open in disbelief as he caught my eye. I knew he was dying to know what was going on, but at the same time he wasn't going to interrupt. By the time I'd brought the mugs to the table, Dane had disappeared.

I asked the cop if he wanted a knife and fork for the muffin, but he said it was finger food for him and he reached for one. He took a tentative bite and followed it with a swig of the coffee. I waited with bated breath, as if I was in some super important baking competition. He repeated the motions but this time closed his eyes momentarily.

The suspense was getting to be too much, and I wasn't known for my patience. "So?" I said finally.

"It's not the same as the fritter, but close enough to work. And also, really good." He finished it off with another sip of coffee. "So when are they going to be available and where?"

I hadn't thought that far in advance since I was still working on the recipe, but since he'd given them his stamp of approval, I guessed the recipe was okay as is. "How about this," I said. "I'll make them a regular item at Maggie's, along with the usual muffins."

"Deal," he said. "But this will just be between us. I promised the wife no apple fritters. You said these have less sugar and aren't fried, but I'm still not sure my wife would completely approve."

As if I would ever be talking to Mrs. Borgnine anyway.

It was amazing to see the restorative quality of food. The lieutenant's whole demeanor had changed. Then he remembered that we weren't supposed to get along and went back to making grunting sounds.

"So, are you going to tell me what you know?" he asked halfheartedly.

"There are just a lot of pieces that don't seem to fit into any kind of pattern."

He got up from the table and went to the door. "Why can't the perp just give themselves up?"

Had I just made friends with him? I glanced out the window to see if a pig might be flying by.

Dane must have been hiding in the bushes. He was at my door a moment later, knocking frantically.

"Now I've got him as competition for your affection, too?" he teased. "You do know he's a married man and not as much of a catch as yours truly." He assumed a model stance with a merry smile.

He noticed the crumbs on the table. "You lured him in here with food. The muffins you made last night. That was what it was all about?"

"I just thought if there was something I could do to mend fences with him since we all do live in a small town, it would be a good idea. It doesn't make me happy to see him rubbing his temples every time he sees me. Would you like to be known as a headache?"

Dane rolled his eyes. "I hope it worked. Then maybe he won't give me awful shifts when he sees me hanging around with you."

I gave him a look and his smile faded a little. "You might want to deny the romance part, but you will agree that we're friends," he said, and I nodded.

"I think Lieutenant Borgnine has reached a roadblock with the investigation."

"He actually talked about it with you?" Dane sounded incredulous and then disappointed. "That was my thing. If you start comparing notes with him, it's going to take away my edge."

"I noticed that you said 'as competition for my affection, too.' I have told you over and over that Sammy and I aren't anything more than good friends. Plus he seems to have found a girlfriend. Bridget from the café is making a move on him. She's working as his assistant. You said you saw them last night."

Dane's face clouded. "It doesn't sound like you're very happy about Sammy finding someone."

"It's more like she found him."

I'D LOST TRACK OF TIME AND REALIZED THE BUSES would be returning soon. It was certainly nice that Vista Del Mar was so close by. Once Dane jogged off, I double-timed it back across the street. I went directly to our meeting room, quickly and without interruption. But then I stopped in the doorway, stunned by the sight that greeted me.

When I looked back toward the the driveway, I saw that the buses had pulled in and people were getting off. Some of my group were already on the path, approaching the small building where I stood. They were smiling and chatting as they walked. Lucinda threaded through the group and was in the lead. She caught one look at my expression and pressed forward to reach me first.

"Did something happen?"

I stepped aside and let her see in the doorway. She tried to remain calm, but she gasped at the sight, too.

I had encouraged the retreaters to leave their bags while they went on the tour, and now they had all been emptied. Balls of yarn were scattered everywhere; knitting needles, crochet hooks and all the other tools they used were scattered on the table and floor.

Lucinda turned back toward the approaching group. "We have to do something to stop them." But just then the Difficult Duo came through the door.

"What happened?" Rayanne said in an accusing voice. At almost the same moment Crystal and Wanda came in and viewed the scene. I realized there was nothing to do but tell them all the truth. I waited until everyone was there. They were all speechless and just stood against the wall, staring at the mess.

"I'm so sorry," I said, which sounded pretty weak considering the havoc we were looking at. "I don't know what happened."

"Well, I have a pretty good idea," Rayanne said. "We weren't all crazy before like that cop tried to say. Someone did go through our rooms and didn't find whatever they were looking for. So they waited until we were all gone and then tossed our bags. It looks to me like whoever it is has gotten kind of desperate." Rayanne turned and stared directly at me. "You were here the whole time we were gone," she said in an accusing voice.

Lucinda stepped in front of me. "You can't think that Casey had anything to do with this."

Bree, Scott and Olivia chimed in and said that Rayanne was being ridiculous. Dolly suggested that someone go and get Lieutenant Borgnine and tell him about it. Jeff offered to find him.

In the meantime, we all went back outside. The writers had gone into the other half of the building and had shut the door. As we were waiting, Lisa and Derek came up the path.

"What's going on?" Lisa asked, seeing us all standing around. Someone pointed at the open door and she and Derek looked in. They seemed shocked at the sight, but I couldn't help thinking that they hadn't gone on the tour.

Lieutenant Borgnine came up the path with Kevin St. John. Neither of them appeared to be in a good mood. Kevin St. John threw me an angry nod and I was sure he was thinking it was another chink in what was already a bad weekend. The two of them went around the inside of the room and then came outside.

The lieutenant began to ask some questions, like if the door had been left open, or if anybody had anything valuable in the bag they'd left in the room. The one thing he didn't do was rub his temples or glare at me. He scribbled down a few notes and seemed about to say something when Kevin St. John nudged him and pointed at something.

"I think we've found the perp," the hotel manager said. Everyone turned to where he was pointing. Julius had just come out of the brush. He took a look at the group and when he saw me came over and rubbed against my ankle.

"That cat is a menace. I told you to keep him off the Vista Del Mar property." Kevin was glaring at me, and then he turned to the cop. "Can't you call animal control and have him taken away?"

"And do what, put him in cat jail?" Lucinda said, putting her hand on her hip in a defiant gesture.

"Julius didn't do it," I said. "My place is full of yarn and he has no interest in it."

"What if some little animal ran into the room and the cat chased it?" Dolly said in her opera singer voice. She turned to me. "I'm sorry to say that, but you know it could be true."

The two men looked at each other, shrugging and shaking their heads. Lieutenant Borgnine told me to deal with the cat and said that as far as he was concerned the case was closed.

Wanda and Crystal took the group inside and said they'd help get everything in order while I took Julius home.

"I know you're innocent," I said, looking into his arresting yellow eyes and making a grab for him. I was relieved that he didn't fight me and let me carry him home. After we were inside, I went around closing all the escape routes I'd left for him so he could come and go as he pleased.

"Sorry to have to do this. It's only temporary—I promise." To try to smooth it over, I offered him a surprise treat of stink fish. He had figured something was going on and didn't do his usual attack of the smelly food but instead sat by the bowl and watched me leave.

It was a little less chaotic by the time I got back to the

meeting room. Everyone had claimed their projects, and they were sorting out the bags, which wasn't that easy since so many of the bags looked the same.

Crystal and Wanda had gotten together while I was gone and had already agreed to keep the workshop going longer than planned. Bree, Olivia and Scott were helping out with any problems related to the projects. Lucinda was doing her best to act as host while I was gone and had urged them all to help themselves to drinks and cookies.

The thing that saved me was that so many yarn people were cat people as well. They were horrified at what Kevin St. John had suggested and were willing to let it go with the feeling that cats will be cats.

"But I'm sure Julius didn't do it," I said to Lucinda. We were hanging by the coffee and tea service while the others settled into working on their projects again. "Did you notice how Mona slipped out before Lieutenant Borgnine and Kevin St. John got here? Did you see her on the bus?" I asked Lucinda. My friend thought about it for a few moments and then nodded.

"I remember noticing that her hat blew off when we went outside at Bird Rock, but she didn't put it back on until we were back on the bus."

"Really?" I said, surprised, but then Lucinda reminded me that it was cloudy. We went back to talking about the mess in the meeting room. "I think Rayanne was right about what she said. That whoever went through the guest rooms went through this room. But the question is, what were they looking for?"

"It makes no sense. The group agreed that they didn't leave anything valuable in here," Lucinda said.

"That's the obvious thing, but what if whatever the person is looking for doesn't appear valuable, except to them?"

"Spoken like a true detective," Lucinda said. "I wouldn't have thought of that."

I laughed at myself. "It is one thing to think of it, but another to figure out what it was."

19

THE EFFECT OF KNITTING AND CROCHETING WAS amazing. Once the group got lost in their work, everyone seemed to have forgotten there was ever a problem. They all left happy when the workshop ended. I made a beeline for my place. I felt terrible that Julius was being punished for something he didn't do. It seemed like it had been long enough and the group had been so forgiving that I wanted to give him back his freedom.

I was surprised to see Sammy sitting on the back stoop by the door.

As soon as he saw me, he stood up. "Case, you have to help me." I should be used to the nickname by now, but it still seemed funny to have a nickname that was just one letter off from my real name.

Sammy was built like a big teddy bear, and he had very

expressive eyes that showed his emotions. Now they looked forlorn, and despite all my problems with the retreat, I immediately zeroed in on his need and asked him what was wrong.

"It's the show tonight. Here it is, my chance to do some big-time illusions that require an assistant, and I don't have one."

"What happened to Bridget?" I asked, thinking of how she'd acted when I'd seen her in the morning. She'd made it sound like they were a cozy couple.

"I wanted to make things clear to her. I said I was only interested in her as an assistant." His shoulders drooped. "I tried to be as nice as possible, but she was coming on too strong. Out of nowhere she was trying to rearrange my life. It's not my style to be bulldozed like that." He looked at me. "It's got to be a mutually agreeable situation."

He realized he'd gotten off track. "The point is, I made a commitment and I have no one to cut in half." He didn't say anything more with words, but I got the drift from his expression. I knew how much this show meant to him. It didn't matter that he was a highly respected urologist and surgeon—magic was his dream.

"Okay," I said. "What do I have to do?"

"Just wear this and lie there." He presented me with something in a bag and I was almost afraid to look.

I agreed. It was probably the last thing in the world I needed to do right now, but Sammy always came through for me and it was the least I could do for him. And, oh, yes, I was glad about Bridget. Not because I was jealous or anything—I just thought he deserved better.

She probably blamed me for what he'd said, so there went any in I had with her to help with the new muffins.

Sammy hugged me profusely and thanked me for saving the show. I wasn't so sure about that. "Maybe you better wait until after the show to thank me. I hope I don't ruin it."

"You'll be great. I know it." He told me when to be where and left.

As we were talking, I could see Julius through the window. It looked like he was marching back and forth in protest at being locked inside.

I had planned to just stop in at my place for a short time to arrange his escape places and freshen up, but by now I wasn't surprised when things didn't go as planned.

I considered ignoring the phone as it started to ring and the mechanical voice announced that the call was from my mother. Actually, it said "Dr. Feldstein," which could have been either of my parents, but it was always my mother who called. But it didn't feel right, so I grabbed it on the fifth ring.

"So things are going well?" my mother said after I'd mentioned being in kind of a hurry. I realized when I'd talked to her before, Don Porter was alive and well. Could I just leave out what happened to him?

If only I had said, "Fine," in a different tone of voice, I might have gotten off the call without spilling everything. I wasn't proud of the fact that even at the ripe old age of thirty-five I still cared what my mother thought.

She immediately recognized that the way I'd said, "Fine," meant there was really a problem. Like the doctor she was, trying to get at a patient's problem, she started asking questions.

"What is it? Is it the group you have this time?"

"They're fine," I said. Not a lie. They weren't the problem.

"Is it something with that cop who lives down the street? When your father and I came to see you, it was obvious there was something between you. But just remember you'd have to be worried every day if he'd make it home."

I withheld a laugh, considering that most of Dane's duties seemed to be telling jaywalkers to go to the corner to cross the street. My mother immediately transitioned into talking about Sammy. She started to say something good about him but caught herself.

"I know my liking him is like the kiss of death to you. I wish I could tell you to steer clear of him and say it like I meant it. Then you'd probably throw yourself into his arms."

"Oh, Mother," I said in a withering tone. "I think I'm more mature than that." And then I added that I was going to be his assistant in the big show he was putting on for Vista Del Mar.

"Enough with the magic nonsense. See, there *is* something I don't like about Sammy. I'm one hundred percent with his parents on that. He should concentrate on being a doctor and forget all this other stuff. You know you care about him. Otherwise, why would you be acting as his assistant?" I was starting to make disagreeing noises, but she talked on. "He would walk through fire for you," she said. I didn't have a comeback for that because I kind of thought it was probably true. So I diverted her attention the only way I could think of. I told her she was right that there were some problems with the retreat.

"So then, what's wrong?" she said, getting to the point.

I told her the whole story. "Madeleine is depending on

me, and if I don't come through I'm afraid she'll take away the deal I have."

I expected my mother to somehow think that would be a good thing, but instead she was annoyed at the position I was in. My mother and I might argue back and forth, but underneath it all, she was my biggest supporter.

"The best thing you can do is to figure out who killed that travel writer," she said. "You've done it before. Do you have any suspects?" She paused for a moment. "Didn't you tell me there was a woman who was all wrapped up and claimed she was allergic to the sun? You seemed to think she was suspicious."

"Now that you mention her, I heard her hat blew off today when she was outside and she didn't get upset and said that it was cloudy outside."

My mother laughed. "If you're going to lie, you ought to think it through. I'm not a dermatologist, but I do know that even with clouds the rays of the sun get through. My diagnosis would be that she was trying to hide something."

"Thanks," I said, not sure if I really liked my mother trying to assist me. I was so used to her speech about when she was my age she was a doctor, a mother and a wife, and what was I? This new attitude actually made me uncomfortable, and I wondered if she had some ulterior motive. Maybe she'd gone to some seminar on how to outsmart your patients with psychology or something.

I ended the call, telling her I had to get back to my people. I waited a moment to see if she was going to add some kind of reminder that I didn't quite measure up, but she just wished me luck and said good-bye. Was she up to something?

I'd barely put down the phone when it rang again. Julius was sitting down, watching me. As I answered the phone, I walked to one of the windows and lifted it so he could have his freedom again. He jumped on the counter and sniffed the air, but then instead of squirming through the opening to get outside, he jumped down and continued to watch me.

I got it. He didn't necessarily want to go out; he just wanted to know that he could.

"Frank?" I said, surprised. "Is something wrong? Why are you calling me?" My tone was worried. He made such a production when I called him, and here he'd called me twice in one day.

"You seemed to be having trouble with this investigation. I feel like I'm your mentor, so I wanted to help you."

Then I got it. It was a pity call, and I started to put my back up. But then I faced the truth: he was right. I was stuck.

"Am I going to get a little appreciation, Feldstein? I might be your mentor, but it is Saturday night here, and some of us have plans."

"Another date?" I asked, and I heard him chortle.

"Maybe that date never ended." He cleared his throat. "We're not here to talk about my social life. And I don't want to stay on the phone all night." I heard some music in the background. I strained to figure out what it was. The rhythm belonged to another time, and I noted a male voice singing before I recognized that it was Frank Sinatra. I was picturing his lady friend lounging on a couch. Or did he have the same recliner chairs everywhere?

"Feldstein, I'm talking to you. You're not even doing the

customary *uh-huh*s to show you're listening." He spoke in a singsongy voice and I snapped back to attention.

"Sorry," I said. "How about you run that all by me again?"

"I was suggesting you tell me everything you know about the dead guy."

"I can do that," I said. "First, he was a travel writer. I heard that he liked to get the most benefit from trips he took. Like he'd take notes to write different kinds of articles. The hotel clerk said he thought that Don was meeting someone that he didn't know." I repeated the details about the paper from the message board with the name Snow Drop. Frank let out a *hmmm* sound.

"He seemed to be looked up to by the writers who came to this conference, but not very diplomatic when he gave critiques. No one said it exactly, but I don't think he cared if he hurt their feelings. I know he gave scathing critiques to at least two men. One, who I still haven't connected with, made a scene and charged out of the room. The other guy . . ." I stopped as I thought of the bird tattoo on his chest. "Well, he claimed to have been upset but then decided Don was right, and he rewrote the piece and took it to Don's room, which also was right around the time Don was probably shot.

"His name is T Dot," I said, then explained his name. "He told me that he didn't tell the cops about the trip to Don's room. He seemed to be worried because he thought someone saw him in the hall and might mention it to the cops."

"T Dot?" Frank said. I had the feeling he was shaking his head with disbelief. "You have to believe that someone who comes up with a name like that thinks he's pretty special and could be someone who freaks out when his work is criticized. He told you he was going to give the guy a rewrite. Or maybe the plan was to give him a piece of his mind and then a bullet to the chest. As for telling you about it, it sounds like he was worried that he'd been seen."

"He seemed like such a nice guy," I said, and I heard Frank chortle again.

"Feldstein, if you're going to track down a killer, you have to keep your perspective. You don't have to dislike someone to think they did it. By the same token, if you do like someone, it doesn't let them off the hook."

"What about the person Don met?"

"You should definitely try to find out more about that. And the other guy who got his work pulled apart—how hard can it be to find him? Do you have any clue about who he is, like a name, a birthmark on his cheek or something?"

"He's wearing one of those army surplus jackets, like a bunch of the guys here. But his has some initials on the front, which I think are a KC. I explained that Madeleine had remembered the initials because she said they reminded her of me. "But even if I find him, it's not like he's going to tell me that he killed Don," I said.

"But he could tell you something else without even realizing it. Look what T Dot told you." Frank chortled some more about the name.

"I think you know what you have to do," he said finally. "So what's on the agenda for tonight. Some kind of soiree?"

I told Frank about the open mike event, followed by a magic show and capped with square dancing. He reacted only when I mentioned my part in the magic show.

"Geez, Feldstein, I'm really sorry I'm missing your debut. I just hope the Amazing Dr. Sammy remembers he's doing a trick and not surgery."

As Frank signed off I heard him say to someone, "I'm all yours now, Cream Puff." *Cream Puff, really?*

I finally took the costume out of the bag and gagged. It was a one-piece thing that was flesh colored, except for the middle part, which looked like a tuxedo bathing suit. There was also a pair of tall black boots. What had I agreed to?

I wasn't going to show up wearing it for the whole evening, but I also didn't think I'd have time to change, so I stripped and pulled on the ridiculous outfit and put a loose-fitting stretchy black dress over it. The boots were a little stiff, but they worked okay with the dress.

Julius had been watching the whole thing. He didn't seem to approve, and I half expected him to put up both his paws, as if to say, "Are you sure you know what you're doing?"

20

IT WAS DARK WHEN I WENT ACROSS THE STREET.
By now I knew the way so well, I didn't need the flashlight
to find my way. I'd put a black fleece over the dress and
added a red scarf. Both felt good as the chilly breeze blew
in from the water.

I had thought it over and decided that it was better not to
try to find KC in the Sea Foam dining hall after seeing how
Kevin St. John had reacted to Lucinda hanging around his
writers. If he'd seen through her trying to appear she was
helping out, there was no chance he wouldn't figure I was
up to something. It was still free time before dinner and I
thought I'd wander around the grounds and see if I could
find the green jacket with the initials. Well, really I was
after the wearer of the jacket. I passed a few people walking

toward one of the guest buildings. Only one wore one of the green jackets, but the front of it was blank.

I looked in on the Lodge next. I was surprised at how crowded it was. The fire going in the massive stone fireplace and the warm glow given off by the amber-colored leaded-glass lamps managed to make the cavernous room seem almost cozy.

The area with the couches and easy chairs had been taken over by Olivia, who had a whole group working on squares. Their yarn covered the table in their midst with spots of color. The writers were scattered all over. Some were shooting pool or playing table tennis. A bunch of people were gathered around a long table hunched over their laptops. They'd all hung their jackets on the backs of their chairs. I noticed that several of them were the army surplus style. Jeff Hunter's beat-up leather jacket stuck out like a sore thumb. All their screens were covered with writing, including Jeff's. He seemed deeply engrossed in something and didn't notice me until I stopped next to him and asked what he was up to.

He sat back from the computer and gestured toward the screen. "I thought about what I said during the workshop about being on the road and someone suggesting I write about it. They all helped me with the format," he said, indicating his tablemates. "And I signed up to read it at the open mike event."

While I was talking to him, I was glancing at the jackets hanging on the chairs, hoping to see a *KC* on the front of one. "I don't mean to be rude," Jeff said, going back to hovering over the screen. "But I want to give this another read-through."

"Of course," I said, backing away. I did another turn around the table, trying to be unobtrusive as I checked the jackets once again. No letters, just one button that said, I HEART POODLES.

The pool and table tennis players had left their jackets in a heap on a chair. I pretended to be clumsy and knocked into the chair, sending the jackets to the floor. None of them even noticed as I examined each jacket as I picked it up and put it back. I came up empty again.

I was beginning to face the fact that there was no guarantee the man with the right jacket was even in the Lodge, when the door opened and a man walked in. I automatically looked at what he was wearing and felt my heart quicken as I saw the green color of his jacket. There was something lighter on the front.

Before I could get a good look, he moved on and went toward the line of phone booths. By the time I'd crossed the room, he'd gone into one and shut the folding door.

I hovered around outside the booth, trying to appear nonchalant as I peered in the small window to get a closer look at the jacket. I'm afraid my effort to be nonchalant didn't work very well, and after a moment he opened the folding door and glared up at me. "What's the problem?" He turned and checked the phone booths behind him, which were all empty. "Can't you use one of those?" he asked in a short tone.

"Right," I said, backing off. Rule number one of getting someone to talk to you was not getting off on the wrong foot.

He watched me until I picked one of the booths and went inside. The good thing was that I could see him when he left the phone booth; the bad thing was that I could see that all the phone booths were now full and a line had formed.

Then I realized it might not be such a bad thing. The same people who were looking into my booth with impatient stares were doing the same to him. I hoped it would make him as uncomfortable as it was making me and he'd hurry up. I had picked up the receiver and was pretending to talk, while at the same time thinking about how I was going to engage this guy in conversation.

The line was getting longer and the pressure of watching people shift their weight impatiently was getting to me. Finally, I abandoned my booth. I was hoping the guy in the green jacket would feel the same pressure, but when I passed the booth he was in, he seemed deep in conversation.

At least I'd found him, and I tried to make a mental note of what he looked like so I could pick him out from the crowd in the dining hall. In the few moments I'd had to take in his appearance, I'd noted he had dark wavy hair and a fashionable amount of stubble on his face.

I hung around near the wooden counter that separated the lobby-like area of the room from the business section. A new clerk was on duty and I hoped that Gill was home, finally catching up on his sleep.

At last the door folded back and my target came out. All the work I'd done for Frank had been on the phone, and snagging someone in person was much harder. What was I going to say to get him to stop, let alone talk to me?

I caught up with him as he went across the room to the

door that went out over the deck. "I'm sorry for hanging outside the phone booth," I said. "I was trying to watch how you did it." I let out what I hoped sounded like an embarrassed laugh. "I had no idea how pay phones work anymore."

His face softened into an understanding smile. "Right. No more dropping in a coin." He'd stopped now and turned to face me fully. I thought about Frank's advice to flirt to get information. But my flirting skills were pathetic and way too obvious.

"I couldn't believe the phone took a credit card," I said in a friendly voice. "You just seemed like you knew what you were doing with the phone. Again, I'm sorry if I bothered you."

I had heard that apologizing was a good way to get on people's talkative side. More than once, I'd started one of the phone calls for Frank by saying that I was sorry to bother them, but I was looking for so and so, or I needed some kind of information. I wouldn't say it worked like a charm. Some people were too grumpy to care, but for most people, after that initial apology they were willing to help.

It seemed to work with this guy, too. "If I'd known you were having trouble, I'd have given you a tutorial." He reached out his hand. "I'm Van."

"Is that just Van, or do you have an initial first?" I said, thinking of T Dot.

He laughed good-naturedly. "That is just so pretentious." We shook hands. "I've seen you around. Are you with the writers' conference?" Oh, no—he was being friendly now, and maybe even a little flirty. He was much better at it than I was. But most of all, he was likeable. I hadn't asked him the first question about Don's death and already I didn't want him to be the killer.

I explained who I was quickly because I wanted to get back to having him do the talking. I'd overheard some of the writers talking to one another and I'd noticed they all used the same good opening question. "So, what do you write?"

It worked with him just as I'd seen it work with others. His face lit up as he began to talk. "I write nonfiction." He paused and smiled at some inner thought. "Although it's not completely nonfiction, I guess. I write copy for brochures and freebee magazines. In other words, advertising. It's nonfiction with a slant toward the positive on whatever I'm pitching."

"So then you're in a different place than most of the people at your conference," I said, and he nodded.

"Yes and no. I think everyone is here about learning. I really came just because of Don Porter. I wanted to hear him talk." He stopped and seemed to be considering his words. "It's terrible about what happened to him."

"Did you get what you came for? I mean, did you go to his workshop?" I was trying to keep him talking.

He seemed to come to an inner conclusion. "If I'm going to bend your ear, the least I can do is buy you a coffee." He looked at his watch. "There's still time before dinner." He held out his arm in the direction of the café. I certainly wasn't going to say no after that move.

The same older man who'd been there in the afternoon was behind the counter. I was glad that Bridget wasn't working. I was sure she blamed me for what Sammy had said to her. Who knew what kind of scene she would make. He ordered two coffees from Bridget's replacement and chose a table near the windows. It was in its own little area, with no other tables nearby. With the darkness outside, the interior seemed too brightly lit, which made it feel hollow. Dolly offered me a wave from across the café. She was sitting with the woman who had the short knitting needles stuck in her bun.

"Okay, I'm ready to have my ear bent," I said.

"Like I said, I came here for something specific. I landed a gig writing the copy for a travel company. I might have overstated my qualifications to them to get the job, if you know what I mean. But writing is writing, right?" He punctuated it with shrug and a smile. "I brought along several pieces and I was hoping for a few pointers from Don." He took a sip of his coffee and glanced around the room. "I didn't really want to do the whole workshop thing. I thought we could talk professional to professional." Van put his head down in what seemed like embarrassment. "I actually followed him when he went off to the lighthouse. I caught up with him when was about to sit down on the bench that overlooked the rocks and water. He was very disagreeable and snarled at me. I thought it might be because he seemed to be struggling with something in his messenger bag, and I offered to help."

I was trying not to appear to be listening as closely as I was. "Did you see what he was having trouble with?" I asked.

Van shrugged. "It seemed like a big fuss about nothing. All I saw was a tote bag." He looked around the café and saw one of the tote bags the writers had been given. "It was like that, but there was something bulky inside it."

He stopped himself and looked at me. "That really has nothing to do with anything. The reason I wanted to talk to him was to explain my situation. When that didn't work out, I went to the workshop and read one of the pieces to the group. I started to explain it was like jazz, but Don shushed me and insisted the work had to stand on its own. Since he didn't understand that it was really improvisational advertising copy, he ripped it apart, and, well, I got steamed. I mean, really, who was he, anyway?"

Van's voice started to rise in anger, but he caught himself. "I was really afraid someone who was there was going to mention it to the cops."

"Then you didn't?" I asked.

"No, absolutely not. The last thing I need is to be considered a suspect. If anyone else told the cops about the minor blowup, I figured the cops haven't put it together with me." He realized he might have said too much. "I hope that doesn't mean you're going to rush off and fink on me."

"Of course not. Why would I help them?" I said. That was certainly the truth. Even with my new and improved relationship with Lieutenant Borgnine, I wasn't about to feed him information. Van reached over and patted my hand in appreciation. I happened to glance toward the entrance just at that moment, as Dane came into the café. His eye went right to Van's hand on mine, and the flare in his eyes was unmistakable as he came straight over to our table.

Van must have seen the uniform and freaked, because when I turned toward where he'd been sitting, the spot was empty.

"Who is he and what was that about?" Dane asked, his brows together in concern.

"It's not what you think. He was telling me about his experience with Don Porter."

Dane appeared wary. "It seemed to me that he was making a move on you."

"He wasn't." I changed the subject and told him about my new job for the night.

"This I've got to see," he said with a grin.

Our conversation was interrupted as the bell announced dinner. Dane went off to his cop business and I joined Dolly and her companion, whose name I now knew was Wilma, to walk to dinner.

The Saturday night dinner was always fancier than dinner on the rest of the nights. If Sammy hadn't been doing his big magic show, he would have been circulating doing table magic. Dolly, Wilma and I all took our usual seats at the same table we'd been sitting at all weekend. Lucinda slipped into the seat next to me. Even with all the ups and downs, it seemed like the weekend had done her good. The table quickly erupted in small talk.

I tried to take part, but I kept going back to the conversation with Van. I started to dismiss him as a suspect but realized it was only because I'd liked him. Frank's words about not letting my personal feelings get in the way of investigating echoed in my head. I went through the whole conversation again. It had sounded like he'd been depending on getting hints from Don and instead got torn apart. The fact that he was a professional probably made it sting even more.

It was true he had explained away his behavior, but it could have been just a cover-up.

Lucinda nudged me. "Let's get our dinner." She stood up and waited for me to join her. She saw the boots I was wearing, and the dress, neither of which were my typical clothes. "What's going on?"

I gave her a quick explanation as we walked back to the cafeteria line. When we'd gotten our food and were on our way back to the table, I felt a tug at my sleeve and stopped abruptly.

"Can I talk to you? Can I talk to you?" DeeDee said in a low voice. I wondered what was up now. Lucinda had missed me stopping and was already back at the table.

I stepped out of the way of the cafeteria traffic and put my tray down on an empty table. Poor DeeDee was definitely tense. She kept moving her head and looking around. The movements were jerky and her hair swirled across her face.

"Okay, what is it?"

"I want to apologize," she said. I could see she was going to repeat the phrase, but she managed to stop herself. She seemed a little stuck after that, so I tried to make it easier by asking what it was that she was apologizing for.

"I want to apologize for Rayanne being so difficult and making all those threats. I know when you understand why, you'll forgive her," DeeDee said. "You know how she complained that the man who died was not nice to her at the lighthouse?" She waited for me to nod to show I remembered before she continued. "She was upset because he was her cousin. That's why she's been so testy all weekend."

"What?" I said as what she'd said registered. "Don Porter was Rayanne's cousin?"

DeeDee suddenly tensed, and when I followed her gaze I saw that Rayanne was coming toward us. She didn't seem happy—as if that was anything new.

DeeDee began to speak very fast. "She doesn't want anyone to know that he was family. But I thought you should know so you would understand." Rayanne was even closer now. "Don't tell her I said anything," DeeDee said as her speech picked up speed. "And don't tell anyone else what I said, either. If she finds out I told, there will be hell to pay. We're officemates."

"What's going on?" Rayanne said, looking from DeeDee to me and back at DeeDee with a harsh stare.

"Nothing. Nothing at all," DeeDee said to her friend. "I was asking Casey if she'd seen you, and here you are. Here you are."

"Let's get our food," Rayanne said, snagging DeeDee along with her.

I couldn't move for a minute as questions surged through my mind. Had Rayanne known her cousin was going to be here? Was she the one who'd left the note on the message board and called him Snow Drop? And the biggest one of all—did she kill him?

"What happened to you?" Lucinda asked when I finally got to the table. "You look kind of discombobulated."

"I'll tell you in a minute." I set my tray down and was getting ready to sit when I saw that Borgnine had come in. He stood in the front and scanned the crowd. I was glad when he bypassed my group as he made his way across the room.

I was sure the lieutenant tried to be unobtrusive, but it was hard to miss the gruff-looking man in the rumpled tweed jacket, and a stir went through the dining hall as he stopped at one of the tables and leaned down to talk to someone. I craned my neck to see who it was.

"Oh, no," I said as the lieutenant took hold of Van's arm. As they walked to the door, Van looked back and caught my gaze. If looks could kill, I would have been dead.

"What was that about?" Lucinda asked.

That was a good question. Had Lieutenant Borgnine somehow overheard our conversation in the café? I was in earshot of the other retreaters at the table and didn't want to mention my conversation with Van. They didn't know I was involved with investigating and I decided it was best to keep it that way, so I just said that maybe Borgnine had solved his case and left it at that. Then I joined in with the conversation at the table.

WHEN DINNER ENDED AND EVERYONE SCATTERED to get themselves ready for the evening's events, I dashed across the street. I checked the house for the cat and found Julius on the love seat in the office. "So you're staying inside tonight," I said to the black cat. "I get it. You want it to be your decision." He closed his eyes and then opened them, looking directly at me as if to say, "Now you understand cats."

My reason for being there wasn't to check on the cat, though. I went for the landline and punched in Frank's number. I hoped I wouldn't be interrupting anything with his date. I tried to leave what I might be interrupting as vague in my imagination, not wanting to even picture any intimate moments. The phone continued to ring and I began to get the feeling he wasn't going to pick up. Finally he answered with a breathless hello.

For a second I considered just hanging up and pretending the call never happened, but the way phones were now, there was no anonymity, so I plowed forward.

"Hi, Frank," I said, sort of choking on my words.

"This better be good," he said. "My honey and I were just—"

"You don't have to say any more," I said, cutting him off. "This won't take long. There's just been a development and you're the only one I can discuss it with."

"When you put it that way, Feldstein," he said. "Tell me, but leave out any extraneous details. I want to get back to—"

"*Ssst,*" I said, almost automatically trying to shush him. "I don't need any details."

I heard him laugh. "Makes you uncomfortable to think about me on a date, huh? If you're going to be doing all the PI stuff, you're going to have to toughen up."

"Sure, next time," I said. "So here's the scoop." I told him about DeeDee's apology and that Rayanne was related to the dead guy.

"That's a bombshell," he said. "She could be the one who killed him over something stupid like when they were kids he took her Halloween candy and she's been seeking revenge ever since."

"Good scenario for a murder. It sounds like something the writers here would come up with," I said. "I intend to check it out, but there's something more pressing. I found the other writer. The one who had the public meltdown and stormed out. It seems that the cops knew someone had a meltdown, but not who, and he was glad to leave them in the dark."

"He told you that?" Frank said, sounding impressed. "I'm telling you, Feldstein, you've got the gift of unzipping closed lips."

"Hold the compliments," I said. "It might not have turned out so good for me." I explained Lieutenant Borgnine's appearance at dinner and how he was holding Van's arm as he escorted him out. "It was right after Van spilled the story to me. So he probably thinks I told on him."

"Ouch," Frank said. "The big question is, do you think he killed the travel writer?"

"All I know is that he could have. He tried to explain away his behavior at the workshop, but he could have had a motive. Having his work ripped apart in public could have made him go off the rails and want revenge."

I heard Frank swallow hard. "Not good, Feldstein. A guy who kills for revenge thinks you turned him in. Unless the cop locks him up, he's going to be wandering around that place looking for you. I'm telling you, you ought to be carrying for your own protection."

"I don't do guns," I said firmly. "Nothing is going to happen. All the events tonight are public, and I'll be in front of a lot of people."

Frank picked up on *in front of* and I reminded him about being Sammy's assistant and he chortled.

"Feldstein, you lead an interesting life." I knew he was ending the call. "And now I have to get back to my honey. We were in the midst"—he interrupted himself and told me to let him finish this time—"of a dance lesson. She's giving me a refresher lesson in the Argentinian tango." I heard some music come up just before the phone clicked off.

"I'm not the only one who leads an interesting life," I muttered to myself before rushing back to Vista Del Mar, ready to face my fate.

21

THE SKY HAD CLEARED ENOUGH TO SEE THE MOON. It bathed the grounds in enough light to see the outlines of the trees and underbrush. I had put on a tough front for Frank, but I still kept checking my surroundings as I made my way to Hummingbird Hall. I hoped that Van had broken down and given Lieutenant Borgnine the confession the cop had been wishing for. And that he was safely locked up in the small jail at the downtown police station.

I stopped in the entranceway of Hummingbird Hall. The auditorium had the same Arts and Crafts architecture as the Lodge. The inside was done in dark wood and there was an open framework of wood beams overhead. Like all the other buildings, this one seemed to have walls that were mostly windows. Other than a stage at the front, nothing was built in, so the large space could be arranged for different purposes. At the moment there were rows of chairs divided by a center aisle. The alcoves along the sides had stacked bales of hay as decorations for the square dancing. Kevin St. John was just walking across the stage to the microphone and podium that had been set up in the middle of it. I did a double take when I saw him. Honestly, I had never seen him in anything but dark suits and plain white shirts with a conservative tie, but here he was, in a yellow-and-white-checked shirt and stiff-looking dark-wash jeans. I checked his footwear, wondering if he was wearing cowboy boots, but instead he had on sneakers. He'd completed the outfit with a bolo tie.

I walked behind the bales of hay, going along the side to check out who was there. The first row was almost empty and appeared to have been reserved. As I'd figured, the two groups each had their own areas. There were many more writers than yarn retreaters, and they took up one whole section and half the section on the other side of the center aisle. I glanced over the writers' group, looking for Van, and was relieved not to see him.

Kevin St. John was droning on, but I took in only every other word. I got it—he was welcoming everyone and giving them the layout of the evening. He mentioned the open mike, the magic and the square dancing. I continued to look around to see who was where.

Lisa and Derek had separated themselves from the two groups and were in the last row. Lucinda was sitting on the aisle with my group, and I was confident that she was looking after everyone. I recognized Mona's big hat in the same row and made a mental note to figure out a way to find out what she was really up to. The early birds had spread themselves through the retreaters, and a number of my group were working on their projects. Dolly was sitting with the Difficult Duo, and I hoped her warm charm would cancel out Rayanne's complaining. Trying to find out anything about her dead cousin was going to be a real challenge.

When I located Jeff Hunter, he was getting out of his seat and climbing over the rest of the people in the row. When he got to the center aisle, he made his way to the front and then looked around for a moment before taking one of the seats in the first row.

I retraced my steps and went to the back of the auditorium. "*Psst*, over here, Casey," a whispered voice called. Sammy, decked out in his performance tuxedo, was standing at the very back of the auditorium. The area was covered by a small balcony, and the kitchen crew was in the process of setting up refreshments on several long tables covered in red-and-white-checked paper tablecloths.

His face fell when he saw my long dress. "Case, you changed the wardrobe?" I lifted the dress enough for him to see the boots and the beginning of the body stocking. Poor Sammy seemed so nervous as he gave me an awkward hug.

"I'd only do this for you," I said, thinking of the ridiculous outfit underneath.

The open mike portion began and I watched from the back. The first woman read what she called flash fiction, which she explained was a five-hundred-word story. She read it off her phone, which made her cadence a little off because so little would fit on the screen at one time. Jeff went up on the stage next. He laid his laptop on the podium and readjusted the microphone for his taller stature and then fiddled with the laptop. Even from a distance, I could tell by the jerking of his movements that he was nervous.

When I thought about it, who could blame him? He was putting his work out for all to judge. True, it wasn't like the workshop, where it would have been critiqued—I imagined if anyone said anything here, it would be positive. It made me think of T Dot and Van. But only for a moment. Once Jeff's voice stopped shaking, I got lost in his piece. It was like he was creating word pictures, the way he described the pastel sky in the Mojave Desert at dawn, rainbows on the edge of Las Vegas and the view of the San Fernando Valley that opened up when he came through the Sepulveda Pass. From there he focused in on a particular trip. He'd written up the story he'd told us about how, since he was going anyway, he had taken a dog to his owner and it had led to him adopting a dog himself.

When he talked about traveling, I realized that although their circumstances were different, his experience wasn't too dissimilar to what Don Porter had done. They both traveled with a purpose, and it seemed like they were both always going from one place to another. My train of thought was interrupted when he finished speaking. I let out a sigh of relief when everyone applauded and it sounded like they meant it.

I missed the rest of the readings as Sammy hustled me along the side and into the backstage area.

A large table had two red boxes on the top. Near it was a cart with some shiny squares of metal and a larger piece of metal that appeared to have a sharp edge. They all had black handles at the top. Suddenly the whole thing was becoming real to me and I wondered what I'd signed up for.

"Aren't you supposed to practice an illusion this elaborate?" I said, touching the sharp edge of the large metal square.

"I'm doing all the heavy lifting, Case," Sammy said, running his hands over the boxes on the table. He seemed to be muttering something to himself; then he spoke to me. "I was just going over the patter. That's what it's all about, the patter. You just have to lie there, and as long as I don't cut through it too soon, everything will be fine."

"How about I knock on the box when I'm ready," I said. "So no cutting until I rap twice. Okay?"

"Sure, sure, Case," Sammy said, pacing around the small area.

"Remember, you're a surgeon. You're used to doing dangerous things under pressure," I said, hoping to reassure him.

"Maybe, but I don't have an audience when I'm fixing a bladder." He continued to pace and I continued trying to calm him down. Finally Kevin St. John stuck his head in and said the last person was finishing their piece.

"Take off your dress," Sammy said, then apologized. "I'm sorry, Case. That sounds kind of tacky. And there's something else. Don't even think about what I'm going to tell you to do. And if you notice what you're doing, don't ever tell anyone. The secret to how it's done can never get out." He had gotten very nervous and seemed to be coming unglued. He started muttering to himself that we really should have practiced the act. "It might have been a mistake to agree to this. I don't know if I'm ready." He swallowed a few times. "Maybe I should just go out there now and tell them the show's canceled."

His demeanor was making me a little nervous, but I also had a lot of confidence in Sammy. "No, Sammy. This means too much to you. Take a deep breath and let it out slowly."

He did as I suggested and he instantly seemed a little better. "Oh, Case, you're the best—"

"I know what you're going to say, 'and you're the only one who gets me.'"

The plan was that I would wait backstage until he was ready for me. Kevin St. John introduced him and he went onstage. He seemed to lose his nervousness the moment he was in front of the crowd. He was used to doing tricks with a participant, so he had people come up from the audience. When I peeked out, he was doing the trick with the three shells. The three shells all looked the same and I couldn't imagine how Sammy kept track of the pea. There was no more time to think about it, though, because he had announced his grand finale illusion. That was my cue to push the table with the box onto the stage. It did creep me out a bit, since it looked amazingly like a coffin.

Sammy started into his patter as he took the boxes off the table and introduced me as his assistant. He made some lame joke about me being two places at once and having a split personality. Succeeding with the earlier part of the show seemed to have given him confidence, and he seemed a lot calmer.

I wasn't so sure I was, though, as I climbed on the table and let him put the shackle above my feet and tie my hands together. Then he put the box over me with only my head and hands still showing to the crowd. Now was when I supposed to make the adjustment. It took only a moment for me to get uncomfortable. This was a job for a contortionist. I decided the best way to deal with it was by thinking of something else, or better yet imagining myself somewhere else. I reached for something to hang on to, and suddenly Jeff Hunter's piece came to mind. I'd picture the desert at dawn. But I was too nervous to settle on one image, so I started thinking about the piece as a whole. And then the story about the dog. I wondered if Don had ever been asked to do something like that.

I was so lost in thought that I forgot all about the signal I was supposed to give Sammy. I was definitely not cut out to be a magician's assistant. I wanted the illusion to be over and to get out of the box. I turned my head to look out at the audience, hoping that would help. Wouldn't you just know? Van had just come in the door and was standing at the back of the room examining the crowd. It was just then that he saw me, or at least my head. Sammy was continuing with his patter while I was watching Van come down the center aisle. The way he was walking, it was clear that he was steamed.

Sammy was saying something to me that I didn't focus on, until finally he leaned close and said, "You didn't knock. Is everything okay?"

I apologized and nodded, and Sammy went ahead with the rest of the trick. I was glad that I couldn't see the blade. Even though I knew it wasn't going to really cut me, it made me nervous thinking of what would have happened if I hadn't moved.

He plunged the blade down the center of the box, and then he slid in the metal panels before separating the two halves.

Van was at the foot of the stage now. He glared at me. "How could you? You said it was us against the cops and you wouldn't tell them anything." That wasn't quite what I had said, but I wasn't about to argue. He seemed to be getting more and more upset, and I imagined how he must have acted when Don criticized his piece.

He started to climb on the stage as he continued to yell at me with a menacing stare. I was kind of a captive audience, though I didn't think he could do anything worse than pinch my check. When he got closer, I told him it hadn't been me.

"C'mon, the timing was just a little too close for me to believe that." I was trying to think back to when we'd been talking and who could have overheard. There had been no one sitting close enough. Then I remembered something. *But why?* I thought.

By this time, Sammy had stopped the trick, leaving the two boxes split apart, as if I was still cut in two. He went after Van, telling him to get off the stage. Sammy was tall, with a hulking build, and even though he was totally nonviolent, he looked like he could do some damage.

Meanwhile, it seemed like the audience had all sucked in their breath as Van left the stage and Sammy turned to the crowd. "That's what happens when you have such an attractive assistant. I could see why her boyfriend could get a little steamed over what I did to her."

There was a moment of absolute quiet; then the group

broke out into laughter and then applause. Good for Sammy. He had made it seem like Van's outburst was part of the show. While Sammy was busy taking bows, I was still stuck in the box and getting more claustrophobic by the second. I was rethinking Bridget's backing out. Maybe she had been on to something.

Sammy was still engaging the audience, ad-libbing his patter. I was beginning to feel numb and finally tried to get his attention. I started out softly, but when I saw I wasn't getting anywhere, I got louder.

"Hey, Dr. Sammy—how about putting me back together?" Although I said it like I meant it, the audience thought it was all part of the act and laughed in response.

I saw that Dane had just come into the auditorium. He glanced around, and then his eyes went right to the stage and he started to come toward the front. My blood was going to all the wrong places. I was hot and starting to feel faint. Meanwhile, Sammy was still kibitzing with the audience and making lame jokes.

I don't know if my face was very flushed, or maybe it was the freaked-out look in my eyes, but Dane picked up on it. He got to the stage and jumped up on it. He turned to Sammy and said, "You're under arrest for murdering a trick." Sammy glanced back at me, and then he appeared to notice my discomfort. Dane stood there while Sammy supposedly glued me back together. I was relieved to assume my original position just before he took the box off. The two men helped me up. Sammy and I started to take our bow, but someone yelled that Dane was clearly part of the trick, too. Someone else yelled out that Sammy was like Penn &

Teller with the crazy illusions. Dane joined in on the bow, and then his eyes popped when he saw my outfit.

I knew he was going to tease me about it, but I was too busy trying to get back the train of thought I'd had about Don Porter. Something had flitted through my mind that would have changed everything, but now it seemed to have disappeared.

22

DANE AND SAMMY BOTH TOOK ME OUTSIDE TO GET some air. Now that we were safe from the audience finding out that all the extras hadn't been planned, Sammy asked about the guy who had yelled at me.

"Someone yelled at you?" Dane said, assuming his cop mode.

"You know how I'm asking around about things?" I said. "One of the writers told me something, and he thought I told Lieutenant Borgnine." I turned to Dane. "Maybe you can find out who really told on him. I'd rather not have him scowling at me for the rest of the weekend."

"It's just one more day," Dane teased, then relented. "Borgnine probably won't tell me anything, but I can ask."

"So is this going to be permanent?" Dane asked, looking at my silly looking "tuxedo."

"I'd love to have Case as a permanent part of the show, and after tonight, I want to come up with a whole new act. More comedy." He turned to me. "You would be good with that. You're very funny," Sammy said.

"Not intentionally," I countered.

"I better get back and clear the stage," Sammy said. I could see that he was pumped up from the success of the show. I was going to have to talk to him about my continuing involvement in the act.

I recovered after a few minutes in the night air and went from feeling refreshed to being cold. "I'm not supposed to do this," Dane said, taking off his cop jacket and wrapping it around me. He glanced around to make sure Lieutenant Borgnine wasn't standing anywhere nearby.

He shook his head again at my attire. "It's going to be hard for me to restrain myself from teasing you about that outfit."

"Be my guest," I said, taking a bow. "If you knew what a tight squeeze it was in there, it actually makes sense." I looked down at the boots. "Well, maybe not those."

I could feel my smile fade as I went back to trying to recapture the thoughts I'd had while trapped in half the box, but now that I was out of it, I wondered if they were merely a reaction to the panic I'd been feeling. What I really wanted to know was what had happened between Van and Lieutenant Borgnine.

"I'm going to ask you a favor. It's kind of awkward, but I can't really explain anything about why I want to know."

Dane smiled. "Oh, boy, a secret mission. I'll get out my decoder watch."

"This is serious," I said. "Could you find out what Lieutenant Borgnine knows about Van? Like, is he considering him a person of interest?" I stopped for a moment. "Whatever that means, anyway."

"It's about the same as being a suspect. I like to say it means we're watching you." Dane started to move around and I realized that with the short sleeves of his uniform, he was cold. I took off the jacket and handed it back, saying that I'd left my dress and jacket in the backstage area. "So do you think you can do it?" I pressed.

"For you, anything," he said. His tone wasn't teasing this time, and it made me uncomfortable to know that he meant it. I wasn't playing a game with him, keeping him at a distance. It was a genuine feeling that letting go and falling into the flames would be a mistake. If only he could understand that I was really thinking of him. I liked him far too much to want to start something and then have me mess it up. I couldn't help but look past the moment. For example, if I didn't clear up this murder and Madeleine's worst nightmare happened and it came out that she'd talked to Don on the plane, she could forget all she'd said about our friendship and how much she liked my retreats. Kevin St. John would jump at the chance to stop giving me the deep discount. Who knew? Maybe he'd talk them into raising the cost. My business would collapse. I needed both the retreat business and the baking to keep my head above water.

I knew myself, and at that point I would just throw in the towel, sell my aunt's house and figure out something entirely new to do, somewhere else. And Dane would be collateral damage. If he was just some guy looking for a good time for a little while, it would be different. Behind all the teasing and hotness, he was such a solid guy.

I knew his history. His father had never been in the picture and his mother was an alcoholic, which had forced him to be the man in the family for his sister and mother. I admired how even after her countless failures to stay sober, he never gave up on his mother. And he was still looking after his sister, too. But that was a whole other story. He cared about the teens in Cadbury and did what he could by keeping them out of trouble and occupied in his garage / karate studio. He fed them massive amounts of pasta, too.

I just wished that there wasn't always this thing when he was around. I wasn't sure how to describe it other than it felt like a buzzing though my whole body. So I knew that I was playing with fire when I said okay to having him come by my house later and tell me all he could find out.

"I better get inside," I said, glancing back at Hummingbird Hall. Kevin St. John was responsible for the square dancing, but I felt accountable for my group's participation in it.

When I came out of the backstage area back in the dress over my silly outfit, I walked into chaos. It reminded me of having the set of a play arranged for the next scene. Kevin stood on the stage, directing the staff to remove all the chairs. As fast as the chairs disappeared, the bales of hay were moved in closer. The writers and my group had all been herded to the back of auditorium for refreshments.

I found Lucinda and chuckled when I saw her outfit. My friend, who always wore designer everything, was wearing a billowing turquoise skirt.

"Kevin went all out," she said. "He brought in a whole bunch of skirts and these." She lifted her skirt to show off a many-layered petticoat. "There were western shirts for the men and bolo ties." Then she seemed to remember Sammy's show. "Was all that really part of the act?" she asked, her face sliding into concern. "If it was, you're quite the actress. You look pretty distressed."

I was in the process of admitting the truth when I saw Madeleine come in. What was even more surprising was that she wasn't alone—her sister, Cora, was with her. Madeleine had exchanged her jeans for a denim skirt, though she had left off the petticoats. Cora seemed to shrink back from the crowd. She hadn't altered her clothing choice for the occasion and wore one of her formal suits and had a handbag on her arm. I always called that Queen Elizabeth–style because it reminded me of the way the monarch carried her purse.

Kevin St. John saw the Delacorte sisters from the stage and appeared stricken. He might give off the impression of being the lord of Vista Del Mar, but he knew very well who the real bosses were.

Cora stopped to check out all the activity, but Madeleine came over to me. Her expression dimmed to deep worry. "Casey, anything to report?"

I considered what to tell her. It seemed that things were moving along, but there was nothing concrete yet. "Things are looking more promising," I began. "But don't you think that maybe you've overreacted about Don Porter? Talking to a stranger on the plane isn't such a big deal. Cora probably wouldn't be as upset as you think," I said. "And there is no reason to suppose that Lieutenant Borgnine is going to question you anyway."

My attempt didn't seem to work, and Madeleine grabbed my arm. "Please don't say anything to her. You don't understand. It was all because he saw me knitting. I was using some yarn I bought on the trip." She stopped and checked her surroundings before she continued. "It seemed like it would be no problem." She paused as if she was going to say more, but Cora squeezed between two women wearing so many petticoats that their skirts were almost horizontal and joined us, wrapping us in a cloud of Chanel No. 5.

Cora appeared perturbed as she took in all the activity and then turned to her sister. "I thought that when you started spending so much time here that meant you were keeping an eye on things. This place is out of control." She shook her head with annoyance. "Will you look at her?" She made no pretense of hiding her disapproval as she pointed to Mona, who still wore the big hat, sunglasses and clothes that shrouded her shape. "I tried to say something to her, but she simply walked away," Cora said. "She looked a little familiar to me. What do you think?"

If Madeleine answered, I didn't hear it, because just then Dolly pushed through the crowd carrying a cup of punch. "Darlin', this is just the most fun idea." She took in the two sisters standing with me. She'd seen Madeleine, though only briefly, at the workshops, but it was the first time she was seeing Cora. "That suit looks almost like a real Chanel," she said in her opera singer voice.

"It is a real Chanel," Cora said in a haughty voice. "Which of the groups are you with?"

"I'm with Casey's. I thought this was going to be just a quiet weekend away from the grandkids, but it's been one exciting thing after the other." Her voice dropped. "Though it was terrible about that man's death. I would have been worried, but the policeman with the wrinkled jacket said he was sure that it was personal. You know, not some wild killer on the loose. And then there was the disaster in our meeting room when all the yarn got messed around." She turned her attention to Madeleine. "I guess you missed all of that. Lucky you to have all your yarn neat in your bag."

"We're not going to talk about yarn now," Madeleine said quickly. "Why don't you get some more punch before the dancing starts." Madeleine almost gave Dolly a push in the direction of the refreshments. I was surprised at her prickly behavior, but I was sure it had to do with Cora being there.

Kevin St. John came by our little group just then. He was all smiles and spoke in a cloying tone as he greeted the sisters. "How nice that you've come for the square dancing," he said.

Cora gave him a withering look. Actually, she gave us all a withering look, including her sister. "As one of the owners of this place, I am going to have to step in and take a more active role. Another murder here? Pretty soon Vista Del Mar will be described as the place where people check in but don't check out."

We all looked at her, trying to figure out if she was being facetious and if we should at least smile, but Cora's expression remained grim. Now I understood Madeleine's panic about her sister finding out that she was making friends with strangers. Madeleine was the older sister, but Cora was the tough one.

THE SQUARE DANCING WAS A SURPRISING HIT. Kevin had gotten in a real square-dance caller, and he gave a short lesson first. Since everyone was there just for fun, none of them were too upset if somebody do-si-doed incorrectly. Even though Lieutenant Borgnine wasn't there, Madeleine and Cora stayed only until the dancing began. It seemed to me that it was mostly Cora's idea that they leave. Madeleine glanced back wistfully at the dancers as they headed to the door.

With them gone and the dancing continuing, Kevin St. John caught up with me on the sidelines. He usually managed to hide his emotions, but this time he looked like he'd had the life squeezed out of him. He actually leaned against the stack of hay bales as he stopped next to me.

"You heard it. Cora wants to get involved with running this place." He let his head fall forward in despair. "It's going to be a disaster," he said.

Ha, if he thinks that *is going to be a problem,* I thought. When Gwen finally decided to come forward and let her fellow Cadburians know that she was the love child of Edmund Delacorte and therefore entitled to Vista Del Mar, it was really going to hit the fan.

23

AT LAST, IN THE PEACE OF MY OWN HOUSE, I collapsed on the sofa in the living room. It was a relief not to have to go to the Blue Door that night, but I was too wired from the day to think about going to bed yet. Besides, Dane had said he would come by with whatever he found out.

Julius had jumped up next to me and was curled against my leg. It was nice that someone seemed glad to have me home. I was too keyed up to sit there, though. It seemed normal to be baking late at night, so I went into the kitchen and made a batch of the almost-apple-fritter muffins to tweak the recipe.

The smell of them baking was perfuming the air when I heard a knock on my kitchen door. The top half was glass, just like at the Blue Door, so I saw that it was Dane before I opened it.

He was out of uniform now, in jeans with a hoodie. He came right in and sniffed the air. "You can't help yourself, can you? Sun's gotta shine and you gotta bake." He glanced toward the oven. "Whatever it is smells delicious."

He waited until I invited him to sit and then peeled off the hoodie. It wasn't unusual for him to stop in at the Blue Door when I was baking, but we both seemed to realize this was different.

I was trying not to be awkward, but I wanted this over as soon as possible. I busied myself taking the muffins out of the oven and putting the pan on a rack to cool. "So, why don't you just share what you found out, so that you can go home and get some sleep," I said in a falsely bright voice.

He got up and came behind me, allegedly to check out the muffins, but he leaned against me as he did. "Someone told Lieutenant Borgnine that the guy who yelled at you, Van something, was the one who'd thrown a fit at the travel writers' workshop, but more damning was that he hadn't told the cops about it when he was questioned. Actually, he had denied even going to the workshop."

"That was kind of what I figured. But he didn't arrest him?"

"Van apologized and said that he didn't want to get involved and he'd seen a character on a TV show stay out of a situation by denying even knowing the victim. What was he going to charge him with—watching too much television?"

"Oh," I said. "Did you find out who the someone who told was?"

"Sorry," he said, standing close enough behind me that I could feel his chest rise and fall as he breathed. "The most I could find out was that it was a woman."

His closeness was getting into the danger zone. The feeling his presence inspired was zinging all over me, and part of me wanted to just turn to face him and let things take their course, but my judgment prevailed and I stayed put and stayed on the subject of the investigation.

The trouble was that I was speaking too fast and my breathing was choppy, totally giving me away.

"I don't know why you don't face up to it," he said.

"Yes, you do," I said. "I told you I would just make a mess of things. And there's a reason I may not be sticking around here much longer."

Dane took my shoulders and turned me to face him. "What are you talking about?"

I hesitated. I had been keeping everything about Madeleine strictly to myself. But he'd sort of put me in a corner and I felt I had to explain. I gave him the whole story of how she'd come to me, hysterical about her sister finding out about her talking to Don on the plane.

"That doesn't sound right," Dane said. "I know Cora Delacorte is old-fashioned, to put it mildly, but to get crazy because she found out her sister talked to someone on the plane, even if he did turn up dead . . ." His voice trailed off as he shrugged.

"Madeleine has been staying under the radar as far as Lieutenant Borgnine is concerned. She figures if he doesn't see her at Vista Del Mar, he'll have no reason to connect her with Don Porter. But you're right; it does seem over the top." I thought back to earlier in the evening. "Maybe there's something else going on with the sisters. We had kind of an odd conversation earlier. Cora was throwing her weight around, telling Kevin St. John that she was going to get more involved with running the place." Dane chuckled at the concept. "But then there was something Madeleine said."

"What exactly was it?" he asked. He had put a little distance between us as the subject of our possible relationship got shoved to the side.

I searched my mind for her exact words. "She said something about him seeing her knitting and then she said she didn't think it would be a problem. The question is, what was she saying wouldn't be a problem? Now that I think about it, that doesn't seem to go with a mere conversation. Maybe there was more that went on between them." I was talking to myself now. "That must be it." I turned to Dane with a smile. "Thank you. I wouldn't have gotten to that without you."

"Glad I could be of service," he said. "Now, what was it we were talking about?" He struck a thoughtful pose that was all for show. "That's right, we were talking about us. Look, I'm a big boy and I don't need you to look out for my better interests. Besides, what makes you so sure that I'm looking for something long-term? Before you came along, I was known as the heartbreaker of Cadbury, tossing women aside like used tissues." He was trying to keep a straight face, as if I would believe that anyway.

"You were not," I said, taking a playful swipe at him.

"Try me and I'll show you."

"Not tonight," I said, walking him to the door.

"You know where to find me." He pointed in the direction of his place. "I'll be at heartbreak hotel down the street." He was lingering by the door, looking way too appealing.

Reason seemed to have gone out the window, and I leaned in and gave him a quick kiss, and then panicked. "Forget I did that," I said as I pushed him outside.

He stopped outside the glass and looked back with a grin. "You're weakening. You can't resist my charm forever."

"In your dreams," I said, trying to sound sarcastic. I reached to the wall and hit the switch, turning off the kitchen light. Why did that make me think of something?

24

SLEEP DIDN'T COME EASY. I WAS WIRED FROM Dane's visit, and everything from the weekend was swirling around in my head. Julius had settled into a perfect little niche next to me and gave me a dirty look when I pulled back the covers to get up. The one thing I had learned since beginning the yarn retreats was that not only was knitting relaxing, but the rhythm and monotony of doing the knit stitch row after row also seemed to help me to think.

I went into the office and found the tote bag with the project I had started. *Started* was the keyword here. I had picked the smallest and most basic one. I was going to make a washcloth with cotton yarn and bigger needles so it would go more quickly. So far I had just done a few rows.

Julius came in to see what was going on. I guess it didn't interest him because after a moment he went back to parts unknown as I began to work the needles. The project was so simple I had even been able to help Rayanne with it. The process was to simply knit two stitches, yarn over and then knit across. At some point when the triangle got big enough, I'd have to start decreasing, but I had a ways before I got there.

As the needles moved, my mind went elsewhere. It seemed like the best thing I could do was to examine everything I knew and see if anything new emerged. Madeleine came into my thoughts first. After thinking over what she'd said, again, I remembered that she had gotten cut off right after she'd said she didn't think *it* would be a problem. Could she have meant to say something more? There had to be more to her relationship to Don than she had let on.

I tried to remember everything that T Dot had said. There was the issue of a tote bag that was in Don's room when T Dot was there, but not when the cops investigated. What was in the tote bag and what had happened to it? There were so many tote bags floating around the place.

T Dot put himself near Don around the time he must have been shot, when everyone was at the Roast and Toast. He'd told me only because he was worried that someone had seen him near Don's room.

The tiny triangle was getting bigger as I knitted and thought. I was glad that Frank couldn't see me. He'd think I was like Miss Marple. Frank wasn't a fan of fictional detectives. "It's not like the real world," he'd told me when I'd first started the temp job. But he had spoken well of Sherlock Holmes and said that there was something to his lateral thinking. Frank had this crazy of way of explaining it. "It's like this, Feldstein. Sometimes you have to flip the picture."

I almost wanted to call him and ask him more about what that meant. But it was practically the middle of the night here and even later in Chicago so I was on my own.

How could I flip the picture, as Frank put it? Suddenly something popped out at me. How about this for flipping the picture? I was so busy thinking about T Dot being in the vicinity of Don's room that I had never considered the woman he said had seen him. She had also been in the vicinity of Don's room around the time he was shot.

I made a mental note to talk to T Dot again in the morning. All he had said about her was that she was wearing a scarf. Maybe if I got him to look around the dining hall at breakfast, he could pick her out.

By now my eyes were heavy and I knew I could sleep. I put my knitting away and found the light switch to shut off the lights. Why was the switch making me feel like I was missing something?

I MIGHT HAVE HAD TROUBLE SLEEPING THE NIGHT before, but I certainly wouldn't have had trouble sleeping late into the morning. The big alarm clock started going off across the room making it clear that wasn't going to happen. *Sunday morning,* I thought with mixed feelings. Usually by Sunday the retreats were winding down and there was a feeling of completion. I was always relieved and at the same time sorry to see them end. But this time there was no feeling of completion. After the false start to the program, my retreaters hadn't gotten very far in their new projects. At least they seemed to be easy enough that they'd be able to finish them when they left. But the biggest thing was Don Porter's death. Lieutenant Borgnine had talked to Van but then let him go because there wasn't anything to charge him with. But did that mean that Borgnine really thought Van wasn't involved in Don Porter's death?

What would happen when the retreat and conference ended and everyone scattered? I supposed the case would stay open. What would happen with Madeleine? I didn't think that Lieutenant Borgnine would connect her with Don Porter, but that didn't mean that she would stop worrying. In other words, it was going to be hanging over my head unless the case got wrapped up in the next few hours.

"That's it. I have to do something." To add emphasis to my words, I pounded my fist on the bed. Julius turned his head toward me and opened his eyes as if to say, "What is going on?"

I showered and dressed in record time and was on my way across the street, determined that Don's death was going to be solved before the retreaters and writers scattered. Anyone seeing me walk down the driveway would have seen the determination in my step.

As I walked onto the Vista Del Mar grounds I was deep in thought. It felt like I was laying out pieces of a puzzle, trying to see how they fit together. I recalled that the desk clerk had thought Don went to the lighthouse to meet someone. And he'd seen a bag like the one given to the writers in Don's messenger bag. That made me think of the now-you-see-it, now-you-don't tote bag in Don's room that T Dot had mentioned. I remembered now that I had seen Don at the lighthouse when I'd escorted my group there.

My thoughts drifted to how Dane had come up behind me and put his hands on my shoulders and our silly conversation about the bench where we'd had our famous make-out session. I was seeing the bench in my mind's eye, and it triggered me to remember that I'd noticed a bag there. I'd even joked to Dane about it.

When I pictured it in my head, I realized it was a tote bag. Another now-you-see-it, now-you-don't tote bag, because when I'd looked back it was gone.

I began to connect the dots. Don's messenger bag had a bag inside. Maybe the tote bag I'd seen next to the bench. Maybe it was the tote bag that T Dot had seen in Don's room and that was gone when the cops went through the room.

My thoughts were interrupted when the door to the Lodge opened and Lieutenant Borgnine came out. To say he looked like hell was an understatement.

It wasn't hard to figure out why. He'd probably barely slept all weekend as he tried to close in on Don's killer. I gave him a sympathetic smile as I approached.

His response was a grunt and a sigh. His head was down and he was about to pass me but then stopped short. "I don't suppose you have anything to share," he said.

"You mean about the investigation?" I asked.

"I mean about your investigation. You don't cover your tracks very well."

"What do you mean?" I asked surprised.

"How about Van Simpson wanted to know if you were an undercover officer working for us." He let out a mirthless laugh. "As if we could have an undercover officer in Cadbury. The way everybody knows everybody's business, there's no chance the town wouldn't figure it out." He let his words sink in before continuing. "So it was obvious you questioned him. I'm just wondering who else you questioned."

He'd opened the door about Van, so I picked up the thread. "What about Van? I noticed that you didn't arrest him."

The lieutenant let out a really heavy sigh. "My cop gut tells me he's the one, but I didn't have enough to arrest him. And now all these people are going to check out and go back where they came from." He leveled his stare at me. "So you see, it's your civic duty to help me." He let out another sigh. "I don't know why you're even involved. This Porter guy had nothing to do with your group." He studied my face for a moment. "Or is it that you're just some armchair detective who can't resist getting involved?"

I was going to say something about that being my civic duty in a sarcastic tone, but he looked like he was about to fall asleep standing up, so I decided not to take his swipe personally. But I also didn't want to answer, so I totally ignored the question.

"You look like you need a little pick-me-up," I said, giving his jacket a tug so he'd follow me. We might be at odds most of the time, but I couldn't help but feel for him.

He followed along behind me like a sleepwalker. "In the old days in L.A., staying up like this when I was on a case was nothing. I might have gotten a little rusty." I took him back to the Lodge and into the café. I sat him down, then ordered him a black eye, thinking the coffee with two shots of espresso might help clear the fog for him.

In search of some *and* to go with the coffee, I went back to my place. Julius was asleep on the kitchen table and gave me a confused look when I rushed back into my kitchen and grabbed a couple of the almost-apple-fritter muffins I'd made the night before.

The lieutenant already had the coffee when I returned, and his face actually lit up when I put the two muffins in front of him. "I tweaked the recipe a little. Tell me what you think."

He bit into one and instead of a sigh let out an *ah*. It was gone in a couple of bites. "Even better than the others," he said. "Though the wife probably wouldn't approve." He went for the second one, and I started to ask about Van.

"What makes you think it was him?"

"Like I said, it was my cop gut. The guy seemed to have been offended by Porter. I got the feeling he saw himself on the same level as the travel writer. Just guessing, but I bet first being blown off when he tried to talk to him and then having his work torn apart in public awakened some secret feeling of being a failure, or a fraud—something he couldn't bear."

I was impressed with his insight and maybe a little surprised. I think the surprise showed in my face because he rolled his head at me in annoyance. "You're not a cop for all these years without learning something about what makes people tick." He picked up the crumbs of the muffin. "But I've got nothing to pin it on him. If you happened to hear anything like maybe someone saw him coming out of Don's room with some feathers sticking to his clothes . . ." He left it hanging, but I got the drift.

He got up and picked up the empty coffee cup and the wrappers from the muffins. Both seemed to have done him some good, and he appeared more alert. Even so, I had wondered if his cop gut might just be the product of exhaustion. We walked out of the café into the larger room of the Lodge. Some people had begun to come in as it got closer to the time for the breakfast bell to ring. The door by the driveway opened and Madeleine came in. She stopped just inside and glanced around the room. When her gaze reached us, her expression changed to shock and she seemed to look for a place to hide. She darted into one of the phone booths and shut the folding door.

I had no problem separating from Lieutenant Borgnine. Even though he had sort of asked for my help and was appreciative of the apple muffins, I didn't think he wanted to be seen fraternizing with me. I waited until he had left the building and then I tapped on the door of the phone booth.

"The coast is clear," I said when Madeleine opened it. She seemed relieved but also took a moment looking at the interior of the phone booth. "This brings back memories," she said, touching the door.

It seemed like she was going to take her time exiting the tiny space, and I wanted to get on with talking to her. I had to endure a few minutes of her walking down memory lane first, though. The phone booth had apparently reminded her of the old days at Cadbury Drugs and Sundries. When she started talking about the soda fountain with the chocolate phosphates, I stepped in to speed things up.

"That sounds lovely," I said, holding out my arm to help her out of the booth. I led her to the seating area, which thankfully was empty. I sat us close together on the couch to keep our conversation private in case anyone came in. I knew she wouldn't talk if she thought anyone was around.

"Madeleine, last night when we were talking about Don, you said you didn't think *something* was going to be a problem." I watched her expression to see if she knew what I was referring to. I saw her gulp, which I was pretty sure meant she did.

"You said your sister would be upset if she found out you talked to a strange man on the plane. But there's more to it, isn't there?"

Madeline pushed her bobbed brown hair behind her ears. It seemed like a nervous gesture and maybe a way to buy time. She was about to start talking and then stopped herself, as if she was trying to decide how to tell the story.

"After I did it, I thought it might have been a mistake, and I vowed I would never tell anyone." She rolled her eyes skyward. "Someone like you would just think I was foolish, and my sister would think I'd lost my mind, even if Don Porter hadn't been killed."

"You do remember that you're the older sister," I said, trying calm her. "And you are an adult." It was hard to keep a straight face when I said that, considering she was in her seventies.

"You're right, of course, but Cora has always sort of handled things. She thinks my change of wardrobe is foolish and she was completely against me going off on the trip to Peru. I have been doing my best to hold my own, but if she knew what I did, I'm afraid she'd think I was incompetent and try to get power of attorney. Now that my world has opened up, I simply will not go back."

I patted her hand to offer support. I hadn't realized it was that serious. "It would be easier to help you if I knew the whole story."

"Oh, dear," she said in almost a wail. "If I tell you, you must promise to keep it to yourself and not to judge me too harshly."

I held up my hand in a mock Girl Scout salute and promised on my honor to do everything she asked.

"Okay, then," she began. She swallowed a few times before continuing. "We were on the plane from Lima to San Francisco and Don started up a conversation with me. He was certainly interesting, with all of his travels. Somehow I mentioned that the trip to Peru had been such a big deal for me since I'd never strayed very far from Cadbury. When he heard I was from Cadbury, he asked if I knew of a place called Vista Del Mar. Of course I said not only did I know of it, but that my sister and I owned it. That's when he mentioned coming for the writers' conference."

She digressed and told me about the meal they'd had and the turbulence they'd hit. "It really made me nervous," she said. "I was so glad that I'd brought my knitting along. It was a good way to stay calm." Time was running out and I wanted to tell her to get to the point, but it was not the way to deal with Madeleine. I had to just let her go at her own pace until she got to whatever she'd been holding back.

Meanwhile, people had started to come into the Lodge. I didn't notice who they were—I was just glad they'd stayed away from the seating area so far.

"It was all because of my knitting that he asked me," Madeleine said. "It seemed like such an innocent favor, and he'd been so nice on the plane."

"Favor?" I said. "What kind of favor?" Now we were getting down to it, and I sat up and leaned toward her in anticipation.

265

"He'd bought a bag of yarn for a relative, and he asked me if I'd take it through customs for him. He said that he was concerned they'd think it would seem odd for him to have it and ask a lot of questions and maybe take the yarn apart. But since I had all my knitting stuff, it wouldn't seem odd for me to have brought back yarn."

"And you did it?"

"Yes," she said, getting flustered. "But then I kept thinking of the recording they play at the airport about not taking packages for strangers. And that's just what I did. Well, he wasn't quite a stranger, but almost. I was certainly glad to hand the bag back to him when we got to Vista Del Mar. If Lieutenant Borgnine found out I'd done that, who knows what he would do. And Cora would find out and then she'd say I didn't have enough sense to go off traveling on my own."

"It was just a bag of yarn?" I asked.

"I didn't look through it, but yes, that's all it was."

"Really?" I said, sounding disappointed. "That's all?"

25

I MADE MY WAY TO THE DINING HALL AS THE BELL
began to ring for breakfast. I'd tried to get Madeleine to
come with me, but she was too worried about running into
Lieutenant Borgnine and had gone to the café instead.

I was looking forward to everybody being gathered in
one spot, hoping I could clear up more of the questions I'd
thought of the night before. Breakfast started late on Sundays, and everyone seemed in a more leisurely mode, except
me. I wished the line for the dining hall would move faster.

When I finally got inside, I went right to my regular table.
Lucinda was already there, dressed in a gray Eileen Fisher
outfit, fluttering around greeting the retreaters and doing
her hostess routine.

I would have loved to go right to the cafeteria line. The
smell of breakfast foods had my mouth watering in anticipa-

tion. There were always waffles with melted butter on Sundays, along with baked French toast and eggs benedict. But my attention was across the room with the writers. Van didn't look my way when he came in. He seemed hunched over and tense, and I noticed that he had brought his suitcase with him. That usually meant a guest had already checked out and was planning to leave right after breakfast. What could I possibly get on him in the next hour or so to give Lieutenant Borgnine what he needed to arrest him? Of course, that was assuming the lieutenant's cop gut was right.

It didn't matter anyway, because I saw that Lieutenant Borgnine had come in and was hanging around the entrance. Maybe he had some new information and was going to nab Van when he went to leave.

In the meantime, I went across the room to talk to T Dot. I had no problem finding him. All I had to do was look for a pair of hooded eyes peeking out from his chest. He was on his way back to his table with a plate heaped with food when I stopped him.

"How's it hanging?" he said as a greeting.

I skipped right to the point. "I remember you said that you were concerned because a woman had seen you near Don Porter's room around the time he was shot."

He sucked in his breath and looked around nervously. "Did she tell the cops?" He looked at me. "Are you a cop?"

"I don't have the answer for your first question, and the answer to the second one is no." I glanced around at the room full of diners. "You didn't seem to have much of a description of her other than she had on a scarf." He nodded in recognition. "I just thought maybe if you looked around now, you might be able to point her out."

"Why would I do that?" he asked, striking a defiant pose.

"It's not about her pointing out that you were there as much as you pointing out that she was there." I don't think he completely understood other than that it wasn't about him being in trouble, but he was a little more agreeable.

"Look, I didn't really see her very well," he said.

"What if I pointed someone out? Could you tell me if she's the one?" He shrugged as an answer but agreed half-heartedly to try.

I pointed across the room to Rayanne. He leaned forward to get a better view of her sharp features. I wasn't happy when he shrugged. "I don't really remember how she looked. We just exchanged a few words." When I asked him what she'd said, he grumbled about his breakfast getting cold and started to walk away. He said something that I didn't quite get. It sounded like *sort of vice*, or *saying twice*.

When I went back across the room, I noticed that Van and Lieutenant Borgnine were both gone. What did that mean?

I wasn't very good company when I finally got my plate of food and joined my group. They were all talking about yarn and the retreat, while I was trying to make some order out of the craziness in my head.

Lucinda seemed to have a sixth sense that I was busy working something out, and she continued to act as hostess and left me alone.

I sat at the table nursing my coffee after the whole place had cleared out. The retreaters were off to their last chance at free time before the final workshop. Then it would be lunch and good-bye.

I cut through the Lodge and saw that Madeleine wasn't in the café, but Sammy was. He was standing over one of the tables with a crowd around him. When I got closer, I saw that he was doing the trick with the shells again. Only he'd changed his patter and the observers were all laughing as he lifted the shell they were sure held the pea. Something made me stop and watch for a few rounds.

How were those people ever going to figure out which shell the pea was under when the shells all looked the same and he kept moving them around? Suddenly I thought of the crime scene and realized why I'd been reminded of something when I shut off the lights. What if there was something Don was trying to say by reaching for the light switch, something very literal.

Suddenly all the puzzle pieces started to come together. I wasn't sure of all the details, but there was something I had to check. I slipped out of the Lodge and ran back to my place. My hand was shaking as I unlocked the converted guest house and went inside. Thanks to the as-usual cloudy sky, the light was low in there, but I hesitated to turn on the lights. The tote bag of yarn was where I'd left it after Madeleine had given it to me. What if Madeleine had mixed things up and this was actually the bag of yarn that she had carried through customs for Don?

I thought back to how she'd given it to me almost as soon as she'd gotten off the bus, and only later had Don come looking for her.

I took it over to the window where the light was brighter

and took out all the skeins. There didn't seem to be anything special about them other than they seemed handspun. I poked through them to see if something was hidden inside but came up empty. Then one of the labels slipped off the ball of yarn and fell to the floor. I looked it over as I picked it up. There was the usual information about how many yards each skein held, what the yarn was made of, and the color with the dye lot. Then I noticed there was something handwritten as well. I checked the other skeins and saw there was something different written on each one. I noted that there was a small letter at the top of each skein. As I saw the *a*, *b* and *c*, I figured out the letters must be a way to show the order. I lined the skeins up in alphabetical order and tried to make sense of what was on the labels. It looked like some kind of formula.

Now I got it. I had a new perspective on the trip to the lighthouse and a lot more besides—including understanding what T Dot had really said to me at the Lodge. I had to find Lieutenant Borgnine. I had to show him what I'd found and tell him what I'd figured out. Most likely he was still somewhere on the grounds of Vista Del Mar.

I turned to go just as the door opened. "There you are, darlin'," Dolly said, coming inside.

I froze. Her voice was friendly enough, but I'd figured out that T Dot hadn't said *saying twice* or *sort of vice*, but *singing voice*. There was only one person's voice that described, and she was standing in front of me.

"I was just going to clean up this mess and go back across the street." As I was speaking I tried to grab the labels, but all I got was a ball of yarn before she pushed me out of the way.

"At last," she said, scooping up one of the labels and reading over it. She grabbed the cloth tote and began to stuff the yarn and labels into it. I took advantage of her distraction and rushed to the door, but she was amazingly fast for an older woman with so much heft and I realized her slow movements before had all been an act.

"I don't think so," she said, slamming the door and then standing in front of it to block my path. Her voice had gone from friendly to icy cold and her expression had hardened. It was hard to believe she was the same woman who'd been so friendly and accepting all weekend, but then that was obviously all an act, too.

She saw me looking at the tote bag she'd slipped onto her arm.

"I know you're on to it," she said.

"I don't know what you mean." I tried to keep my voice steady. "If that yarn means so much to you, take it and go. No questions asked."

"I read lips," she said. "I saw what you said to the kid with the bird tattoo on his chest and his comment. I knew you were doing some kind of investigating, and after what he said, you'd figure out the woman in the hall was me. When I saw you coming over here, I thought we could have a little *talk* before you did anything with the information. But this," she said, holding the bag up to her chest, "is a real lifesaver. I didn't know what I was going to tell the people I work for when I didn't have it."

She began to mutter to herself. "I was so sure that Don Porter double-crossed me. I guess whatever he was trying to say about some woman was true." She stared at me. "I'm not even going to ask how you ended up with it."

"Then you were the one who left the message for Don Porter, but called him Snow Drop?"

"I didn't know who I was contacting. Yes, I left the message. The deal was I was to leave a bag with the payment and Snow Drop would take it and leave the bag with this yarn in its place." She went back to muttering to herself. "When I looked at those labels and there was nothing but yarn information—" She seemed to be reliving her distress. She swallowed it back and addressed me. "He didn't know who I was, but I was watching the bench when he made the switch. I went to his room and demanded he give me the payment back since he hadn't delivered his end of the bargain." I watched her shoulders drop in dismay. "He said it was already gone."

I remembered what Maggie had said about seeing him in the coffee place with his computer. "So the 'payment' was really access to something, like maybe a bank account?"

"Yes, a routing number, an account number and a password written on the labels in my bag of yarn. When I got to him, he'd already moved the money to another account and destroyed the labels with the numbers," she said, and suddenly I understood why he arranged for the cab to the airport for the next day. He'd gotten what he wanted.

"And you took that bag of yarn from his room?" I thought of the cloth tote T Dot had seen and that was gone when the cops went through the room. Something else occurred to me. "And you left the yarn in the gift shop."

"I was afraid the yarn might connect me to him somehow, and I didn't know how else to get rid of it."

"So, then you were the one who went through the rooms and all the bags in the meeting room?" I asked.

"No," she said curtly. She seemed annoyed with herself that she hadn't understood that Don was trying to tell her that the bag was somehow switched. "Enough of all this talky-talky. I have to get a move on now." She looked me in the eye. "Sorry to do this, but you know too much now." There was a small gun in her hand, pointed directly at me. Frank would be upset at my lack of knowledge of what kind of gun it was, but what did it matter? They all did the same thing.

Dolly looked around the room and saw a throw pillow on a chair but waved her hand in dismissal. "That pillow business didn't work very well. I guess we could do it here without trying to cover the sound. There's nobody around."

She moved away from the door and pushed me toward the center of the room. I looked for some escape, but there seemed to be none as she raised the gun. I held my breath and closed my eyes—

Suddenly I heard the door open and voices coming toward us. When I opened my eyes I saw that Derek and Lisa had come in and they both had guns that were much bigger than Dolly's.

Derek took a step toward Dolly. "I'll take that," he said, reaching for the tote bag. But Dolly had already erased the space between us and I felt something at my temple.

"One more step and she gets it," Dolly said. Then she gave me a shove. "We'll be going now." How had this gone from bad to worse? And did Derek and Lisa even care if she shot me in the head? There was only one thing I was sure of. If I took a step out the door, I'd never be coming back. I thought of Julius sitting on the stoop waiting for me. And when I didn't come back he'd think I'd abandoned him, just like whoever had owned him before.

A stupid idea came to mind. I didn't know if it would work, but at this point what did I have to lose? "Do you have a plan where we're going to go?" I asked, trying to keep my voice from trembling.

"Shut up," Dolly said, but when she didn't make me move, I realized I'd hit a nerve. I heard her muttering to herself about various options. Lisa and Derek held steady. Finally, Dolly seemed to have decided on a plan, and she motioned for me to move.

I looked down at my feet. "I can't go," I said. "My shoe is untied."

"Who cares? Now, move," she ordered.

"Okay, but if I don't tie my shoe, my foot is going to slide and I won't be able to walk very fast. I might even trip. Since those Crocs of yours don't have laces, it's probably hard for you to understand." Dolly seemed to be thinking it over. "You can tie it for me if you want," I said.

"You didn't really think I'd fall for that?" she said with a mixture of a groan and a laugh.

"Okay, then it's on you if I slow your getaway," I said.

"Fine. Go on and tie your damn shoe." She gave my arm a shove.

I bent down, knowing she was watching, but between the chiffon scarf she had wound around her neck and her girth, her view was blocked. I had already come up with a plan, but now I had to carry it out. It was taking longer than expected and she was getting impatient when I kept saying that the laces had slipped out of my hands and I had to try it again. Finally, I stood.

"That took long enough," she said with annoyance and gave me a shove. "Now, move. I took a big step forward and she tried to do the same, but with an *oof* sound she started to fall forward.

She tried to steady herself and dropped the gun and the bag before she hit the ground. But a moment later she was up and ran out the door, leaving behind her shoes.

I was surprised when neither Derek nor Lisa made a move to go after Dolly. "What's going on?" I said.

26

I DIDN'T GET AN ANSWER UNTIL WE'D ADJOURNED
to the Lodge and we were on the other side of the registration
desk in the business office of Vista Del Mar. Kevin St. John
was standing—well, really pacing. Lieutenant Borgnine had
an impassive expression as he waited for an explanation.
Dane, in uniform, was standing with his arms folded.

Derek and Lisa had put their guns away, and now they
took out their badges. "Sorry we couldn't tell you all we're
FBI," Derek said.

"And you're not really married," I said.

"That wasn't a lie," Lisa said. "We are married."

"Just not to each other, right?"

"What gave us away?" Lisa asked. "So we'll know for
next time."

"You couldn't seem to agree if you had kids," I said and she winced.

The others in the room seemed less concerned about their marital status than hearing why they were there. Lisa and Derek confirmed what I already knew and then filled in some of what I didn't.

"We were on the lookout for this," Derek said, holding up the tote bag. "The formula on the yarn wrappers is for an undetectable explosive and was on its way to a terrorist cell. We knew there was going to be a handoff here, but not who, where or when.

"Once we saw the Snow Drop note on the message board, we went to the lighthouse at the appointed time to watch. We hadn't expected so many people to be there. We saw Porter pick up a bag and leave one in its place. We had hoped to intercept the drop, but we got distracted by a big dog loping across the grass and jumping on us. When we looked back at the bench, the bag was gone. Because of who was there, we figured it had been taken by someone staying at Vista Del Mar. Our goal was to find the bag with the formula."

"Then you were the ones who went through all the rooms, and then all the bags at my workshop," I said.

"Yes," Lisa said. "Please tell your cat we're sorry he got the rap for it."

"When Porter got killed, we figured something in the deal had gone wrong. I have to say, by this morning we were feeling pretty desperate about finding the formula. So, when we saw Dolly Erickson going up your driveway, we got suspicious about what she was up to."

"Lucky for me you did," I said.

Derek smiled at me. "I think you would have done okay even if we hadn't. How did you do what you did?"

I'd brought Dolly's shoes with us and I held out the pair of pale blue Crocs and showed how the straps had been pushed forward and there was something binding the straps together.

I still had the ball of yarn in my hand from when I'd tried to get hold of the labels. The tail of it was connected to the Crocs. Then Lisa figured it out. "It's finger crochet. You used finger crochet to make something to tie her shoes together. I wish those women who thought it was useless could see you now." Lisa gestured with her hand. "Show them how you did it."

I cut the yarn free and then demonstrated making a length of chain stitches using my finger as a hook. Lieutenant Borgnine looked skyward and shook his head. Kevin St. John kept trying to say something, but in the end all he did was sputter. Dane smiled and mouthed, "That's my girl."

Derek turned to me. "You wondered why I didn't go after Dolly—" He pointed past the counter to the main area of the Lodge just as a breathless and disheveled-looking Dolly came through the door. "The people she works for don't like screwups. They tend to reward it with a slow and painful death. I knew when she thought about it, she'd realize being locked up was a better option." Just as he finished, Dolly walked up to where we all were and asked to be taken into custody.

"You still haven't told us," Derek said, stepping closer to me, "how you ended up with the formula."

I was trying to think of an answer when I saw that Madeleine had left the café and was crossing the room. As she passed the registration desk, she glanced over the counter and saw all of us and started to pick up her pace. But then she reconsidered and made her way around the counter and said that as an owner of Vista Del Mar, she was entitled to know what was going on.

Kevin St. John immediately stepped in and tried to shield her. "That's okay, Ms. Delacorte. We have everything under control."

"You're right. You should know," Derek said, ignoring the manager. He explained the whole story. Poor Madeleine. When she heard about what was in the bag of yarn, she seemed almost faint. But then Derek got to the end and said it was down to the question of how I'd gotten possession of the formula.

"Is she in trouble?" Madeleine asked.

"Maybe," Derek said. Madeleine considered what he'd said for a moment, and I wondered if she would tell the truth or not. She seemed to have come to a conclusion and stood a little straighter as she turned to Derek with a resolute expression.

"Don't blame her. It's my fault." She seemed embarrassed as she explained about carrying the bag of yarn all the way to Vista Del Mar. "I gave it to Casey by mistake and gave Don Porter the yarn I'd bought for her." She looked around the room at all of us. "I understand I did something terrible." Madeleine took a deep breath, closed her eyes and held out her hands as if she expected to be handcuffed. When nothing happened, she finally opened her eyes.

"It clearly wasn't intentional," Derek said as she retracted her hands. "And if you hadn't done what you did, we might not have kept this formula from getting where it was supposed to go. Who knows how many lives could have been lost?"

"What about Don?" she said.

"He was a bad guy," Derek answered. "It was all about money for him. He obviously didn't care what kind of havoc he would cause. And he manipulated you. I think you've learned your lesson and you understand that those recordings at the airport mean something."

While they were talking, Cora had come into the Lodge and finally did hear what Madeleine had wanted to keep from her. The younger Delacorte sister's lips were pursed when she came around the counter, and she started to scold Madeleine in front of everyone.

Instead of seeming defeated by her sister's comments, Madeleine actually stood taller. "I am old enough to make my own decisions, whether it's clothes or travel. I don't need your okay."

Cora was speechless.

Now that everything seemed settled, Derek and Lisa left with Dolly. They didn't even need to handcuff her. Lieutenant Borgnine seemed relieved that Don's death was settled. There was no mention of his cop gut and how it had pointed to Van.

I did finally understand who'd tipped Lieutenant Borgnine off about Van keeping stuff from the police, though. Dolly had been across the café and I remembered that she had told me she could read lips.

*   *   *

BY THE TIME I GOT TOGETHER WITH MY GROUP, they were all in our meeting room for the last workshop. Crystal and Wanda were circulating among them, trying to make sure everyone knew how to finish their projects on their own. Even so, both of my helpers were giving out their e-mail addresses in case anyone got stuck.

"Where have you been?" Lucinda said. "There are other people missing—where are Dolly and Lisa?"

"It's a long story," I said, and they all gathered around me. Lucinda looked like she would burst by the time I got to the end.

"I am definitely not telling Tag about the exchanging bags and a secret formula. He's paranoid enough already."

Crystal was particularly pleased that the finger crochet she'd taught might have saved my life. She definitely gave Wanda an I-told-you-so look.

The Difficult Duo were amazingly quiet. I noticed that once it came out what kind of person Don Porter really was, Rayanne didn't volunteer that he was her cousin and DeeDee kept jerking her head from side to side, probably regretting that she'd mentioned Rayanne's relative to me.

Jeff said he was glad he had only been a courier for a dog.

I went up to Mona. "I know your secret." Under all her layers. I heard her gasp. Just before I'd left Derek and Lisa, it had occurred to me to ask them about Mona, since it seemed while they were looking for the formula, they had gotten background information on some of the people in both groups. Mona had been a red flag with all her garb, and they'd checked out who she was.

"Please don't say anything," she said in her low voice. "It's better that it should come from me."

"No problem," I said. With all the issues I had getting along with Kevin St. John, I didn't want to be the one to tell him his mother was one of my retreaters. Her behavior all made sense once I found out who she was. No wonder she asked so many questions about him, seemed to be watching him, but at the same time avoided getting too close. I suppose she was afraid he might recognize her. I'd even heard Cora Delacorte say that Mona looked familiar.

She assured me she was there for only good reasons. She'd come to see how he was doing. She regretted abandoning him and leaving him with her mother to bring up. She'd disguised herself because she wasn't sure she'd have the courage to face him. But she'd decided to tell him who she was and try to make amends.

Mona was likely to find Kevin needing her support. He'd been so full of himself at the beginning of the writers' conference, but after this weekend, he wasn't so sure he wanted to handle events. It was easier just to be the innkeeper. Plus he now had the prospect of Cora and Madeleine being in the middle of Vista Del Mar's business.

As it got to be time to wrap up the workshop, everyone got nostalgic and there was a lot of exchanging of information and promises to keep in touch. Surprisingly, they all wanted to be notified of my next retreat. One comment said it all. The woman with the knitting needles stuck in her hair pulled me aside.

"Who would have thought that a retreat in this rustic spot would turn out to be so exciting?"

The early birds and Lucinda were the last to leave. I thanked Bree, Olivia and Scott for all their help and said I wished I'd been able to spend more time with them.

"That's okay," Olivia said with a warm smile. "It sounds like you were off saving the world."

The airport shuttle picked everyone up and Lucinda and I watched until it turned onto the street and drove out of sight.

"Well, it's home to Tag for me," she said. The restaurant was closed on Sundays and I knew he probably had everything waiting at home for her return. She had said a weekend away always reignited the spark between them. She grabbed the handle of her bag and headed for her car, and I walked home.

When I saw Julius sitting on the stoop waiting for me, I rushed up to hug him. I was glad he didn't know how close it had gotten to me never coming back. It was going to be a stink fish fiesta.

A car pulled into my driveway and Sammy got out. He had a huge grin on his face. "Case, you won't believe it," he said. "I don't know how it happened, but word spread about my comedy magic act and I got an offer to do a private party at one of the Pebble Beach resorts. I know this is just the beginning. But I can't do it without you. Are you in?"

I couldn't let him down. "Okay, but I need a better costume."

His face lit up even more. "Whatever you want. And this time we'll be sure to practice. I'm going to make you levitate."

I rolled my eyes. What had I gotten myself into?

He followed me inside while I gave Julius the special treatment. He would have hung around longer, but I told him I had calls to make and then it was off to the Blue Door to bake.

I called Frank first.

"Feldstein, wow, it sounds like you really got into the deep end this time. So those writers were all innocent?" he said.

"Yes, but it was thanks to the stuff T Dot told me and your idea about flipping things that I figured out it was probably the most unlikely person at my retreat. The other guy probably still blames me for Lieutenant Borgnine giving him the third degree. But he's gone by now, anyway."

"Glad I could help," he said. "If that's it . . ." I heard a woman's voice calling him Frankiepoo. *Frankiepoo?* I tried not to laugh. "Well, keep in touch. And job well done." There was a click and he was gone.

I called my mother before she could call me. She was absolutely silent while I told her the whole tale. "Not what I expected," she said. "I admire how clever you were, but I can't say it makes me happy that you had to escape someone trying to shoot you." She let out a sigh. "I guess that means you'll be keeping your deal with Vista Del Mar. I know you really like what you're doing, but I think if you came back here it wouldn't be the worst thing."

"Never say never," I said. Just before she hung up she said something that totally shocked me. "I just want you to know that I'm really proud of you." Then she clicked off.

And then it was time to go to the Blue Door. Since the restaurant was closed on Sundays, I went in a little earlier than on other days. Even so, the streets of Cadbury were already ultra quiet.

I opened the door and turned on the lights. The dining room was all set up for the coming day. I carried the bag of supplies for the muffins into the kitchen. It was exciting to think I was going to debut the almost-apple-fritter muffins. With soft jazz playing on the radio, I began to take out the ingredients for the Blue Door desserts. I'd just finished grating the carrots for the cake when I heard a knock at the door.

I took a peek and saw Gwen Selwyn with her face pressed against the glass. I was surprised to see Crystal's mother and let her in. Her brows were furrowed and she clearly had something on her mind.

"What is it? Is there a problem at the yarn store? Is everyone all right?"

She started talking before I finished. "I'm ready to let it out who my father really was. I'm sure it's going to cause problems. I need to start by telling Crystal. I feel silly to have to ask this, but could you help me do it?"

I readily agreed, but as I looked past her through the window, I felt like calling out for all the Cadburians to put on their seat belts, because they were in for a rocky ride.

We agreed on a time to talk to Crystal, and she left in far better shape than she'd come.

I went back to my baking and was mixing the batter when I heard someone else at the door. When I checked, I saw Dane standing on the porch.

"I had to make sure you were okay. How do you manage to get in so much trouble?" he said with a teasing grin. He was out of uniform now and carrying a plate covered in foil.

"I don't know what you mean. It was just another Sunday in Cadbury," I joked.

"Yeah, and you probably missed a few meals. I had the karate kids over and made them a mountain of pasta. I figured you might need some." He lifted the foil and the rich tomato-garlic smell made my mouth water.

He took me into the dining room and picked a table by the window. "I'm sure no one minds if you take a break. And I'm sure you need one."

I knew he was right. I'd been running on nerve all day, and now it was wearing off. The food was delicious as always, and I really appreciated his thoughtfulness. He sat watching while I ate.

I was waiting for him to start with the teasing again, but he had a serious look on his face. "I'm really glad everything worked out. It seems like your worries about Madeleine pulling the plug on your deal are over."

"It looks that way," I said, scraping up the last of the sauce.

"So, that means you'll be staying in Cadbury," he said, and I nodded. "Then I guess all your fears about loving and leaving me are history, too." I froze, figuring what was coming next. How long could I keep on fighting the obvious?

All there was to say was, "Yes."

Wanda's Four-for-One Knit Patterns

All four patterns start the same way. They begin with four stitches cast on, followed by a row of knit stitches, and then rows of knit stitches with an increase, which creates a triangle shape.

The washcloth and baby blanket are both squares. When the triangle reaches the decided width, the following rows decrease a stitch until there are just four stitches left. They are bound off and the yarn fastened off. All ends are woven in.

Supplies

Washcloth: 1 skein Lily Sugar 'n Cream, 100% cotton, approx. 120 yds (109m); U.S. size 10½ (6.5mm) knitting needles

Baby blanket: 4 skeins Cascade Yarns Pacific Chunky Color Wave, 60% acrylic, 40% merino wool 120 yds (110m); U.S. size 10½ (6.5mm) knitting needles

Triangle Head Scarf: 1 skein Lily Sugar 'n Cream, 100% cotton, approx. 120 yds (109m), U.S. size 10 ½ 13 (6.5mm) knitting needles

Shawl: 2 skeins Lily Sugar 'n Cream, 100% cotton, approx. 120 yds (109m), U.S. size 13 (9mm) knitting needles

Tapestry needle for weaving in ends

Recipe

Crochet hook size G/6-4.25mm for making ties
for Triangle Head Scarf
All the patterns start the same way. Cast on 4
stitches.

Row 1: Knit 4.

Row 2: Knit 2, yarn over, knit across.

Washcloth: Repeat Row 2 until 8 inches wide. Continue with Row 3.

Row 3: Knit 1, knit 2 together, yarn over, knit 2 together, knit across.

Repeat Row 3 until there are 4 stitches left, bind off and weave in ends.

Baby blanket: Repeat Row 2 until 36 inches wide. Continue with Row 3.

Row 3: Knit 1, knit 2 together, yarn over, knit 2 together, knit across.

Repeat Row 3 until there are 4 stitches left, bind off and weave in ends.

Triangle Head Scarf: Repeat Row 2 until 21 inches wide, bind off and weave in ends. Ties: Cut 50-inch length of yarn. Use crochet hook to attach to side point of scarf. Make chain stitches down, fasten off and weave in ends. Repeat on the other side.

Shawl: Repeat Row 2 until 36 inches wide, bind off and weave in ends.

Lieutenant Borgnine's Almost-Apple-Fritter Muffins

5 eggs
½ cup milk
½ cup brown sugar with 2 teaspoons cinnamon
   mixed in
1½ teaspoons vanilla
2½ cups egg bread cut into small cubes
1 ½ cups diced honey crisp apples

Preheat oven to 350°F (180°C) and line 6-muffin tin with paper baking cups.

Whisk eggs, milk, cinnamon-sugar mixture, and vanilla in a large bowl. Stir in bread cubes and apples. Spoon into prepared pan, filling cups to top. Bake until a knife comes out clean, approximately 25 minutes. Makes 9.

Ready to find
your next great read?

Let us help.

Visit prh.com/nextread